Here

Here

Women Writing on Michigan's Upper Peninsula

Edited by Ronald Riekki

Michigan State University Press | *East Lansing*

♾ The paper used in this publication meets the minimum requirements of ANSI/NISO Z39.48-1992 (R 1997) (Permanence of Paper).

Michigan State University Press
East Lansing, Michigan 48823-5245

Printed and bound in the United States of America.

21 20 19 18 17 16 15   1 2 3 4 5 6 7 8 9 10

Library of Congress Control Number: 2014949059
ISBN: 978-1-61186-163-1 (pbk.)
ISBN: 978-1-60917-458-3 (ebook: PDF)
ISBN: 978-1-62895-230-8 (ebook: ePub)
ISBN: 978-1-62896-230-7 (ebook: Kindle)

Book design by Charlie Sharp, Sharp Des!gns, Lansing, MI
Cover design by Erin Kirk New
Cover image of Miner's Castle, Pictured Rocks National Lakeshore

Michigan State University Press is a member of the Green Press Initiative and is committed to developing and encouraging ecologically responsible publishing practices. For more information about the Green Press Initiative and the use of recycled paper in book publishing, please visit *www.greenpressinitiative.org*.

Visit Michigan State University Press at *www.msupress.org*

Contents

Winter/Talvi

Spring/Primavera

Summer/Niibin

Foreword

Alison Swan

A couple of years before Henry David Thoreau launched his experiment in self-improvement at Walden Pond, Massachusetts, fellow New Englander and transcendentalist Margaret Fuller undertook a summer tour of the Great Lakes. Her goals were similar, her tack quite different, for it's clear from her book, *Summer on the Lakes, in 1843,* that meeting people was a highlight. Fuller encountered Michigan's Upper Peninsula briefly. She left this report of shooting the pre-locks rapids of the St. Mary's River with two "Indian canoe-men" whom she clearly admired: "It is, no doubt, an act of wonderful dexterity to steer amid these jagged rocks, when one rude touch would tear a hole in the birch canoe. . . . I should like to have come down twenty times that I might have had leisure to realize the pleasure."[1]

Water, of course, defines peninsulas, and the largest surface supply of fresh water in the world defines the Great Lakes State's two sprawling peninsulas. Even the boundary with Wisconsin is just about 50 percent river: Brule and Menominee. I had to look that up. Even though my mom, her parents, and their parents were Yoopers (as I write, this word is being added to the Merriam-Webster dictionary), I grew up in the southeastern corner of Michigan's Lower Peninsula (*not* the "L.P." for those of you who aren't already in the know), close to Lake Erie, which defines the southern boundary of the Great Lakes basin. The westernmost reaches of the U.P touch the southern shore of Lake Superior about 600 miles from there.

I'd hazard a guess that when most people think of the U.P., they think of the Great Outdoors, that larger-than-life entity immortalized in the best-known literature of the U.P.: Ernest Hemingway's Nick Adams stories and Jim Harrison's poems and novels. They probably don't think of Fuller's, as she called them, "poetic impressions,"[2] and while they might think of Lake Superior, they probably don't know of Janeen Rastall's term for it, "deep-hearted," or of Lisa Fay Coutley's characterization of it: "doesn't take any shit . . . wears stilettos in ice storms, does crosswords in pen," and "eats red meat." (Perhaps "Lake" is the wrong term!) In recent years this freshwater sea has become famous. U.P. glamour shots are disseminated to the world and attract outdoors lovers to country that's wild and beguiling, all right, but not necessarily in the way Chamber of Commerce images might lead you to believe.

Little ancient forest remains. In certain places one must still guard against stepping through thick underbrush into a long-abandoned mine shaft. There are abandoned farms, ghost towns, and almost-ghost towns. On the other hand, hundreds of thousands of acres of second- and third-growth forest (and hundreds of miles of logging roads), with their resident moose, black bear, and wolves, do offer up a wild playground. There are hundreds of miles of lightly developed shoreline. And—this *is* rare—there is quite a lot of distance between most of these places and the closest outlet of this or that retail or restaurant chain. Many people, including a number of the writers collected here, find all of this refreshing. "We have the best life, / the best wind, / the best large birds," asserts the narrator in Catie Rosemurgy's "Summer in Gold River." Others, including many of the characters and narrators in the poems and stories that follow, find the large distances oppressive, especially since industries such as logging and mining send the majority of their profits out of the communities where they are made. Caitlin Horrocks's narrator in "The Sleep" describes a sentiment that makes people leave: "'What's to love?' our children [ask], in surly disbelief: What kind of morons hustle for jobs that don't even pay for cable television?"

And then there is the weather, which "mocks the powerful inventions of the century," as described in Ellen Airgood's "Winter Wind." All that Lake

Superior water means voluminous snowfall and icy summer wind. Snow regularly begins in September and falls into May. "The snow fell day after day so that it seemed there would be no more room for it," reports the narrator in Gloria Whelan's *Once on This Island.* Hard frosts can run into June and return in September. In between, everything from mosquitoes to white pines has to complete the year's growth and reproduction, so when the air finally softens with humidity and heat, it also prickles with stinging and biting insects and swells with pollen. There are a few paradisal weeks at the end of summer, but in general, life in the U.P. is not for the faint of heart or anyone married to comfort.

It goes without saying that those who stay are hardy. Ellen Airgood's narrator in "Winter Wind," for example, "lit the kerosene lamp, drew nearer to the fire, and was able to smile a little through my shivering teeth at our canniness in not relying too completely on modern things." What's not been well acknowledged is that such a rugged landscape and its scrappy inhabitants provide excellent habitat and company for writers. In the stories and poems collected here you will find quite a lot more trouble than pleasure; trouble, it seems to me, that's exacerbated by the U.P.'s isolation and isolating weather, trouble that's met with wry aplomb: betrayal, lost children, abuse, rape, addiction, and the like. "There are those of us / who drink ourselves to death and those who take a lighter hand," says the narrator of Emily Van Kley's "Vital Signs," "but even teenagers know better / than to believe in immortality." The trouble is not without its levity. Residents of Horrocks's fictional U.P. town, Bounty, literally hibernate, rather successfully, and the schoolgirl friends in Carroll Watson Rankin's *Dandelion Cottage* struggle with a child-size version of poverty—in a life-size playhouse.

One of the U.P. places my brothers and I take our children to play is the same woods where our young selves came to know nature. A couple of abandoned cars and numerous long-discarded cans stud the forest understory. All are rusted, but not so far gone that we can't recognize a 1930s roadster and beer cans so old they were opened with sharp-tipped church keys. My brothers, our kids, and I might say, "What's to love?" So much! Truly dark nights where stars are uncountable and wolves howl, for one thing, and for another, house-sized rocks that Superior crashes over, deep woods full of quiet, fresh water full of pan fish, a wooden screen door opening into our grandma's tidy and, so far as we knew, untroubled kitchen—and brushes with relics from families, including our ancestors, who once walked the same paths we do.

Images of just this sort of haunted wild beauty dominate the poems collected here. "This place is where the eagles dance and connect with the Anishinabe / This place is held close to our hearts / Generations have connected / Through the dances of old and / The powwows now held there" (Sally Brunk, "Lac Vieux Desert"), and, "When I carry / The woes of the world / Into the woods / Branches reach out / And brush them gently off" (Stellanova Osborn, "Censors").

The world limned in *Here* feels intimately known in a way that's generally unavailable to travelers. These authors seem mainly to be writing from home, in both the domesticated and undomesticated senses of that word; home with all its resonances, from sheltering and nurturing children, to enduring depravation, to finding solace on a familiar windswept beach. Readers are invited to meet people, with all their messes and beauties, as well as other-than-human wild nature, which comforts as well as thwarts. Bame-wa-wa-ge-zhik-aquay, whom many know as Jane Johnston Schoolcraft, sings a sort of hymn that *does* invoke the Great Outdoors and the emboldening influence of wild nature: "Here in my native inland sea . . . all is glorious, free, and grand."

One hundred and seventy years after Margaret Fuller traveled the Great Lakes, we have this essential collection of poetic impressions from North America's freshwater heart. How lucky for us that these women, true intimates of the U.P., have put down their words.

NOTES

1. Margaret Fuller, *Summer on the Lakes, in 1843* (Champaign: University of Illinois Press, 1991), 150.
2. Ibid., ix.

Introduction

When I have been asked to name the most important Upper Peninsula authors, I have often answered with the big three of fiction writer Ellen Airgood, poet Catie Rosemurgy, and multiple-genre writer Bame-wa-wa-ge-zhik-aquay (a.k.a. Jane Johnston Schoolcraft). It's a different answer from the typical patriarchal trinity of Jim Harrison, John D. Voelker, and Ernest Hemingway I've heard so many people reiterate.

In the significant U.P. book *The Sound the Stars Make Rushing Through the Sky: The Writings of Jane Johnston Schoolcraft,* Bame-wa-wa-ge-zhik-aquay is labeled as the first known Native American woman writer and literary writer, "by some measures the first known Indian poet, the first known poet to write poems in a Native American language, and the first known American Indian to write out traditional Indian stories."[1] As well, her stories were source material for the epic poem *The Song of Hiawatha.* When we talk about the beginnings of Native American literature, that discussion starts with a female author in Michigan's U.P.

I collected top three lists from a variety of distinguished Yooper authors to find out their favorite U.P. books. Catie Rosemurgy's writing appeared on those lists more than any other writer in these pages. One could make the argument that she is the most respected poet currently writing about the U.P. She's an author's author, a poet's poet.

As far as I know, Ellen Airgood is the only author signed to a major publisher who resides in and writes about the U.P. and is not university affiliated. That university outsidership is critical, as it connects her even more intimately with the region. She lives and works in Grand Marais, and the combination of her U.P. authenticity and the rarity of having a true Yooper whose works are published by a major publisher gives her a voice I view as maybe the most valuable of any U.P. fiction writer writing today. The U.P. seems necessary to her being—and the voice of the U.P. seems to have an indissoluble tie to her writing.

The U.P.-dedicated works of Sault Ste. Marie's Bame-wa-wa-ge-zhik-aquay, Escanaba's Rosemurgy, and Grand Marais's Airgood trump the occasional and sporadic U.P. writings of Hemingway or Harrison, who would themselves, I'm sure, definitely not self-classify as U.P. authors. Not to say that their works aren't stunning and important to the history of U.P. literature. They are. But I want to reformulate the conversation. Voelker-Harrison-Hemingway cast a massive shadow, but I want to shift the sun. This book, I'm hoping, will give a more real, diverse discussion to the all-time great U.P. literature. The canon is opening.

As a matter of fact, I'd like to highly discourage people from seeing this book as a definitive closed list of U.P. literature (or U.P. women's literature). The book is really an expansion of *The Way North: Collected Upper Peninsula New Works* and just the beginning of upcoming Michigan State University Press volumes of U.P. literature that will make for an even larger, more thorough literary canon when read together, especially with, of course, the long list of books individually published by the authors.

Fittingly, the anthology's structure reflects Mother Nature, the four seasons being such a critical part of the region's incredible uniqueness. Certain pieces felt wintery to me, others full of summer (in both literal and metaphorical senses). My hope is that you'll be taken on a journey through the writings and can experience a true multi-vocal perspective on U.P. life, all of its months of emotion, from its far shoreline edges and Lake Superior breakwater of Anne Sexton's "The Break Away" to the deep internal "gaping mine in the earth" in Jane Piirto's "Eighteen Maple Trees." You'll see the gorgeous parts, the ugly parts. This is not the tourist perspective. The book, hopefully, mines much deeper than that.

Travel through the 1810s of Gloria Whelan, the 1840s of Bame-wa-wa-ge-zhik-aquay, the 1900s of Carroll Watson Rankin, the 1920s of Janet Loxley Lewis, the 1950s of Stellanova Osborn, and the now of Ellen Airgood. Travel through Lorine Niedecker's Sault Sainte Marie, Ellen Airgood's Grand Marais, Charmi Keranen's Seney, Manda Frederick's Marquette, Jane Piirto's Ishpeming, Sharon Dilworth's L'Anse, April Lindala's Baraga, Mary Biddinger's Copper Harbor, and the plethora of dangerous and beautiful waters surrounding those cities and these pages—Saara Myrene Raappana's "skunk-hot lake," Gloria Whelan's "solitary rivers edged with ice," Barbara Henning's "Lake Superior winds [that] clank the chimes," Anne Sexton's "moon in the pond," and Lorine Niedecker's entire "world of the Lake." I promise these writings will take you there and, in the words of Elinor Benedict, even far "beyond the lake."

I know for myself, reading April Lindala made me teary.
Reading Sally Brunk made me angry.
Reading Catie Rosemurgy made me smile.
Reading Bame-wa-wa-ge-zhik-aquay put me in awe.
Reading Roxane Gay made me jealous.
Reading Sharon Dilworth made me laugh.
I hope you'll have your own roller coaster of emotions.
Enjoy these pages. I did.

I'm sharing with you where I came from. The essential women's life narratives of a land.

NOTE

1. Robert Dale Parker, ed. *The Sound the Stars Make Rushing Through the Sky: The Writings of Jane Johnston Schoolcraft* (Philadelphia: University of Pennsylvania Press, 2007), 2.

Summer

Niibin

[Here in my native inland sea]

Bame-wa-wa-ge-zhik-aquay

Here in my native inland sea
From pain and sickness would I flee
And from its shores and island bright
Gather a store of sweet delight.
Lone island of the saltless sea!
How wide, how sweet, how fresh and free
How all transporting—is the view
Of rocks and skies and waters blue
And all unites in sweetest strains
To tell, here nature only reigns.
Ah, nature! here forever sway
Far from the haunts of men away
For here, there are no sordid fears,
No crimes, no misery, no tears
No pride of wealth; the heart to fill,
No laws to treat my people ill.

But all is glorious, free, and grand,
Fresh from the great Creator's hand.

Announcement

Elinor Benedict

Friends, for better or worse, white birches
and blue waters have taken me. Even
that half-year of ice got me under
its cover and made me give in. You ask
in a whisper, *Why does she surrender
like this, wherever she goes?* I answer,
*Let's face it: I lose my head with my
body.* Once it was blue mountains
that took my breath, the way they kept
reaching for sky. Then single green oaks,
bright in black fields. Here, after sleeping
with snow, white trillium and starflowers
wink among hemlocks, wild raspberries
taste of perfume, lemony aspens and birch
beckon toward fall. I suppose you could say
fidelity means nothing to me. But listen:
faith and geography are no blood enemies,
no blood kin. To the north wind's music,
I've married the country again.

South of Superior excerpt

Ellen Airgood

THE NEXT AFTERNOON MADELINE POPPED THE BUICK'S HOOD AND wiggled the battery cable, a trick Arbutus had suggested, saying she'd never owned a car under twenty years old in her life and knew all the tricks. The engine turned over and Madeline felt a rush of satisfaction. She shut the engine off again and headed across the empty lots to see Mary.

Mary was lounging beside her display, her feet propped on a crate, carrying on a conversation with a man Madeline had waited on at lunch. He was an investment banker from Manhattan who'd come north for the trout fishing. "Pull up a stump," Mary told Madeline, pointing at a spare lawnchair. "You want a pop, there's some in with the fish. Jack, you keep away from there."

All perfectly illegal, Madeline thought contentedly. No way was it USDA approved to sell home-caught fish from an iced-down cooler you had to swat your dog away from, but one good thing about McAllaster was, nobody cared, or almost nobody. The tourists loved the local color, and the locals would live and let live, mostly. The Bensons and people like them, people who wanted things more modern, more homogenized, more like wherever it was they'd come from, well, to Hell with them. Maybe they were within their rights—and Madeline had to admit she still thought that cutting off credit on delinquent accounts was not unreasonable, no matter what Gladys said and no matter how much she herself disliked them personally—but the Bensons' influence didn't extend this far, at least. Not yet.

Maybe McAllaster could resist gentrification. The north side of Chicago hadn't, as Madeline knew from Emmy's own experience struggling to stay in their apartment as the price of everything soared. A working-class neighborhood went upscale and pretty soon the people who'd made it what it was had to leave, unable to afford the cost of living and the homes they'd grown up in, homes where they'd raised families of their own. But here—maybe the harshness of the landscape and weather and economy would stop some of that, or slow it down. And besides, it wasn't all bad. She *liked* pesto and hummus, and if Gladys hadn't been at war with the Bensons, she'd have been in there buying those things.

Madeline shucked off her shoes. It had been busy today, challenging, and she felt pleasantly worn out. She smiled at the banker but didn't join in the conversation. Working at Garceau's, she was seeing that McAllaster was nowhere near as remote as she'd thought. There'd been a movie star out on Desolation Bay the other day, holed up on his oceangoing yacht. He hadn't gotten *off* the yacht, but still. Today alone she'd waited on a tiny indie rock band from Detroit, an elderly Japanese woman who spoke no English, and a rodeo clown from Wyoming, as well as this Manhattanite.

He and Mary were delighted with each other. Watching him lean toward Mary, his eyes bright with appreciation of the story she was telling, Madeline wished she'd brought her sketchbook. Maybe she could've shown how they were the same and different all at once. She half-drowsed while Mary talked to a couple of retired schoolteachers from Detroit who remembered her from last year. They bought two gallons of syrup and three fillets of fish, and Mary tucked seventy dollars into the front snap pocket of her overalls. "I gave 'em a break for getting two gallons at once," she said when they'd gone. "I could've got eighty for that and the fish but it don't hurt now and then in business to give a good deal."

Madeline agreed. Their conversation wandered from there, from fishing and making maple syrup to Mary's memories of the old lumber camp days. Madeline loved hearing about that. This was turning out to be a perfect afternoon. After a while she thought about having a ginger ale. She sat up to pull one from the cooler just as Mary said, "Listen, now, I've been thinking, and

I've been going to tell you—" A county sheriff's truck eased to a halt in front of them and Mary didn't finish. A tall man in a brown uniform approached with languid steps.

"What do you want?" Mary asked in her road-gravel voice.

"I'm afraid I've got to ask you to pack up and leave, ma'am."

"Is that so?"

"This is Village property, Mrs. Feather, and you haven't got permission to peddle here."

"I ain't a missus as you well know," she said, looking up at him without moving. "And as far as I know, it ain't Village property, either."

"The Village is responsible for the upkeep of this parcel in the absence of the deeded owner."

"In other words, Lillian Frank ain't bothered to mow these lots in thirty years and don't give a damn what happens on 'em. Isn't that what you mean?"

"In the absence of the deed-holder, the Village may elect to perform certain upkeep."

"Running me off, that's upkeep?"

"Ma'am, regardless of ownership, the Village has an ordinance barring unlicensed peddlers."

"Oh for God's sake, Jim, stop calling me 'ma'am.' Since when do they have this so-called ordinance?"

"Since the fifteenth of May, as I believe you've already been informed by letter."

"I ain't gotten no letter."

"I've been informed that a letter was duly written and sent."

"Well I ain't duly received it, you young son of a pup—"

"Let me see that ordinance of yours in writing." Madeline felt shaky with anger. Here they were, enjoying the day, selling a little syrup, a little fish, visiting with the tourists, and along comes this jackass to ruin things.

The man barely glanced at her. "I don't need it in writing."

"You're going to have to do better than that," Madeline began.

"Ah, don't bother," Mary said.

"Mary—"

"Give me a hand packing up, Madeline."

"I appreciate your cooperation, Mary."

"I knew you when you was a snot-nosed kid couldn't balance a bike and don't you forget it, Jim Nelson. Don't you *Mary* me."

"Well, I'm sorry that you feel that way," he said.

He drove to the fruit man's stand, all of a hundred feet or so, to deliver the same news. Madeline stood with a gallon of maple syrup heavy in each hand, watching. Albert threw his hands up in the air and his face flowered into anger. He shook a finger in the sheriff's face, and the sheriff leaned forward and put one hand on the butt of his gun. Gus came around from the back of the van and began to shout. Madeline couldn't hear his words, just the nasal whine of his uplifted voice. She saw how ludicrous he looked—the bandy-legged old reprobate in his pointy-toed oxfords and silky windbreaker probably out on parole for some unsavory activity. The breeze lifted a plume of Gus's hair up and held it there. The sheriff advanced and suddenly, a balloon pricked with a pin, Albert subsided. His shoulders sloped and his big hands fell to his sides.

"This is terrible," Madeline said. "It's not right."

"He's just doing his job," Mary said with resignation that surprised Madeline after the way she'd argued with him. "You know his mother died when he was just a boy."

Madeline did not know what to say to this apparent non sequitur.

They were quiet after that. When Mary had driven off in a cloud of exhaust, Madeline spent a long time leaning against her car, gazing at the hotel, feeling blue. Sad, mad, lonely. She hated seeing Albert and Mary defeated, hated not being able to help or change anything. Abruptly she headed past the bank of lilacs and through the orchard to the back door. This was a bad habit, but last night she'd found no way to confess and now she couldn't make herself stop. There wasn't any harm in it. She just had to spend a little more time in there. It was a haven, a place to leave the real world behind for a little while and surround herself in dreams, like wrapping up in a blanket.

GLADYS WAS SLAMMING THINGS AROUND IN THE KITCHEN WHILE Arbutus sat at the table worrying at a napkin with her fingers when Madeline got home. Greyson was perched atop a stack of catalogues, coloring. Randi must've dropped him off again.

"What's wrong?" Madeline asked, taking in the glum scene.

"Gladys is mad," Greyson said.

"I see that. But at what?"

Gladys had been pulling pots and pans out of the low cupboard where they were stored and piling them up on the counter, smacking each item down with force, but she stopped then. She placed both hands on the countertop and pulled herself up, and turned to look at Madeline. Madeline saw at once that something really was wrong, this wasn't just indignation. It was something worse, something deeper.

"What's happened?"

"It's Emil."

"Oh no." Madeline imagined him dead, cold in his bunk in the trailer.

"They're after him now, when will it stop?" Gladys slammed a palm on the counter, but she looked defeated.

"Who, the Bensons? After him for what?"

"Not them, but their crowd. The zoning commission and the Village board. They've condemned his trailer, they say he has to be out within the month."

"They can't do that."

"Apparently they can."

Arbutus nodded, looking woebegone. "There's a letter," she said. Greyson gave them all a serious, gauging look, then went back to his coloring.

"But that's his home."

"Tell them that. They say it doesn't meet minimum codes, it's an eyesore, it's unsafe, there's no septic, no approved water, and bingo, it's condemned, they want it hauled out of there. At his expense, mind you, or they'll do it themselves and bill him for it. *That's* a joke. Emil doesn't have a pot to pee in and come next month he won't have a window to throw it out, either. Here, read it yourself. He gave me the letter they sent."

Arbutus slid an envelope across the table toward Madeline.

"Well, he's got to protest it, that's all," Madeline said, skimming over the letter. "He's got to stand up and say no."

"Lot of good that'll do, have you ever been to one of their meetings? It's all mumbo jumbo." Gladys scraped a chair away from the table and dropped onto it. Greyson slid his picture around in front of her for her to see and she nodded absently. "That's nice, dear."

"It's an intergalactic galaxy monster. Purple Man."

"Is it?"

"Maybe he could help, he can do anything."

Gladys traced the arc of Purple Man's arm upraised in battle. "Maybe, dear."

Greyson slid the picture back around to himself and began coloring again.

"There's got to be something Emil can do. He'll have to get a lawyer."

Gladys's laugh was dismal. "On his income? He doesn't get Social Security, he never paid in. He lives off those skins he trades, and now and then his sister down in Flint sends him some money. She went down there in sixty-seven and got a job in the Buick plant, she's got a retirement. But not Emil."

Madeline rubbed her face, trying to think. "Are they going after Mary Feather's place, too? Whose idea is this, anyway?"

"That zoning committee that got put together last year, I always thought they were up to no good. And no, they won't touch Mary. They wouldn't dare. She's off their map, anyway—Emil's in just close enough to town. And he's got the view, that's what they're really thinking of. Cal Tate's got a chunk of land up there on the ridge. If he can get Emil cleared off and make his own piece that much bigger, he can sell to city folks to put up their big fancy weekend houses. A playground, that's all this is to them. Doctors and lawyers from other cities, that's who'll buy up there. Cal's probably got a whole subdivision planned."

"But that's not right. He can't use his position to line his own pockets."

Gladys and Arbutus gave Madeline ironic looks.

"Edith Baxter is the head of it, meddling old busybody," Gladys said. "I never had any use for her, she always did think she was better than six other people put together and she's got the brain of a goat. Raised here just like us, too."

Arbutus nodded at this. "Yes. And Harvey."

"That's right. Harvey Wines. He's new in town, hauled along his big ideas, wants to change everything so it's just like where he came from, I wish he would've stayed there. And Cal, of course, he put the condos in a few years back, he's worth a couple of bucks. There's a few others, too. Well, Tracy York. Her mother and me were the best of friends, she must be turning in her grave to see what Tracy's done, putting her name to that letter."

"Now, Glad," Arbutus said in a placating tone. "Tracy can't help who she is any more than any of us can."

"So you say. I'm tired of making excuses for her. She ought to be ashamed."

Arbutus sighed.

Madeline was reading the signatures on the letter. "But these people must know Emil, they must've known him since they were children, some of them."

"Yes," Arbutus said, and Gladys nodded grimly. "That's right and it makes me sick to think of it. This town is changing beyond recognition. Makes you want to throw in the towel."

"No. No way. Emil's got to fight it. That's his *home.* He *owns* that land. I think he needs a lawyer." Madeline felt fierce. Mary and Albert, and now this.

"Madeline, I would be surprised if Emil can even read beyond cat and hat and dog. He doesn't have what you'd call a job, he never really has, aside from working in the lumber camps back when he was younger. He traps some, like I said. Hunts. Does the firewood. Gets a little from his sister and a few others around. He brought the letter to me to read, they sent it to him certified at the post office and it scared him. They didn't even have the courtesy to go talk to him in person, the cowards. You know what they want, don't you?"

Madeline shook her head.

"They want to put him in the home down in Crosscut, the one for the feebleminded, the one—" Gladys cut herself off, shook her head. "It's for his own good, they say. Ha. That home is fine for those who need it, but Emil doesn't belong there, he's a whole different story." She gave a bitter laugh. "Well, that's the whole problem. Emil's different, and they just can't stand that. They can't *let* anyone be different. Now you tell me, how is Emil going to stand up for himself against them?"

"I don't know." Madeline frowned at the letter again. "But that's his home. He'll have to fight back somehow. We'll have to help him."

GLADYS HEARD MADELINE'S DETERMINATION WHEN SHE SAID THEY'D have to help Emil. She watched her lean over Greyson's picture, giving it every bit of her attention. *Oh, Gladys,* she said to herself. *What a foolish old woman you are. What are you waiting for? There's nothing to fear in Madeline Stone. She is not Jackie. And even if she was, you'd have to tell her about Walter.*

She'd almost let the cat out of the bag this afternoon, talking about the powers that be wanting to send Emil down to Crosscut to the home for the feebleminded. The home where Walter was. That was no way to tell Madeline she had a great-uncle living.

But what *was* the way? She'd left it too long, and it would only get more awkward every minute. She should have done it right off, like Arbutus said. But she hadn't known Madeline then. She'd wanted to protect Walter in case Madeline turned out to be just like her mother. Careless of people's feelings. Cruel, when she wanted to be. Always a taker, never a giver. Walter was such a sweet soul, there was no way Gladys had intended to subject him to anything like *that* again.

Gladys sighed, caught in the web of her doubts and uncertainties and her own procrastination. Now it was going to be difficult, but she'd made this bed, so she would have to lie in it. *Show some spunk, old woman,* she told herself. *Stop dawdling.*

Fall

Automne

For Those Who Dream of Cranes

Elinor Benedict

STONINGTON, MICHIGAN

In late August near home, as the sun
drops its red coin into a slot of
black trees, sandhill cranes float
down into the new-mown hayfield
where they pace and strut, nearly
tall as deer, dark gray, ghostly,
making no sound as they feed, ready
to leave for winter. Last spring
you heard them coming, a muttering
beyond the lake like something small.
Closer, they grew monstrous, voices
loud as dry wood dropped in a box.
They passed over, bound for their hidden
nesting place. Tonight you watch them
again before they vanish tomorrow,
coming, going, sure as the sun.

All I know of white,

Saara Myrene Raappana

I learned from my mother when she dyed
my communion dress green.
Her thimbled, spit-wash thumb, her tisk.
White shows every spot, she said.
At home, Dad said, *Kissa died* and then
kept on—shrank from the weed eater's touch,
sang the hymns of put-off projects. August
was a skunk-hot lake. I held my breath,
let horse flies bite. Above the bone grin
of his clerical collar, Dad's face lobstered
in the heat, ran sweat rivers down
the La-Z-Boy wagonwheel plush.
Shoeboxed, dirt-brindled, that old white cat
went rot-humid all day in the parched clematis.
I shoveled the hole alone. I watched shadows
close on her like arms crossing to hide
a lost button, a patch of blemished skin.

Lake Superior Confesses to the Shore of Keweenaw Bay

Catie Rosemurgy

No one can make me give up my rowboats. Those tiny kisses
break into blue, red, and yellow flowers
when I hold them close. The balsam fir

and the northern white pine try to be straight
and judgmental. They crowd around and whisper.
Now and then one of them turns the color of rust.

They think they are all the needles
ever lost in haystacks. So serious, serious
about dirt and air, about being solid in between.

I'm a very slow-filling bowl, a massive shudder
over each grain of sand.
I'm wave after wave of proof

that you can grow accustomed to futile desires
as long as you occasionally get to hear
the sound of splitting wood.

I crash because I need
whatever grit the rocks can spare. I only bother
with seven-foot waves because I hope

to drag a common loon, a common goldeneye,
a blue-winged teal, any solid piece of sky,
down inside me to mark the place

where my heart would be. The couple on the beach
watches me. My utter lack of hands
must break their hearts. They must feel it.

Meanwhile, I'm lying. Shipwrecks
I've hired in secret
caress a hundred feet of me at a time.

An ore boat has been touching me
in the same place for eighteen years. Of course I reach out,
but not because I've hated myself

ever since I misplaced the sun. Not because I want
to steal a molecule of daylight, tuck the truly
rare pearl inside me, feel it

gradually sink through me,
until it discovers where I end.
I wouldn't mind systematically tearing the earth apart,

searching through a blue sky for the crucial atom,
and then watching a summer day collapse.
But I take and take what I can get.

Lopsided

Barbara Henning

I cut Patti's hair for her first school picture, lopsided. Our mother had just died. Forty-nine years later we sit on the hill blowing a flute a stick a sax When a mother dies, the young children adapt, their personalities taking various forms based on particular gaps. Five thousand orphaned children scavenge the streets in Baghdad alone. On Patti's porch in Marquette, we watch women in white shorts play tennis while Lake Superior winds clank the chimes. Without a house or food to survive. Through the little cluster of forest we walk down hill to the most magnificent blue. The dog races in a circle in and out of the icy water. My cell phone bangs. Magnifies the wetness. Five thousand orphaned children scavenge. A friend's eating a veggie burger right at that moment at B-line in Tucson with my recommendation. And he likes it. And then the connection dies. Why am I here, I think, when I could be there? Because if I were there, I'd be thinking, why am I here when I could be there.

Seney

Charmi Keranen

It's slow going

waiting for the rock
to become a fish

the log
to become a grebe

the eagle's nest hovers
naked and known

but who in their right mind
would leave

the SUV to fight the deer flies

100,000 ticks per moose

~

We used a retractable razor blade
to scrape the inspection stickers

from each window carefully

safe for another year

yes, there was a forest fire

a virgin pine burn

then blue buckets of berries
all those following years

the town was skirted
like a woman

you're dying to surround

Hemingway said

"Big Two-Hearted

was more poetic"

Lake Superior

Lorine Niedecker

In every part of every living thing
is stuff that once was rock

In blood the minerals
of the rock

~

Iron the common element of earth
in rocks and freighters

Sault Sainte Marie—big boats
coal-black and iron-ore-red
topped with what white castlework

The waters working together
        internationally
Gulls playing both sides

~

Radisson:
"a laborinth of pleasure"

this world of the Lake

Long hair, long gun

Fingernails pulled out
by Mohawks

~

(The long
canoes)

"Birch Bark
  and white Seder
    for the ribs"

~

Through all this granite land
the sign of the cross

Beauty: impurities in the rock

~

And at the blue ice superior spot
priest-robed Marquette grazed
azoic rock, hornblende granite
basalt the common dark
in all the Earth

And his bones of such is coral
raised up out of his grave
were sunned and birch bark-floated
to the straits

Joliet

Entered the Mississippi
Found there the paddlebill catfish
come down from The Age of Fishes

At Hudson Bay he conversed in latin
with an Englishman

To Labrador and back to vanish
His funeral gratis—he'd played
Quebec's Cathedral organ
so many winters

Ruby of corundum
lapis lazuli
from changing limestone
glow-apricot red-brown
carnelian sard

Greek named
Exodus-antique
kicked up in America's
Northwest
you have been in my mind
between my toes
agate

Wild Pigeon

Did not man
    maimed by no
        stone-fall

mash the cobalt
    and carnelian
        of that bird

~

Schoolcraft left the Soo—canoes
US pennants, masts, sails
chanting canoemen, barge
soldiers—for Minnesota

Their South Shore journey
        as if Life's—
The Chocolate River
        The Laughing Fish
and The River of the Dead

Passed peaks of volcanic thrust
Hornblende in massed granite
Wave-cut Cambrian rock
painted by soluble mineral oxides
wave-washed and the rains
did their work and a green
running as from copper

Sea-roaring caverns—
Chippewas threw deermeat
to the savage maws
"*Voyageurs* crossed themselves

tossed a twist of tobacco in"

~

Inland then
beside the great granite
gneiss and the schists

to the redolent pondy lakes'
lilies, flag and Indian reed
"through which we successfully
passed"

~

The smooth black stone
I picked up in true source park
the leaf beside it
once was stone

Why should we hurry
Home

~

I'm sorry to have missed
Sand Lake
My dear one tells me
we did not
We watched a gopher there

Dusk

Stellanova Osborn

A voluble lone duck disdains
The river's quiet mood.
I watched. I thought, a beaver swimming—
But it was just a block of wood.

Sudden Calm at Maywood Shores

Elinor Benedict

For seven days the wind has plowed the waves
in restless rows across the moving field
of Little Bay de Noc. While maples yield
their yellow leaves, my boundary red oak saves
its multitude of shamans' leather hands
until they twist and gesture in the wracking
air that turns the lake to earth, attacking
grass with wars of acorns across the lands
below the limbs.

These days of agitation
shake the universe beneath my hill
and make me fear this landscape never will
be calm again. And yet—my little nation
feels just now a sudden quilt of grace
uncanny in its drop from no known place.

The Next Thing that Begins

Amy McInnis

In the garden, knelt,
although the soil underneath
is damp, and one fold
bares a breeding place for mosquitoes
invisibly young.
Because of their bites
you stand, quickly rub your arms.
A strange motion, so unlike
each night, when in sleep
you stretch your arms
and rub one, the other,
slowly, up to the elbow,
the dry sound that skin
makes on skin
not enough to wake you.
In the morning, we have laughed,
wondered if you dream
of being a surgeon
but I've never left it
dreamt. Something
swarms in the night air,
bites tenderly, like snow.

Once on This Island excerpt

Gloria Whelan

AT FIRST WE WERE SURE THE WAR WOULD BE OVER IN THE SPRING AND we had only to get through one more winter. But soon the frightening news spread over the island that the British troops had marched into our capital city of Washington. There they entered the White House and finished the dinner President Madison and his wife, Dolly, had been forced to leave behind as they fled the city. The British then proceeded to burn down much of Washington. "After such news surely there can be no more meetings between you and Lieutenant Cunningham," I said to Angelique.

She was stubborn. "Lieutenant Cunningham would not burn a building down for anything."

We had no time for quarrels. Without Jacques we labored from sunup to sundown at work we were not used to. To split wood I had to wield a heavy axe. When the first snow fell Angelique was outside with the snow shovel. It was a great relief when the Sinclairs kindly offered to take the pigs so we would not have to sell them. Mr. Sinclair promised, "We will only keep them until your papa comes home. Then you shall have them back." In return for their kindness we made them agree to accept one of the pigs for their own.

They offered to care for Belle also. "Let them have her," Angelique pleaded. "That way we won't have to be bothered with milking and making butter."

"I couldn't let them take Belle." The only time of day when I could safely cry, without making Angelique sad as well, was when I was in the shed milking Belle. I would rest my head against her warm flank and cry as much as I liked. I knew from the melancholy look in Belle's large brown eyes that she understood how I felt. Besides, the Sinclairs would not rub her under the chin every day, which was her favorite treat.

"You have to lug gallons of water to Belle three times a day and you have to milk her twice a day. And Mary, think what it will be like to have to clean her shed each night."

"I won't give up Belle. You take care of the hens and I'll take care of Belle." Up until the snows came I could roll the wheelbarrow from the shed and pitch the manure over the fields. Once the snow covered the ground there was nothing to do but make a huge manure pile behind the shed as Jacques had always done. When I came home each afternoon from my task, Angelique was waiting for me with a tub of hot water and a bar of soap.

Only days before the lake froze over, a boat arrived with mail. At last we had a letter from Papa.

My dear children,

I have only time for a hasty note. Our defeat on Michilimackinac was a great disappointment. Had it only been otherwise I might now be with my beloved family. Last winter our forces here in Detroit were greatly weakened by an epidemic of cholera. Hundreds of our soldiers died, so many that there were not enough caskets in which to bury them. I thank God that I was spared, but it was necessary for me to remain here, for our forces protecting Fort Wayne are few in number.

You must get through one more winter: I am sure that with the help of Jacques, who can do a man's work, you will manage. When the war comes to an end you can be sure I will take the first means of reaching the island and my children, whom I think of and pray for each hour of the day.

Your loving Papa

We read the letter so many times it began to give way at the folds. What would Papa say if he knew Jacques had left us? I resolved that when Papa returned, the farm should be just as he wished.

Winter came on in a rush. The snow fell day after day so that it seemed there would be no more room for it. Each morning Angelique and I had to dig a path from our cabin to Belle's shed and the henhouse. The snow hung down in scallops from our roof. It piled up from the ground.

One morning we awoke to find that the snow from the roof and the snow from the ground had met and we could no longer see out of our windows. "We shall drown in the snow," Angelique groaned. "The cabin will be buried and we will not be found until spring."

We took up our shovels, and putting on all the clothes we had, we pushed open the door and went outside into the winter morning. Angelique could not leave the chickens without food and water. I had to milk and feed and water Belle, who was restless from her long imprisonment in the shed. She stamped her hooves and swished her tail so much I tied it up to keep it from tipping the milk pail.

Buildings made of stone are not very warm. With nothing to heat it but Belle's warmth, it was so cold in the shed that I had to break a layer of ice on Belle's water bowl. Angelique carried the eggs from the henhouse to the cabin inside her bodice so they would not freeze.

I made a frightening discovery that morning. Belle's hay was giving out. In his hurry with the harvest Jacques had left some of the hay uncut. Soon Belle would run out of food. No one on the island had hay to spare. The fort had bought or confiscated as much hay as they could find. It was only through Lieutenant Cunningham's efforts that our own small supply had not been taken.

I was horrified to hear Angelique say, "It would be better to kill Belle while she is fat than wait until she starves to death."

Desperate, I recalled something. "When Belle was out in the pasture I saw her chewing on twigs and branches like a deer," I told Angelique. "There are no leaves now but there are buds on the trees."

I set out into the woods on snowshoes carrying the saw and a basket. Once I was a little way from the farm, the world became perfectly still and white and so bright I became dizzy. The snowflakes fell on my eyelashes so that my lids became heavy and I could hardly see. My tracks on the path disappeared. I thought of Jacques. It was as though he were right there with me. He would be out in the winter snows, going from Indian camp to Indian camp for furs. He would travel long distances on solitary rivers edged with ice. At the end of his long journeys he would return to no warm cabin. I knew our winter was not so hard as his.

Belle ate the tree loppings I cut for her each day. Without the hay to feed on she gave very little milk, but the weather was so bad we were not able to get down to the village to sell what little she gave. Angelique and I ate eggs and cabbage and kale and carrots. We were nearly out of flour so bread was a Sunday treat. A little venison remained from Jacques' deer and the Wests had given us maple syrup, which we sometimes had on our porridge.

On the first day the weather cleared we went down into the village to trade eggs for flour, only to find there was no flour to be had. The winter was as hard for everyone as it was for us. It was harder for those who had no farm produce to fall back on as we did.

When next we went into the village we brought a basket of turnips and cabbage and carrots to leave with Pere Mercier to give out to those who were in need. "We suffer here in the village," he said, "but I hear it is even worse at the fort. There were no boats to supply them this fall and there is nothing in the village to buy. The soldiers have had to kill their horses for something to eat." I thought of the handsome horse the commander rode and wondered how he could make a dinner of it.

That afternoon we had a visit from Lieutenant Cunningham. He came through the door shaking the snow from his coat and stamping his boots. It was the first time Angelique had seen him since the battle. He took her hand and held it for a long while. And she let him. Urging him to warm himself at the fire, she said, "Let me make you some blackberry tea. There are corn cakes left from our dinner and honey."

The lieutenant eagerly sat down to feast on the food Angelique put before him. He appeared so hungry I said nothing about his eating the last of our honey. Angelique sat across from him looking as though there was no finer sight in the world than that of a man licking honey from his fingers. If it had been me, she would have scolded me for my bad manners.

He must have guessed what I was thinking for he said, "I apologize for my behavior. You will forgive me when you learn there is little to eat at the fort."

I couldn't help asking, "Is it true you are eating up all your horses?"

"The horses were gone long ago. It is for that reason that I am here. There are unscrupulous men on the island who come by night to steal the animals from the farms. They then sell them to the quartermaster at the fort for high prices. We are so desperate for food no questions are asked as to how the animals are come by. Today in the fort I overheard two of these scheming men ask how much a cow would bring. Knowing you have one I wanted to warn you. I would offer to protect your animal myself but we are not allowed out of the fort at night. I am sure Colonel McDouall would never stand for such behavior, but no one has the courage to tell him of the thefts, nor the proof to set before him."

I was horrified. "How could they get Belle to the fort?"

"I'm afraid they would shoot her and butcher her. Knapsacks on the backs of two strong men would carry a good deal of meat. Now I must get back." We thanked him and Angelique urged him to come again for a meal.

"What can we do?" Angelique asked after he left. "Perhaps we could ask Mr. Sinclair's help."

"He must guard his own animals. We'll have to think of something else." I hurried out to the shed to reassure myself that Belle was all right. As I rubbed her under the chin an idea came to me. The door into the stone shed was made of a thick slab of wood. It was fastened by sliding a heavy bar across the door. I put Belle's halter on and led her outside. At first she would not walk through the snow, but with gentle urging she stepped along and seemed almost frisky at being out of doors. Her warm breath made little clouds of fog and every so often she would stop to nip playfully at a snow bank. At last we were at the door of the cabin. I opened it and as I began to pull her inside Angelique screamed.

"Mary! What are you thinking of? We cannot have a cow in the house! You must be out of your mind." She picked up a broom and began to shoo Belle away.

"Put down the broom. It is only for one night. We can't let those evil men murder her. I'd rather they shot me." Quickly I told Angelique my plan.

At first she refused to go along with it. "If they catch us they will murder us."

I pleaded and pleaded, all the while drawing Belle farther into the cabin until I could close the door behind her. The moment I let her loose she began to chew a bunch of dried herbs that hung from one of the cabin beams.

"Stop it, Belle." Angelique swung the broom. "That's my rosemary." She looked about the cabin for a place to put Belle, but there was no place suitable for a very large cow. Belle, however, looked quite happy in her new home, which was much warmer than her stone shed.

We dragged her to a corner of the cabin and tied her securely. Hastily we carried away everything within her reach. When we were done Angelique sank down on a chair.

"If you don't want to do it," I said, "I'll do it myself."

"Mary, what have we come to? A cow in the house and you wanting to risk your life? I would never forgive myself if something happened to you."

In spite of her protests, when the time came, Angelique was ready. I think she was willing to go along with my plan just to be sure that Belle would not be spending more nights in our cabin. As the last bit of daylight disappeared we hurried into the henhouse. By opening the door a crack we could easily see the cow shed, which was just across the path.

The hens were used to Angelique's daily visits. After some fluttering and squawking they returned to their roosts and settled down again for the night. As we huddled together to keep warm we could not tell whether our shivering was from cold or fright. We didn't dare whisper for fear of being heard so we had to pass the time in silence.

I had no idea of how long we had been there when we heard muffled voices. Peering out of the crack in the door we saw two men with a lantern approaching the cow shed. We clutched one another and the movement stirred up one of the hens, who squawked. The men stopped in their tracks and looked toward the henhouse. When after a minute the men heard nothing more, they must have decided it was their approach that had disturbed the hen.

One of the men held up the lantern while the other pulled the bar from its slot and opened the door. Together they slipped into the shed. As Angelique and I dashed toward the shed I could hear one of the men exclaim, "The cow is gone!" Quickly I slid the bar back into its slot, sealing the door. We held our breath. For a moment there was silence. Then there were sounds of pushing and heaving against the door. Then silence again. More heaving and striking of the door with heavy boots. There were cries of, "Let us out! We're gentle folk that don't mean harm to a living soul! We wouldn't touch a hair on your head."

A moment later we heard terrible shouts. "Let us out or we'll crush every bone in your body! We'll boil you in oil! We'll tear you apart!"

When we were sure that there was no way the two men could break through the stone shed or the heavy wooden door. Angelique and I returned to the house, where Belle had made herself too much at home.

"It will be very cold out there," Angelique said.

"It cannot be too cold for those evil men," I replied. "Anyhow it will only be until morning."

We were too agitated to sleep so we barred our door and waited for daylight. When it came I wrapped myself up, and putting on Angelique's boots, which were in better condition than mine, I set out for the fort.

The sentry, a soldier I did not recall seeing before, looked both cold and sleepy. "I wish to see Colonel McDouall," I said in my haughtiest manner.

"Our commander has better things to do than come running out to see you." In a brusque voice he added, "Get along now."

"Please tell the commander I have locked up two criminals who have been doing business with his fort."

At this the sentry's eyebrows flew up and his mouth hung open. "What's that?"

I repeated my message, pleased at his reaction. He gave me a long unbelieving look but finally he called to a soldier inside the fort and repeated my request. This soldier looked equally skeptical but went off toward the commander's quarters. As we waited, the sentry kept his eye on me as if I were a snake that might strike at him the moment he turned his back.

My courage began to fail me. What if the commander didn't believe me? And even if he did, he might not care. He might even be angry that the fort would not have a cow to eat.

Colonel McDouall was a smallish man for a commander. His uniform was none too neat, his jacket was unbuttoned and his hat sat on one side of his head. His manner was stern. "Speak up, miss. What do you want?" he asked.

"There are two men who have been stealing farm animals and selling them to your quartermaster. Last night they came to steal our cow but we locked them in the cow shed. They are still there."

"What! You accuse my quartermaster of buying stolen property! I don't believe a word of it." He straightened his hat and began to button his jacket.

"Then you had better come and see for yourself," I said.

"Very well. I shall do just that." He turned to a captain who stood beside him. "Captain Thompson, you will accompany me. All right, young lady, lead on. But if this is some sort of mischief, I'll have you over my knee."

I led the way and the commander and the captain followed along, the commander grumbling at every turn. "What thanks is this," he said," after years to my country to be posted in this godforsaken place where instead of marshaling great battles I must attend to the stealing of cows."

When we reached the cabin Angelique came running out to meet us. The men were still beating on the door and crying out. The commander now looked less skeptical. "Is the cow in there with them?" he asked.

"No, sir," I said. "It is in the house."

"The house! Is that customary?"

Angelique was mortified. "No, indeed, sir. It was only for last night."

At the sound of the commander's voice the men had become quiet. The captain was about to unbolt the door when I stopped him. I called out to the two prisoners, "If you want to get out you must answer my question."

There was silence for a moment and then through chattering teeth a voice said, "Ask your question but be quick about it. We are freezing to death."

"You must tell the truth or we won't open the door. You can just stay there. Who were you going to sell the cow to?" I demanded.

"Brown, the quartermaster, of course. Who else?"

At this the commander himself marched up to the door and pushed back the bolt. As the men rushed out they found the captain and the commander both with muskets at the ready. In a stern voice the commander asked if we had a length of rope handy. At first we thought the men were to be hanged before our eyes but the rope was only wanted to truss them. Angelique fetched it from the cabin.

"I am greatly indebted to you young ladies," the commander said. "You have accomplished what my whole regiment was evidently unable to manage. I myself will handle the quartermaster. Now, before we leave I would just like a peek at the cow."

"Oh, sir," Angelique protested. "It is not tidy in the cabin just now."

"Yes, yes. I can understand how that could be. Well, if it is not convenient at the moment, perhaps you will let me call another time.

We both eagerly assured him that he would be most welcome. They were scarcely out of sight when Angelique hurried into the cabin to get Belle out of the house. Belle did not want to leave the warmth of the fireside and it took the two of us all of a half hour of pushing and pulling to return Belle to her shed.

That afternoon a soldier arrived from the fort. "The commander sends his compliments, ladies," he said. He handed us a good-sized packet, saluted, and left us. Eagerly we untied the string. Inside was a large packet of sugar. And not just ordinary sugar but pure white sugar such as I had never seen and Angelique only just recollected from living in Detroit. That night we had a pinch of sugar on everything, even the turnips.

My Upper Peninsula

Mary Biddinger

We were all suffering from a kind of incandescence.
Would rather fling all the freshly baked rolls
down the stairs than face the accuser.
I wondered if I was moldering. My mother
didn't even recognize the ravioli that I edged
with my spinner. I'd filled it with scraps of cloth
anyway. All the girls in my class had hair like Journey
and mouths the slashes of red a wolf leaves behind.
Save me, oh god of direct and swift evacuations.
Some day I would be lecturing a class of students
or getting tangled in the horizontal blinds
in the middle of an emphatic statement. Nobody
there to wield the tin snips. My pack of girls only
a trigger on a night at the county fair, the reek
of funnel cakes scissoring long-sleeve blouses
into the ratty tanks we'd stash in our purses for later.
There was something dangerous under our skin.
I ask my class again to mark up this draft of the globe.
They've never been drunk in Nice and vomiting across
multiple electrified rails. In a dream, the double that is more
authentic than the original walks down a street with me.

We stagger in unison. We've both had to begin the dessert
again from scratch, not being able to resist a swift punch
to the center of the springform pan. We'd both rather
surrender all of the wooden coins before anyone asks.
Is there anything more exhilarating than a good wait
in damp clothing, or the moment you open your mouth
and realize you know the language after all, you can call
off the dogs or invent the numbers for the pay phone,
and the man who shows you to your room won't leave out
a tour of the aluminum shower down the hall.
He whispers you can both fit in there. He'll write down
every stranger who leaves a card at the front desk.

Sweet Grass Spirit

Clara Corbett

Sometimes the sweet grass   is not to be found   nor picked

But just to be smelled   in the breeze   where it stands

The sweet fragrance of our ancestors   permeates this land

We know who we are   how many times   our feet

walked the paths   that they made

How many lost   how many found

reunited again   in the sweet grass.

You Aren't Sure & I May Not

Emily Van Kley

You aren't sure & I may not
be made of the right kind
of mortar, but how else
to answer the ice
axe of memory, the urge—
part mechanism part
scarsong—which says return
is instinct & instinct
is absolution & absolution
is all we know of quench.
We go. All praise to
your iron smile & hips
solemn as a staircase,
your anointed fingers,
the complicity of denim
& windows white
with hometown frost.
Praise the place where
I could not have met you.
Praise the tiny city down
twelve miles of ice-rutted

highway, all I knew of
cosmopolitan, its several
thousand inhabitants, stone
courthouse scrimmed
in copper, square-jawed
houses on streets named
Magnetic, everything
built when the mines
seemed eternal &
earth was another word
for come right in. Before
the blast that siphoned
an underground river
into the Barnes-Hecker,
filling the throats
of 51, ripping
at the boots of the sole
survivor who terrored up
800 feet of ladder to
the one bright scratch
of sky. Before the new
mines, sliced open like boils,
those too containers for
ache. & when we arrive
if the people are insular,
if they are hard as the jeweled
snout of a Northern Pike, if winter
is a shut vault with the lock
cycling & we never
learn to hunt deer or any
more minor creature—
does it mean we wouldn't

flourish? Couldn't we find
a house with cut-glass
windows & let it go to ruin,
tear up the lawn for garden,
watch our collard greens palm
the sun? At night, wouldn't
I close my mouth around
your knuckles, taste broccoli
flowers & the sand which drifts
everything, the frozefish tang
of Superior mawing the harbor
five blocks down? October
fold us into the creed-cold
winter, snowstorms
like the shed blood of nations.
Sundays spend in the pews
with the fierce & lowly.
Nights slake & burn.

Vital Signs

Emily Van Kley

Of many hometowns, this is the bleakest: main street
gap-toothed with abandoned buildings, three restaurants,
two gas stations, hockey rink, bakery, lakeside foodstore
where there may or may not be potatoes

at the end of a dust-scarved shelf. There are those of us
who drink ourselves to death and those who take a lighter hand,
but even teenagers know better

than to believe in immortality. The evidence is everywhere:
field by the church named for Johnny Mazes whose snow machine
defected in the close woods, whose helmet split

down the middle where there was no seam. Anne Fear
whose young body pin-balled the cab of a flipped van
and who woke with a cheesecloth memory. Softball
tournament named for the beautiful Ahonen twin

whose twenty-year-old heart fell away in the shower, halved shell
on the shore of an inland sea. For the misanthrope, there are

Superior's silt-blasted wrecks, water so cold even wood won't rot
decently. Flooded mine buildings thrusting their acidy tongues down

and down. Too many deer make for a starving winter,
which means you clutching your rifle in thin fall snow
are an instrument of some vital love.

North Country

Roxane Gay

I HAVE MOVED TO THE EDGE OF THE WORLD FOR TWO YEARS. IF I AM not careful, I will fall. After my first department meeting, my new colleagues encourage me to join them on a scenic cruise to meet more locals. The *Peninsula Star* will travel through the Portage Canal, up to Copper Harbor and then out onto Lake Superior. I am handed a glossy brochure with bright pictures of blue skies and calm lake waters. "You'll be able to enjoy the foliage," they tell me, shining with enthusiasm for the Upper Peninsula. "Do you know how to swim?" they ask.

I arm myself with a flask, a warm coat, and a book. At the dock, there's a long line of ruddy Michiganders chatting amiably about when they expect the first snow to fall. It is August. I have moved to the Upper Peninsula to assume a postdoc at the Michigan Institute of Technology. My colleagues, all civil engineers, wave to me. "You came," they shout. They've already started drinking. I take a nip from my flask. "You're going to love this cruise," they say. "Are you single?" they ask.

We sit in a cramped booth drinking Rolling Rocks. Every few minutes one of my colleagues offers an interesting piece of Upper Peninsula trivia such as the high incidence of waterfalls in the area or the three hundred inches of snow the place receives annually. I take a long, hard swallow from my flask. I am flanked by a balding, overweight tunnel expert on my right and a dark-skinned hydrologist from India on my left. The hydrologist is lean and quiet and his knee presses uncomfortably against mine. He tells me he has a wife back in Chennai but that in Michigan, he's leaving his options open. I am the only woman in the department and as such, I am a double novelty. My new colleagues continue to buy me drinks and I continue to accept them until my ears are ringing and I can feel a flush in my cheeks, sweat dripping down my back. "I need some fresh air," I mumble, excusing myself. I make my way, slowly, to the upper deck, ignoring the stares and lulls in conversation.

Outside, the air is crisp and thin, the upper deck sparsely populated. Near the bow, a young couple makes out enthusiastically, loudly. A few feet away from them a group of teenagers stand in a huddle, snickering. I sit on a red plastic bench and hold my head in my hands. My flask sits comfortably and comfortingly against my rib cage.

"I saw you downstairs," a man with a deep voice says.

The sun is setting, casting that strange quality of light rendering everything white, nearly invisible. I squint and look up slowly at a tall man with shaggy hair hanging over his ears. I nod.

"Are you from Detroit?

I have been asked this question twenty-three times since moving to the area. In a month, I will stop counting, having reached a four-digit number. Shortly after that, I will begin telling people I have recently arrived from Africa. They will nod and exhale excitedly and ask about my tribe. I don't know that in this moment, so there is little to comfort me. I shake my head.

"Do you talk?"

"I do," I say. "Are you from Detroit?

He smiles, slow and lazy. He's handsome in his own way—his skin is tan and weathered and his eyes are almost as blue as the lake we're cruising on. He sits down. I stare at his fingers, the largest fingers I've ever seen. The sweaty beer bottle in his hand looks miniature. "So where are you from?"

I shove my hands in my pocket and slide away from him. "Nebraska."

"I've never met anyone from Nebraska," he says.

I say, "I get that a lot."

The boat is now out of the Portage Canal and we're so far out on the lake, I can't see land. I feel small. The world feels too big.

"I better get back to my colleagues," I say, standing up. As I walk away, he shouts, "My name is Magnus." I throw a hand in the air but I don't look back.

IN MY LAB, THINGS MAKE SENSE. AS A STRUCTURAL ENGINEER, I DESIGN concrete mixes, experiment with new aggregates like fly ash and other energy byproducts, artificial particulates, kinds of water that might make concrete not just stronger but unbreakable, permanent, perfect. I teach a section of Design of Concrete Structures and a section of Structural Dynamics. I have no female students in either class. The boys stare at me, and after class, they linger in the hallway just outside the classroom. They try to flirt. I remind them I will assess their final grades. They make inappropriate comments about extra credit.

At night, I sit in my apartment and watch TV and search for faculty positions and other career opportunities closer to the center of the world. There's a pizza restaurant across the street and above the restaurant, an apartment filled with loud white girls who play rap loudly into the middle of the night and have fights with their boyfriends who play basketball for the university. One of the girls has had an abortion and another isn't speaking to her father and the third roommate has athletic sex with her boyfriend even when the other two are awake; she has a child but the child lives with her father. I do not want to know any of these things.

Several unopened boxes are sitting in my new apartment. To unpack those boxes means I will stay. To stay means I will be trapped in this desolate place for two years, alone. I rented my new home—a former dry-cleaning business converted into an apartment—over the phone. There are no windows, save for the one in the front door. The apartment, I thought, as I walked from room to room when I moved in, was like a jail cell. I had been sentenced. My new landlady, an octogenarian Italian who ran the dry cleaner's for more than thirty years, gasped when she met me. "You didn't sound like a colored girl on the phone," she said. I said, "I get that a lot."

The produce is always rotten at the local grocery store—we're too far north to receive timely food deliveries. I stand before a display of tomatoes, limp, covered in wrinkled skin, some dotted soft white craters ringed by some kind of black mold. I consider the cost to my dignity if I move in with my parents, until I feel a heavy hand on my shoulder. When I spin around, struggling to maintain my balance, I recognize Magnus. I grab his wrist between two fingers and step away. "Do you always touch strangers?"

"We're not strangers."

I make quick work of selecting the least decomposed tomatoes and move on to the lettuce. Magnus follows. I say, "We have different understandings of the word *stranger*. You don't even know my name."

"I like the way you talk," he says.

"What is that supposed to mean?"

Magnus reddens. "Exactly what I said. Unless we have different understandings of the words *I*, *like*, *the*, *way*, *you*, and *talk*."

I bite the inside of my cheek to keep from smiling.

"Can I buy you a drink?"

I look at the pathetic tomatoes in my basket and maybe it's the overwhelming brightness of the fluorescent lighting or the Easy Listening being piped through the store speakers, but I nod before I can say no. I say, "My name is Kate." Magnus says, "Meet me at the Thirsty Fish, Kate." On the drive there, I stare at my reflection in the rearview mirror and smooth my eyebrows. At the bar, Magnus entertains me with the silly things girls like to take seriously. He buys me lots of drinks and I drink them. He flatters me with words about my pretty eyes. He says he can tell I'm smart. I haven't had sex in more than two months. I haven't had a real conversation with anyone in more than two months. I'm not at my best.

In the parking lot, I stand next to my car, holding on to the door, trying to steady myself. Magnus says, "I can't let you drive home like this." I mutter something about the altitude affecting my tolerance. He says, "We're not in the mountains." He stands so close. The warmth from his chest fills the short distance between us. Magnus takes my keys and as I reach for them, I fall into him. He lifts my chin with one of his massive fingers and I say, “Fuck.” I kiss him, softly. Our lips barely move but we don’t pull apart. His hand is solid in the small of my back as he presses me against my car.

When I wake up, my mouth is thick and sour. I groan and sit up, and hit my head against something unfamiliar. I wince. Everything in my head feels loose, lost.

“Be careful. It’s a tight fit in here.”

I rub my eyes, trying to swallow the panic bubbling at the base of my throat. I clutch at my chest.

“Relax. I didn’t know where you lived, so I brought you back to my place.”

I take a deep breath, look around. I’m sitting on a narrow bed. I see Magnus through a narrow doorway standing near a two-burner stove. My feet are bare. A cat jumps into my lap. I scream.

Magnus lives in a trailer, and not one of those fancy doublewides on a foundation with a well-kept garden in front, but rather, an old, rusty trailer that can be attached to a truck and driven away. It is the kind of trailer you see in sad, forgotten places that have surrendered to rust and overgrown weeds and cars on cinder blocks and sagging laundry lines. The trailer, on the outside, is in a fair amount of disrepair, but the inside is immaculate. Everything has its proper place.

“You should eat something,” he says.

I extricate myself from the cat and walk into the galley area. Magnus invites me to sit at the table and he sets a plate of dry scrambled eggs and a mug of coffee in front of me. My stomach rolls wildly. I wrap my hands around the coffee mug and inhale deeply. I try to make sense of the trajectory between rotten tomatoes and this trailer. Magnus slides onto the bench across from me. He explains that he lives in this trailer because it’s free. It’s free because his trailer sits on the corner of a parcel of land his sister Mira and her husband, Peter, farm. The farm is twenty minutes outside of town. There’s no cell phone reception. I can’t check my e-mail, he tells me, as I wave my phone in different directions, desperate for a signal. I ask him why he lives this way. He says he has a room in his sister’s house he rarely uses. He likes his privacy.

"You took my shoes off."

Magnus nods. "You have nice feet."

"Can you take me to my car?"

Magnus sighs, quickly drains the rest of his coffee in the small sink. He is a patient man. I like that too.

On the drive back to town I sit as far away from Magnus as possible. I try to re-create the events that happened between standing in the parking lot and waking up in a trailer with a cat in my lap. I refuse to ask Magnus to fill in the blanks. At my car, he grips the steering wheel tightly. I thank him for the ride and he hands me my keys. He says, "I'd love your phone number."

I force myself to smile. I say, "Thank you for not letting me drive last night." I say, "I don't normally drink much, but I just moved here." He says, "Yes, the altitude," and waits until I drive away. My father would appreciate the gesture. I remember the pressure of his lips against mine, their texture and the smell of his bed sheets. I am in trouble.

In my lab, things make sense. The first snow falls in late September. It will continue to fall until May. I tell my mother I may not survive. I tell her this so many times, she starts to worry. I test cement fitness. I fill molds with cylinders of concrete. I experiment with saltwater and bottled water and lake water and tap water. I cure and condition specimens. I take detailed notes. I write an article. I turn down three dates with three separate colleagues. The hydrologist from Chennai reaffirms the openness of his options in the United States. I reaffirm my disinterest in his options. I administer an exam that compels my students to call me Battle-Ax. I attend a campus social for single faculty. There are seven women in attendance and more than thirty men. The hydrologist is there too. He doesn't wear a wedding ring. I am asked thirty-four times if I am from Detroit, a new record for a single day. I try to remember where Magnus lives and all I recall is a blurry memory of being drunk, burying my face into his arm as we drove, and him, singing along to the Counting Crows. I love the Counting Crows.

THERE ONCE WAS A MAN. THERE IS ALWAYS SOME MAN. WE WERE together for six years. He was an engineer too. Some people called him my dissertation adviser. When we got involved, he told me he would teach me things and mold me into a great scholar. He said I was the brightest girl he had ever known. Then he contradicted himself. He said we would marry and thought I believed him. A couple of years passed and he said we would marry when he was promoted to full professor and then it was when I finished my degree. I got pregnant and he said we would marry when the baby was born. The baby was stillborn and he said we would marry when I recovered from the loss. I told him I was as recovered as I was ever going to be. He had no more excuses and I no longer cared to marry him. I spent most of my nights awake while he slept soundly, remembering what it felt like to rub my swollen belly and feel my baby kicking. He told me I was cold and distant. He told me I had no reason to mourn a child that never lived. He amused himself with a new lab assistant who consistently wore insensible shoes and short skirts even though we spent our days working with sand and cement and other dirty things. I found them fucking, the lab assistant bent over a stack of concrete bricks squealing like a debutante porn star, the man thrusting vigorously, literally fucking the lab assistant right out of her high heels, his fat face red and shiny. He gasped in short, repulsive bursts. The scene was so common, I couldn't even get angry. I had long stopped feeling anything where he was concerned. I returned to my office, accepted the postdoc position, and never looked back. I would have named our daughter Emma. She would have been beautiful despite her father. She would have been four months old when I left.

SNOW HAS BEEN FALLING INCESSANTLY. THE LOCALS ARE OVERJOYED. Every night, I hear the high-pitched whine of snowmobiles speeding past my apartment. There are things I will need to survive the winter—salt, a shovel, a new toilet seat, rope—so I brave the weather and go to the hardware store. I am wearing boots laced high around my calves, a coat, gloves, hat and scarf, thermal underwear. I never remove these items unless I am home. It takes too much effort. I wonder how these people manage to reproduce. I see Magnus standing over a display of chainsaws. He is more handsome than I remember. I turn to walk away but then I don't. I stand still and hope he notices me. I realize that dressed as I am, my own family wouldn't recognize me. I tap his shoulder. I say, "What do you plan on massacring?"

He looks up slowly, shrugs. "Just looking," he says.

"For a victim?"

"Aren't you feeling neighborly?"

"I thought I would say hello."

Magnus nods again. "You've said hello."

I swallow, hard. My irritation tastes bitter. I quickly tell him my phone number and go to find a stronger kind of rope. As I pull away, I notice Magnus watching me from inside the store. I smile.

In my lab things make sense. I teach my students how to make perfect concrete cylinders, how to perform compression tests. They crush their perfect cylinders and roar with delight each time the concrete shatters and the air is filled with a fine dust. There's a lot to love about breaking things.

Everyone I meet dispenses a bit of wisdom on how to survive the "difficult" winters—embrace the outdoors, drinking, travel, drinking, sun lamps, drinking, sex, drinking. The hydrologist offers to prepare spicy curries to keep me warm, offers to give me a taste of his very special curry. I decline, tell him I have a delicate constitution. Nils, my department chair, stops by my office. He says, "How are you holding up?" I assure him all is well. He says, "The first year is always the hardest." He says, "You might want to take a trip to Detroit to see your family." I thank him for the support.

I am walking around the lab, watching students work, when Magnus calls. I excuse myself and take the call in the hallway, ignoring the students milling about, with their aimless expressions.

My heart beats loudly. I can hardly hear Magnus. I say, "You didn't need to take so long to call me."

"Is this a lecture?"

"Would you like it to be?"

"Can I make you dinner?"

I ignore my natural impulse to say no. He invites me back to his trailer, where he prepares steak and green beans and baked potatoes. We drink beer. We talk, or rather, I talk, filling his trailer with all the words I've kept to myself since moving to the North Country, longer. I complain about the weather. At some point, he holds his hand open and I slide my hand in his. He traces my knuckles with his thumb. He is plainspoken and honest. His voice is strong and clear. He has a kind smile and a kind touch. He talks about his job as a logger and his band—he plays guitar. When we finally stop talking he says, "I like you," and then he stands and pulls me to my feet. A man has never told me he likes me. Like is more interesting than love. I stand on his boots and wrap my arms around him. He is thick and solid. When we kiss, he is gentle, too gentle. I say, "You don't have to be soft with me," and he grunts. He clasps my neck with one of his giant hands, and kisses me harder, his lips forcing mine open. The flat softness of his tongue thrills me. He brushes his lips across my chin. He sinks his teeth into my neck and I grab his shirt between my fists. I try to remain standing. I say, "My neck is the secret password." He bites my neck harder and I forget about everything and all the noise in my head quiets.

I slip out of my shirt and step out of my jeans and Magnus lifts me up and sits me on the edge of his kitchen table. He places his large hands between my thighs and pulls them apart. I quickly unbuckle his belt, reach for him and he grabs my wrist. He says, "You don't get to be the boss of everything." I say a silent prayer. I close my eyes and he drags his hand from my chin, down the center of my chest, over the flat of my stomach. He kisses my shoulders, my breasts, my knees. He makes me tremble and whimper. "You don't have to be soft with me," I repeat. Magnus kisses the insides of my ankles and then my lips, his tongue rough and heavy against mine. I try to pull him into me by wrapping my legs around his waist. He laughs, low and deep. He says, "Say you want this." I bite my lower lip. I measure my pride against my desire. When he fucks me, he is slow, deliberate, rough in a terribly controlled way. I bury my face in his shoulder. When he asks why I'm crying, I say nothing. For a little while, he fills all the emptiness.

In the morning, I want to leave quickly even though I can still feel Magnus in my skin. As I sit on the edge of the bed and pull my pants on, he says, "I want to see you again." I say yes but explain we have to keep things casual, that we can't become a *thing*. He traces my naked spine with his fingers and I shiver. He says, "We're already a thing." I stand, shaking my head angrily. "That's not even possible." He says, "Sometimes, when I'm miles deep in the woods, looking for a new cutting site, it feels like I'm the first man who has ever been there. I look up and the trees are so thick I can hardly see the sky. I get so scared, but the world somehow makes sense there. Being with you feels like that." I shake my head again, my fingers trembling as I finish getting dressed. I feel nauseated and dizzy. I say, "I'm allergic to cats." I say, "You shouldn't talk like that." I recite his words over and over for the rest of the day, week, month.

Several weeks later, I'm at Magnus's trailer. We've seen each other almost every night, at his place, where he cooks and we talk and we have sex. We're lying naked in his narrow bed. I say, "If this continues much longer, we're going to have to sleep at my place. I have a real bed and actual rooms with doors." He smiles and nods. He says, "Whatever you want." After Magnus falls asleep, I stare up at the low ceiling, then out the small window at the clear winter sky. I wonder what he would think of Emma, if he could love her. I try to swallow the emptiness. I hold my stomach as hot tears slide down my face and trickle along my neck. Just as I'm falling asleep, his alarm goes off. Magnus sits up, rubbing his eyes. Even in the darkness I can see his hair standing on end. He says, "I want to show you something." We dress but he tells me I can leave my coat. Instead, he hands me a quilt. Outside, a fresh blanket of snow has fallen. The moon is still high. Everything is perfect and silent and still. The air hurts but feels clean. He cuts a trail to the barn and I follow in his footsteps. As Magnus walks, he stares up into the sky. I tell myself, "I feel nothing." It is a lie. When I am with him, I feel everything. Inside the barn, I shiver and dance from foot to foot trying to stay warm. He says, "We have to milk the cows." He nods to a small campstool next to a very large cow. I say, "There is absolutely no way." Magnus leads me to the stool and forces me onto it. He hunches down behind me, and he pats the cow on her side. He hasn't shaved yet, so the stubble from his beard tickles me. He kisses my neck softly. He places his hands over mine, and I learn how to milk a cow. Nothing makes sense here.

HUNTING SEASON STARTS. MAGNUS SHOWS ME HIS RIFLE, LONG, POLished, powerful. He refers to his rifle as a "she" and a "her." I tell him my father hunts and he gets excited. He says, "Maybe someday your father and I can hunt together." I explain that my father hunts pheasant, and by hunt, I mean he rides around with his friends on a four-wheeler but doesn't really kill much of anything and often gets injured in embarrassing accidents. I say, "You and he hunt differently." He says, "I still want to meet your father." "I only introduce serious boyfriends to my family," I say. Magnus holds my chin between two fingers and looks at me hard. It makes me shiver. This is the first time I've seen real anger from him. I wonder how far I can push. He says, "You won't see me for a few days, but I'm going to kill a buck for you." Five days later, Magnus shows up at my apartment still wearing his camouflage and Carhartt overalls. His beard is long and unkempt. He smells rank. He is dirty. I only recognize his eyes. Magnus steps inside and pulls me into a muscular hug that makes me feel like he is rearranging my insides. I inhale deeply. I am surprised by the sharp twinge between my thighs. When he kisses me, he is possessive, controlling, salty. He moans into my mouth and turns me around, pinning my arms over my head. He fucks me against the front door. I smile. Afterward, we both sink to the floor. He says, "The buck is in the car." He says, "I missed you." I want to say something, the right thing, the kind thing. I slap his thigh. I push. I say, "Please take a shower." I don't shower though, not for hours.

I VISIT MY PARENTS IN FLORIDA FOR THANKSGIVING AND MY MOTHER asks why I don't call as often. I explain how work has gotten busy. I explain how snow has fallen every single day for more than a month and how everyone thinks I'm from Detroit. My mother says I look thin. She says I'm too quiet. We don't talk about the dead child or the father of the dead child. There is "this life" and "that life." We pretend "that life" never happened. It is a mercy. Magnus calls every morning before he leaves for work and every night before he falls asleep. One afternoon he calls and my mother answers my phone. I hear her laughing as she says, "What an unusual name." When she hands me my phone, she asks, "Who is this Magnus? Such a nice young man." I push. I say he's no one important. I say it a little too loudly. When I put my phone to my ear, I can only hear a dial tone. Magnus doesn't call for the rest of my trip. We won't speak until the end of January.

IN MY LAB THINGS MAKE SENSE BUT THEY DON'T. I CAN'T CONCENTRATE. I want to call Magnus but my repeated bad behavior overwhelms me. The weather has grown colder, sharper. The world grows and I shrink. My students work on final projects. I have a paper accepted at a major conference. The semester ends, I return to Florida for the holidays. My mother says I look thin. She says I'm too quiet. When she asks if I want to talk about my child, I shake my head. I say, "Please don't ever mention her again, not ever." My mother holds the palm of one hand to my cheek and the palm of the other over my heart. I send Magnus a card and a letter and gift and another letter and another letter. He sends me a text message: I'M STILL ANGRY. I send more letters. He writes back once and I carry his letter with me everywhere. I try to acquire a taste for venison. The new semester starts. I have another paper accepted at a conference, this one in Europe. A new group of students tries to flirt with me while learning about the wonder of concrete. I get a research grant and my department chair offers me a tenure track faculty position with the department. He tells me to take as much time as I need to consider his offer. He says the department really needs someone like me. He says, "You kill two birds with one stone, Katie." I contemplate placing his head in the compression-testing machine and the sound it would make. I say, "I prefer to be called Kate."

THE HYDROLOGIST CORNERS ME IN MY LAB LATE AT NIGHT AND MAKES an inappropriate advance that leaves me unsettled. For weeks, I will feel his long, skinny fingers, how they grabbed at things that were not his to hold. Even though it's after midnight, I call Magnus. My voice is shaking. He says, "You hurt my feelings," and the simple honesty of his words makes me ache. I say, "I'm sorry. I never say what I really feel," and I cry. He asks, "What's wrong?" I tell him about the married hydrologist, a dirty man with a bright pink tongue who tried to lick my ear and who called me Black Beauty and who got aggressive when I tried to push him away and how I'm nervous about walking to my car. Magnus says, "I'm on my way." I wait for him by the main entrance and when I recognize his bulky frame trudging through the snow toward me, everything feels more bearable. Magnus doesn't say a word. He just holds me. After a long while, he punches the brick wall and says, "I'm going to kill that guy." I believe him. He walks me to my lab to get my things.

At my apartment, I hold a bag of frozen corn against Magnus's scraped knuckles. I say, "I shouldn't have called." He says, "Yes, you should have." He says, "You have to be nicer to me." I say, "I do." I straddle his lap and kiss his torn knuckles and pull his hands beneath my shirt and look into his beautiful blue gray eyes and I don't say it, but I think, "I love you."

MAGNUS STARTS PICKING ME UP FROM WORK EVERY NIGHT AND IF I have to work late, he sits with me, watching me work. There is an encounter with the hydrologist. Words are exchanged. Magnus clarifies for the hydrologist my disinterest in curries of any kind. He doesn't trouble me again. While I work, Magnus tells me about trees and everything a man could ever know from spending his days among them. He often smells like pine and sawdust.

IN MARCH, WINTER LINGERS. MAGNUS BUILDS ME AN IGLOO AND INSIDE, he lights a small fire. He says, "Sometimes, I feel I don't know a thing about you." I am sitting between his legs, my back to his chest. Even though we're wearing layers of clothing, it feels like we're naked. I say, "You know I'm not very nice." He kisses my cheek. He says, "That's not true." He says, "Tell me something true." I tell him how I hold on to the idea of Emma even though I shouldn't, how she's all I really think about, how she might be trying to walk now or say her first words. I tell him I think I love him and I love how he likes me. He brings my cold fingers to his warm lips. He fills all the hollow spaces.

Love, with Trees and Lightning

Catie Rosemurgy

I've been thinking about what love is for.
Not the obvious part where he gathers
until he is as purposeful inside her
as an electrical storm, not when he breaks
into a thanks so bright it leaves her
split like a tree. (We all jolt back,
our picnic ten shades lighter, our hands
clapped over awe that's too big for our mouths.)

But the two of them, afterwards,
tasting the electricity, nibbling
the charge on the ions. When her pulse
has already risked coming to meet him
at the window of her skin. When what is left
of his body still feels huge, and he sits draped
in his fine, long coat of animal muscles
but uses all his strength to be almost imperceptible.
They curl up, make their bodies the same size,
draw promises in one another's juices.
"You," they say. I love it when they say that.

Would that they could give a solid reason.
Sometimes they even refuse to try.
They make jokes while cinching their laces.
"I'll call soon," he says. "You're so sweet,"
she says, but the rank sugar of his breath
doesn't summarize the world for her.
"Not you," they say.

And nothing bad has happened.
They just turn the doorknob that has been
shining in their hands the whole time, walk out,
and continue to die. Same as the rest of us.
So maybe love is a form of crying. Or maybe
it's our way of finishing what the leaves have started
and turning a brilliant color before we hit the ground.
Name one living thing that doesn't somehow bloom.
None of them get to choose the right conditions.
Think of chemical fires or ghost orchids.

Maybe one body is simply insufficient.
So they change their minds and decide
to stand by one another's side for years.
They bring flowers and carpet and children
into the act. They refuse to move, ever.
They act as if they've found the only hospitable
spot on earth. I love it when they do that.

Copper Harbor

Mary Biddinger

Freakish, like a tapestry.
The dark smudge of fish
shanties and smokehouses.
An orange nylon jacket

knotted on the breakwater.
We watched tourists, made
change for their twenties.

The seagulls were quick
as equinox, Evinrude,
flypaper lit with a zippo.

All cabins have the same
linoleum. It's universal.
I took prints with knees
and palms. Read your tale

of botanical swerve, flash
and fragment. Artichoke
or parsnip? The ether surge

of a mower on the parkway
slapped us out of reverie.
I asked you the sound

of fishhook through a lip.
You gave me a silver cup
and claw hammer. I woke

all night inspecting corners,
nasturtiums. Your body
an arrow into the lake.

Mad Dog Queen

Sharon Dilworth

THE BATHWATER WAS ALREADY COLD. JIM FLIPPED THE SOAP WITH HIS toe, trying to decide whether to get out or refill the tub, when Beth walked in and told him he had to hitchhike up to L'Anse with her on Friday. It was winter carnival up there, she explained, and this would be her third title. She had been crowned L'Anse's Mad Dog Queen two years in a row. The contest was simple—nothing to do with beauty or talent. The winner was the first woman to down a quart of Mad Dog 20/20 wine. There were two prizes: a ride through town on the winter carnival float alongside the Jack Daniels King and a check for three hundred dollars.

"A drinking contest?" Jim asked. He took the washcloth and covered himself with it, but Beth wasn't looking at him anyway. "Why would you go all the way up there for a drinking contest?"

"I win," Beth said. "I always win." She sat on the edge of the sink, her hip pressed up against the mirror as if knowing he would say yes right away. He usually did anything she wanted him to.

"Doesn't it make you sick to drink all that wine?" Jim asked. He watched her, looking at herself in the steamy mirror. He thought she was beautiful. Where most of the other girls wore their hair long and knotted in ponytails, Beth kept hers short. She said it was New York style. Now, wet from the snow, it hung on her forehead like black string. She combed through it with her fingers.

"I don't swallow," she said. "I open my throat and pour it all down at once." She threw back her head and pointed to the base of her neck, where the skin was still pink from the wind. "You have to keep this part open."

"It sounds kind of disgusting," Jim said. His fingers were soft from the bathwater, numb and wrinkled at the tips. "I can't imagine a bunch of women sitting in a bar slugging down bottles of wine."

"It's only a quart," Beth said. She got up and for a minute Jim thought she was coming over to him. Instead she went to the toilet and pulled some paper off the roll. She blew her nose loudly.

"You have to go with me, Jim. I can't hitch alone."

"Was I your first choice?" Jim asked.

"If I say yes, will you go?" She threw the toilet paper in the trash and reached for her mittens.

"First tell me the truth," Jim said. He let the washcloth float around his feet.

"Okay," she said. "I haven't asked anyone else."

And, totally infatuated with her, Jim said he'd go.

Their first ride out of Marquette got them to Koski Korners at eight-thirty, only two miles from where they'd started. Beth was furious. Her dark eyes glared at Jim in the few rare moments she looked at him. Angry at the late start, the cold, the short first ride, she was also mad at Jim for agreeing with Birdie, the gas station attendant, that they should wait inside instead of on the highway.

"The contest starts at midnight," Beth said. She stood in front of the door with a two-pound bag of cheese popcorn and a fistful of beef jerky. These were her supplies to build up thirst. She wouldn't drink anything, not even water, before the contest. "I'd feel better if we were on the side of the road."

"You plan to walk all the way there?" Jim asked.

"No. I plan to get a ride," she said.

"It's freezing out," Jim said. He pushed their backpack against the frosted glass and crouched down near the space heater. The gas station smelled of rusty fuel and onions, the kind from inside a submarine sandwich. Birdie offered them a beer. His large hands waved to the six-pack on the counter. He had lowered the sound of the portable television set hidden next to the cash register, which was tuned to a show about dressing venison.

"They're not going to wait for me," Beth said. "I mean no one's sitting up in the bar taking attendance. They'll yell 'on your mark, get set, go' and I'll still be a hundred miles away yakking away with you."

"Is that how those contests begin?" Jim asked. He got up and took the beer, pulling his sweater down over his hand before touching the bottle. "On your mark, get set, go?"

"Anyone going up to the Keweenaw'll stop in here," Birdie said. He smiled, his teeth overflowing in his mouth as if his jaw had been broken more than once. "Skytta's Standard closes down at six. We're the last place open till you get up near L'Anse."

"You don't hitchhike from inside a gas station," Beth said. She glanced quickly at Birdie and then turned her back to the counter. "I've never heard of anything so stupid."

"We'll die out on the highway," Jim said. "Let's at least get warm before we go out again."

Jim rarely argued with Beth. She was not the kind of person who would tolerate being wrong. She did things her way and, if people didn't agree, she did them alone. Jim tried to change certain things about her, especially the idea that she wanted him as a friend and nothing more. They slept together only when she had too much to drink. She would wake up on those mornings and tell him she didn't remember doing it. Her boyfriends, the guys she did remember doing it with, had to be from the Lower Peninsula. She wanted to meet guys from Detroit, Flint, anywhere south of Saginaw—the big cities where the guys smelled of machines and soap. Jim was from Escanaba, a small city more than triple the size of her hometown L'Anse, but not far south enough to guarantee her a way out of the Upper Peninsula. Jim had accused her of only going out with guys to find a magic carpet ride across the Mackinac Bridge and she had agreed. "That's exactly what I want," she had said. "Some sort of way out of here." He offered to take her anywhere. "You don't mean it," she said. But he did mean it.

Beth moved stiffly around the small cleared area in front of the coolers. Underneath her jacket she wore two sweatshirts. The green hood of one was bunched up around her neck and she tugged at it, stretching the material so it hung without shape.

"Let's just try the road," Beth said. "If it gets too bad, we'll come back in."

Jim sipped his beer, thinking of ways to stall her. "This here's the reigning winter carnival queen." He introduced Beth to Birdie.

"The Mad Dog Queen?" Birdie asked. "Is that contest tonight?"

Beth wiped the window with a mittened hand and pressed her face up to the glass. She ignored Birdie's question, the same way she ignored Jim. The oversized bag of popcorn was tucked under her arm like a pillow.

"So that's why you're so nutty to get up to L'Anse," Birdie said. The folds of his stomach overlapped as he laughed.

"This is her third year," Jim said. "We've got to make it up there by midnight."

"You've got plenty of time," Birdie said. He pointed to the clock hanging between the windows covered with newspaper comics to block the wind. The clock, an advertisement for the National Ski Hall of Fame in Michigamme, had a downhill racer in the center. His stocking cap stuck straight up, forming the number 1 in the 12.

"Not that much time," Beth said.

"I bet you're a winner," Birdie said. He got up from the stool and leaned over the counter closer to Beth. "You Indians sure can drink."

"What makes you think I'm an Indian?" Beth asked.

"Never heard of a Mad Dog Queen that wasn't one."

"Well, maybe you're wrong about this one," she said. Jim watched her pull her hat down and knew she was covering the black hair on her forehead.

"I don't think so," Birdie said. He winked over at Jim. "I can tell an Indian a mile away. You all got those eyes. Dark as can be. Every single one of you."

"You should talk about us drinking," Beth said. "You're a Finn. Everyone knows they're alcoholics."

She pushed open the door and a sharp blast of cold air ran in. Jim stood up and grabbed the backpack by the strap.

"They got tempers too," Birdie said. He offered Jim another beer for the road.

THE RIDE UP WAS SLOW AND QUIET. THE DRIVER DIDN'T SAY MUCH. He sat hunched over the steering wheel close to the cleared square on the windshield. The rest of the truck was iced up, making it impossible to see out of the dark interior. The dash lights glowed, illuminating the man's hands wrapped around the wheel, his knuckles the color of iron ore. Beth ate through the popcorn bag, wiping the cheese off her hands down the front of her jeans. Jim could feel her hipbone knocking into his where the seat sagged between them. The radio tuned out, leaving only static.

"Your breath is foul," Jim whispered in her ear.

"Wait till I finish these," Beth said. She rattled the packages of beef jerky. "Give me a sip of your beer."

"No. You're in training."

"Just a sip," she said. "All I can taste is salt." She leaned over and licked his neck. "Even on you."

She was always doing things like that. Tonight she would probably get drunk and they would sleep together. On Monday things would be back to normal. She would probably come to his room and start talking about a guy she wanted to go out with from Kalamazoo, never mentioning what happened over the weekend. He just couldn't help himself when she was around. Jim let his mind wander until he could see the straight line of her back, the sharp V of her shoulder blades, the color of her skin so much darker than his. He circled two holes in the side window at eye level and stared out at the continuous line of evergreens bordering the highway.

"Remember about Leena," Beth said. "If she's home, you can just ignore her."

Jim nodded, forgetting she couldn't see him.

"You know what I'm talking about?" she asked.

"Sure. I remember," he said.

Beth had told him about her father's girlfriend Leena more than once. Whenever Jim brought her up, Beth waved the question away. "She's not important," she would say. "She doesn't mean anything to anyone." Beth had told him that Leena moved into the house a year before her mother moved out. Both her parents wanted the divorce, but neither could afford to live anywhere else. That winter her mother had slept on the pull-out couch in the living room; in the spring Leena and her father moved a bed into the room over the garage.

Jim knew about the fights between Leena and Beth's mother. Her mother had been yelling at Leena one day and Leena had turned around and thrown soup down the front of her mother's chest. When Jim asked if her mother had been hurt, Beth told him the soup hadn't been hot.

"His girlfriend can't cook," Beth said. "She only goes into the kitchen when she wants to open the refrigerator door. That soup had probably been sitting on the stove for days."

Jim knew that Beth was afraid of having Leena in the house with her two brothers. "It's bad," Beth told Jim one night. "They're not even sixteen yet."

When Jim pressed her on it, she let him know only a little more. "No one talks about it. They ignore it. Especially my mother," Beth said. "If she knows what's going on, she doesn't do anything."

THEY TOOK THE RIDE ALL THE WAY INTO TOWN TO THE IGA STORE AND then walked up the hill to Beth's house. The snow was knee-deep and Jim had a hard time keeping up with her.

"Leena's going to ask you a million questions," Beth said. She waited for him in front of the house. "Don't tell her anything. If she wants to know something, she'll worm it out of you anyway." Beth knocked once before letting herself in. She turned to him in the dark hallway. "We don't have to stay here. I asked my brothers to help find us someplace to sleep."

Leena was lying on the couch in front of the television set. She glanced up quickly when Beth walked in.

"Where's Dad?" Beth asked.

"Working."

"Where?"

"He's doing snow removal."

"Around here?"

"Maybe if you called once in a while you'd know these things." Leena pushed the white blanket off her legs and turned to face Beth. "That way you wouldn't have to drill me every time you came home."

Beth walked out of the room and slammed a door in the back of the house. Jim stood in the front entrance, making a big deal of wiping his boots on the small rug.

"Who's your friend?" Leena called to Beth. "Does he have a name?"

"Jim." He stepped through the archway, deciding his boots were dry enough to walk on the uncovered floors. The room was practically bare. Besides the couch and the television, there was no other furniture in the room. The one lamp was set on the floor, most of the light coming from an overhead fixture in the kitchen.

"You can sit down if you want," Leena said. She was younger than Jim had expected. Her blonde hair was pulled up in a high ponytail at the back of her head and her skin was pale, typical of the Finns from around L'Anse. "I'm Leena."

Jim nodded. She wore a man's button-down shirt, the tails tied in a knot below her hips. She was big, almost heavy enough to call fat.

"Did Beth tell you about me?" she asked.

"No," Jim lied. "Not really."

"She didn't tell you she hates me?" Leena asked. She put her feet down on the floor, pushing herself forward to the edge of the couch. Her face was puffy, as if they had caught her sleeping.

"No," Jim said. Leena smirked and he wondered if she had expected him to say yes.

"She can't stand me," Leena said. She patted the cushion next to her. "Sit down."

"I think we're leaving right away," he said.

"Is she in town for the chugging contest?"

"Yes," he said. "It starts at midnight."

"She's only doing it for the money." Leena got up from the couch with a cigarette in her mouth and came over to Jim. She handed him the blue plastic lighter and cocked her head to one side, waiting for him to light it for her.

"You'd think if you could smoke those things, you could at least light them for yourself," Beth said. She walked past them into the kitchen. She had changed out of her sweat shirts into a black turtleneck, making her skin look even darker than usual.

Jim lit Leena's cigarette and gave her back the lighter. She tossed it across the room, where it landed on the couch.

"It's true," Leena said. "All you want is the money."

"So what?" Beth asked.

"Well, maybe there's a lot of other people in this town who would like to be the winter carnival queen," Leena said. She blew smoke out of her nose and her mouth as she spoke. "I don't know why you have to keep coming back here and ruining everyone else's chances. You're the one who says you hate this town."

"The boys told me they'd be home," Beth said. She spread her makeup on the kitchen table and wiped the small compact mirror on a T-shirt hanging from the chair. "Where are they?"

"Your dad's up in the Copper Country doing snow removal," Leena said. She bent over the table, inspecting Beth's makeup. "He's been there since last Thursday."

"All right," Beth said. "But what about the boys? They knew I was coming home. Why aren't they around? Did they go out?"

"How would I know?" Leena asked. "They don't tell me anything." She picked up some of the makeup and carried it over to the window. As she looked at her reflection, she put on a thick layer of mascara, the cigarette glued to her bottom lip.

"All the attention you give them, couldn't you at least find out where they're going?" Beth asked.

"Your mother came and took all the furniture," Leena said. She stared at herself, turning her head slightly to one side. "I'm sure the boys helped her move everything out."

"It was her furniture," Beth said. "You knew she was going to take it one of these days."

"Not all of it was hers."

"She left what wasn't."

"Did you know she was going to come and take everything?" Leena asked. She put the mascara tube back on the table and reached for something else.

Beth slapped her wrist. "Leave it alone."

"Did your mother tell you she was coming over to take the stuff?" Leena waited until Beth was busy with the brush, combing out her hair, before picking up another stick of makeup.

"Maybe," Beth said.

"You let her know next time she steps foot in this house, I'm going to have her arrested," Leena said.

"It's her house," Beth said. "She bought and paid for it with her own money."

"It would have been nice if someone had let me know about her coming and stealing all the furniture," Leena said. She went back to her reflection in the window. "That way I would have been prepared for it. I almost died when I walked in and everything was gone."

Jim got tired of standing. He pulled out one of the chairs and sat down near Beth.

"What time is it?" She grabbed hold of his wrist and turned it to look at his watch.

"Almost eleven," he said.

Leena untied her shirttails and tucked them into her jeans. She unzipped her pants in the middle of the kitchen. "Maybe I'll go down to the bar with you two," she said.

Beth put her makeup back in the flowered case and rolled her eyes at Jim. Leena was quiet as if she expected Beth to tell her she couldn't go.

"You don't mind if I go to the contest with you, do you, Jim?" Leena put her coat on just as Beth was getting hers. "If Beth is in the contest, you'll just end up sitting alone anyway."

Beth pulled her hat on and walked out the front door, not waiting for either of them.

Jim got up and followed her out.

"Let her go," Leena said. "We'll be down at the bar soon enough. We'll see enough of her tonight."

He caught up with Beth on the street. "Wait a minute," he said. "What do you want me to do?"

"You might as well wait for her now," Beth said. "She's going to go no matter what."

"It's not my fault," Jim said. "What was I supposed to do?"

"You didn't have to talk to her," Beth said. "I told you to ignore her. That was the first thing I told you."

Beth went on ahead. Jim let her go. He let her get away with so much. But he wouldn't give up—not yet. Jim saw her slide down the path and reach for a branch to hold her balance. The trees were covered with ice and he was surprised when it didn't snap off in her tight grip.

IT WAS CLOSE TO ONE O'CLOCK WHEN THEY FINALLY YELLED, "ON YOUR mark, get set, go." The bartender had dropped the two cases of Mad Dog, carrying them up from the cold storage in the basement. Half the bottles broke, the cherry wine spilling everywhere. He tried to substitute blackberry Mad Dog, but some of the women protested, saying that two different flavors wouldn't be fair. One might be easier to swallow than the other. There was some talk about breaking into the liquor store down the street to replace the smashed bottles, but the judge argued that there had never been a rule about the wine having to be the same. The contest was the first woman to down the quart. Nothing had ever been said about flavor.

"There she is, front and center. Just like she always is." Leena nodded toward Beth, who stood in line with the other women on the dance floor, waiting for the contest to begin. The bar was hot with so many people. Beth fanned her face with a piece of paper.

Jim slid off his stool, giving it up to Leena. She had refused to sit down, waiting until Jim was sitting before pushing her hip against his leg, moving in on the stool.

"Does she think she'll win again?" Leena asked.

Jim drank his beer and shrugged. The coaster stuck to the bottom of his mug and he flipped it back on the bar.

"You can talk to me," Leena said. "Beth doesn't care if you talk to me."

Jim poured more beer in his mug and held the pitcher up for Leena. She pushed her glass over to him.

The bar smelled like cherry cough syrup. Jim kept his eyes on Beth. She had her hair tucked behind her ears, making her look young. Jim took another swallow of his beer and walked over to her.

"Good luck," he said. The noise in the bar was overpowering. She looked at him for a long moment and he wasn't sure if she was going to talk to him.

"I wouldn't stand so close if I were you," Beth said. "They go wild if they lose."

"What about you?" Jim asked. "Are you going to get wild?"

"I'm not going to lose," she said. She leaned forward to speak to him while the woman next to her was yelling about drinking choke cherry wine. "But I'd like to get drunk."

"I'd like to see you get drunk too," he said.

"I'm sure you would."

"Do you want anything now?" he asked.

"I'd like this thing to get going so I can win and get out of here."

"How can you be so sure you'll win?" Jim asked. Her breath smelled like the stale cheese popcorn and she backed away as if she knew what he was thinking. He stepped closer to her.

"I didn't come up here to lose," she said.

The judge came by and collected the papers from the women. Jim looked at Beth in question.

"It's our head measurement," she said. "For the crown."

Jim laughed. He reached for her hand. She was sweating. He hadn't expected her to be nervous about the contest. He liked the feeling he had of protecting her, though he wasn't sure he was really doing anything. Beth wasn't the kind of person who seemed to need much protection.

"Why don't you tell Leena to get lost?" Beth said.

Jim kissed her and she pushed him away. He tried again and she let him kiss her for a couple of minutes.

"I mean it," Beth said, moving her face away from his. "It'll be big trouble if you give her a drop of attention. Pretty soon she'll be walking around with a swelled head and no one will be able to talk sense to her."

"I didn't know I had that kind of effect on women." Jim laughed.

"With someone like Leena, a dog could get her acting crazy."

The judge came back around and told the women to line up. The photographer from the *Baraga Bugle* was there to get a couple of pictures.

Jim went and sat down at the opposite end of the bar from Leena. He offered to buy the bartender a shot and the bartender gave him a free shot with a beer chaser. They toasted. The bartender had white tape around his hand and held the beer mug with two fingers, his pinky wrapped immobile.

"You going to need stitches on that?" Jim asked.

"I don't think I got any glass in it," the guy said. He finished his shot and beer before Jim had taken a sip. Jim wondered if he was training for the Jack Daniels contest.

The bartender leaned over to speak to Jim. "Do you know how much money I just made?" he asked.

Jim shook his head.

"Twenty bucks."

"For what?" Jim asked. For a split second he thought it might have something to do with Leena.

"The cases of Mad Dog," the bartender said.

The near-bald judge got up on one of the tables and called everyone's attention.

"What?" Jim asked. He turned his stool and saw Beth step up to the table.

"Yeah," the bartender said. He poured another half shot in both their glasses. "Some lady from Baraga paid me twenty bucks to drop the cases."

"I don't get it," Jim said. He swallowed his shot quickly.

"She gets sick on cherry," the bartender said. "But she really wants to win the contest."

The judge held the stopwatch over his head and called for quiet.

"Ladies, pick the bottles up," he yelled across the room.

Beth picked up the quart with one hand and gathered her hair off her face with the other. She held her hand on the back of her head as if giving herself support.

"Unscrew the caps," the judge screamed. "Get ready." He stared at the stopwatch. "On your mark, get set." He waited a second. "Go!"

Jim watched Beth. He saw her throw back her head and pour it all down at once. He knew she won when the judge jumped from the table and grabbed her arm. She threw the bottle to the ground. The judge held her arm over her head and said something, but the breaking of the glass muffled his words.

Leena came up behind Jim. She put her arms across his shoulder. "I don't know how, but she wins every year."

Jim inched away from her. "Do you want a beer?" he offered.

Leena nodded. "They shouldn't even let her enter," she said. "She should be disqualified the way she treats this town."

Jim lost track of Beth on the dance floor. Leena followed his stare across the room. "The Finns are going to go crazy. They wanted to win this year, but no one can pull that crown off that Indian's head. I guess it just goes to show you who the real drinkers are around here." Leena's makeup smudged under her eyes, her pale skin showing the blotted color.

"Maybe next year," Jim said.

"The Indians despise the Finns," Leena continued. "It has something to do with the land they say we took about two hundred years ago."

"I don't know," he said. He had heard the story from Beth. The Indians had been forced to move across Keweenaw Bay when the Finns came in to settle. Most of the Finns went to work in the copper mines, but some of them stayed and farmed the Indians' land. Jim didn't think Beth really cared about something that happened so long ago. He once asked her if that was why she had a grudge against Leena and she laughed. "That's why the Finns think we can't stand them, because they took our land. But we don't like them because they're stupid."

"Of course, that's not the only reason Beth hates me," Leena said. The bottles were still smashing on the floor and Jim had a hard time hearing what she was saying. "She thinks I'm turning her brothers away from her. But it doesn't have anything to do with me. They're wild."

The bartender came over and poured Jim another beer.

"Now that crazy woman wants her money back," he said. "Just because she lost. I told her there was no guarantee on the deal, but she's stubborn."

"They're Indians," Leena said. "You know what they had in the living room when I first moved in?" She didn't wait for Jim's answer. "A spittoon. Right in the living room and when they watched TV they would spit in it. It made me so sick I had to throw it out. Now they spit in the sink, in the glassware, everywhere."

Jim drank his beer slowly, waiting for Beth to come over. He saw her and she held up her thumb. He raised his glass and she nodded.

"Are you in love with her?" Leena put her hand over his. He moved it to drink his beer.

"Why?" he asked.

"Because I can tell you right now, she's not in love with you."

"How can you tell that?" Jim asked. The woman next to him pushed up against him and he was caught off balance.

"Easy," Leena said. "If she was in love with you, she never would have brought you home. She never would have let you see where she came from."

Jim had already thought of that, so it didn't bother him to hear it from Leena. He wasn't sure he really believed her.

"And she sure wouldn't have let you see her chug a quart of Mad Dog," Leena continued. Jim moved away from the bar with his mug. The dance floor was covered with glass. The smell of the different flavors was suffocating. Beth was leaning on the railing talking to a group of guys, one of them probably the reigning Jack Daniels King.

The bathroom was empty. Jim stuck his mug on the sink and went into the stall. It was cool and quiet compared to the bar area. Only a couple of hours before, they had been complaining about the cold. Now his shirt was soaked with perspiration. He finished and went over to the sink. He closed his eyes and relaxed for a minute in the darkness. He was tired.

Leena walked in. He saw her blonde ponytail in the mirror.

"Is there a line for the girl's bathroom?" he asked.

She came over and put her arms around his neck.

"Don't," he said. "What are you doing here?"

He grabbed her wrist with his wet hands. She held tight, her own hands clasped together, pulling down his head.

"Don't worry," Leena said. She pushed her face against his, her skin brushing his cheek. "Beth's busy getting her photograph taken for the newspaper."

"Let's go," he said. He pulled her hands apart and threw her away from him. Her head hit the paper towel dispenser as Beth walked in.

"Get out of here," Beth said. Jim bent over the sink and spit. The taste of whiskey was too thick in his throat.

Leena rubbed her head and glared at Beth.

"Get out of here," Beth yelled again. She moved toward Leena and Leena ran out.

"Do you know who she is?" Beth asked. She put her back to the door, blocking anyone's entrance.

"She walked in," Jim said. He washed his hands, letting the water pick up the spit on the side of the sink.

"She's my father's girlfriend," Beth said. "She sleeps with my father."

"She walked in and started making the moves on me," Jim said.

"Because you were paying her all that attention," Beth said. Jim had never seen her this frustrated and he wanted to believe that she was jealous. "You could have left her alone. You didn't have to talk to her."

"You're right," he said. "I should have ignored her."

"She's a Finn," Beth said. "Do you know what they do?"

Jim shook his head. "No. What do they do?"

"They store up for the winter like squirrels. They think squirrels have the right idea. In October they start eating as much as they can. They think that's smart. But do you know where that gets them?"

"No," Jim said. He went over and put his arms around her. "Tell me."

"It makes them fat," she said. "Really big and fat." She was crying. Jim stroked her hair, pulling it from behind her ears. It fell in her face.

"Don't you see?" she asked. "If she tried something on you, then she tries things with my brothers."

"No," Jim said. "No, she doesn't." Jim held her close and she cried into his already damp shirt.

"She'll do anything to spite me," Beth said. "I told you to leave her alone."

"I'm sorry," Jim said. "I just didn't understand." He felt very close to her and hugged her into his chest. She let him hug her.

"I want to go back tonight," she said. She stood up straight and looked at her reflection in the mirror. Jim wiped a tear from one cheek and she turned her head so he could get the tears on the other cheek.

"I want to hitchhike back to Marquette," she said. "Will you go? I don't want to spend the night here."

"If that's what you want," Jim said. "You know that."

"I want to get out of here."

LEENA WAS NOT AT THE BAR WHEN JIM WALKED BACK TO GET HIS JACKET.

Beth crossed the dance floor and went to the fridge for her check. Jim spotted Leena near the jukebox in the front of the bar; when Beth was ready to leave, they went out the back door. They walked down the alley in silence.

"What about the ride on the float?" Jim asked. They turned the corner and the frozen Keweenaw Bay spread out in front of them, the white dead water illuminated in the dark night.

"I guess they'll have to find someone else to do it," Beth said. "It's not all that much fun anyway."

"Pretty cold up there?"

"It's freezing."

To the west, the gold painted statue of Bishop Baraga, the patron saint of L'Anse, watched over them from the low hills of the Porcupine Mountains. Their footsteps were muffled on the frozen gravel off to the side of the highway. The red taillights of the car flashed on fifty feet in front of them and Beth took off running. Jim ran, one more time, trying to catch up to her.

My Lake

Lisa Fay Coutley

My lake has many rooms and one, which is red
with a door that's always open but chained.
My lake owns boxing gloves. She owns lingerie.
She can swing, she can cha-cha, she can salsa
and tap but refuses a simple slow dance. My lake
learned early to rest the needle without a scratch.
She has been classically trained in lovemaking.
When she wants to ride a roller coaster, she does
it alone. When she lets her hair down, men go
blind. My lake doesn't take any shit. She wears
stilettos in ice storms, does crosswords in pen.
She eats red meat. Her porch needs painting,
her flowers need weeding, but my lake reads
palms in twelve different languages. If my lake
puts her hand to your chest, she decides. At times,
whole days can pass when she won't let anyone
near her. She freezes just before she murders
her own shore. It's been years, and still my lake
won't name the delicate sound of ice taking,
then brushing away. She might say it's the train

of a wedding dress, or the rain falling on a glass
slipper. There are times she sees the grace of two
loons gliding—their bodies a duet over breaking
water, and she slows herself. She makes a cradle.

Winter

Talvi

Winter Mines

Sharon Dilworth

Everyone's heard by now that Barbara Wyatt swallowed a half can of Drano. My husband says, in this town, news like that doesn't need any help getting around—people just want to talk about it. Nancy Whitney was in the supermarket on Third Street this morning and she told me she heard Barbara did it in front of a full-length mirror. They found her on the bathroom hamper where she had ripped off her sweater and torn her blouse trying to release the burning pain in her stomach. By the time they got her to the hospital, her lips, which had touched the can, had swollen black.

Nancy was sweating in her down jacket in the supermarket. She rubbed her pregnant belly in circular motions.

"I knew Barbara was depressed," she said. "But I didn't see anything like this coming. I don't think there was any warning at all."

"I didn't talk to her that much," I said. "Not since she moved back to town."

"It's the winter," Nancy said. "I know it's the winter. Fifty-seven inches of snow fell last month alone. And the winds have been coming off the lake at such high speeds that everyone's having trouble just standing up."

Nancy and I tried to hug good-bye, but her eight-month pregnancy wouldn't let us get very close. She went to stand in the ten-item-or-less line with the bag of birdseed and a gallon of milk and I pushed my grocery cart to the household supply aisle. I picked up a can of Drano. The red cap is fastened so tightly that a knife is needed to break the seal. On one side of the can a skull is sketched next to a poison warning: "Contains sodium hydroxide (caustic lye) corrosive. May cause blindness. Always keep out of reach of children. Store on high shelf or in locked cabinet. Harmful or fatal if swallowed."

I wondered how much of the can Barbara had swallowed and I wondered if she knew how much it was going to hurt. Had there been a moment when she wanted to stop what she had done?

My husband doesn't want to hear about Barbara Wyatt. He can't think about anything depressing.

"Please," he asked me this morning. "Don't talk about her in front of me. I don't see why you keep talking about her."

"Barbara was a friend of mine," I said. "I want to talk about her."

"All right. But not with me. Not right now. I can't listen to other people's problems," he said. He brought a roll of paper towels to the kitchen table and folded two separate sheets in half and then again so the coffee mugs wouldn't mark the wood table. He spent yesterday afternoon scrubbing the table with toothpaste trying to get the ring marks out of the wood. I can still smell the mint.

"I don't have time to get involved with everyone else's problems," he said.

"I'm not asking you to get involved with anything, I just want you to listen to me."

"Let's talk about normal things. Nothing depressing," he said. He drank his coffee in long swallows.

"It shouldn't affect you."

"I don't want to talk about someone's suicide."

"But you don't talk to me about anything else," I said. "Everything depresses you."

"A lot of bad things have happened this year," he said. He spooned some jelly on his toast and spread it out evenly with his knife.

"What? What bad things have happened to you?" I asked. I got up from the table and dumped the rest of my coffee down the sink. He refuses to keep coffee with caffeine in the house. He says it aggravates him, but I can't get used to the taste of coffee with nothing in it.

"I'm not going to fight with you," he said.

"Nothing in your life has changed." I repeated the same thing I've said to him since Christmas. "Your life is exactly the same as it is every winter."

"Don't be ignorant." He got up from the table and left the kitchen, leaving the toast on the plate.

"What's so different about your life right now?" I called.

"I won't fight with you," he shouted. I could hear him walking around the living room.

"We're not fighting. I just want you to talk with me."

He didn't answer, but I continued. "You're making everything up in your mind. You're the one that's making yourself depressed. Nothing's happened. Nothing's changed."

When we fight, he shuts up. He won't argue with me. He says it's just a waste of time, because I refuse to look at things the same way he does. In the mornings he makes a list of what has to be done around the house. He spends every weekend scrubbing with bleach and ammonia. During the week he works on projects he finds for himself, like mending holes in the summer screens or rearranging the boxes of junk in the spare bedroom.

Even though he won't answer me, I know I'm doing right. Nothing has changed. The mines closed the same time they do every year, the week before Thanksgiving. There's a lot of talk about the mines not reopening, but that goes on every year. I don't think it's any worse than it was last year. Someone said something to my husband and he's convinced that the mines are closed forever. He's acting like he doesn't have a job. During Christmas vacation he decided not to leave the house. He says when he goes out he runs into people, like the bartender at the Third Base Bar, who ask him what he thinks about the mines. Last time he went out the guys at the liquor store bet him fifty dollars that the mines would stay shut once the snow melts. My husband says it's too hopeless to talk about.

THE WOMAN AT THE CHECKOUT COUNTER ASKS ME IF I WAS A FRIEND of Barbara's.

"In grade school," I tell her. "We were real good friends in grade school."

"I thought I remembered you two coming in here." The woman sits back on a stool she has behind the counter and shakes her head. Her sweater is buttoned up around the neck and she wears brown driving gloves to punch the cash register keys. The front door of the store automatically opens and closes, letting the wind in. I button my coat.

"That was a lot of years ago," she says without looking at my groceries. "Didn't she leave town for a while? I remember something about her getting a job somewhere else."

"She just moved back here." I pick up a newspaper for my husband. It is the newspaper from downstate, which never writes about what's going on in the Upper Peninsula. It's the only newspaper he'll read.

"I feel so sorry for her family," the woman says. "What they must be thinking right now. It really makes you wonder."

I don't remember the woman changing over the years. I've been going to the store every day and she has always looked the same to me. Her gray hair frames her face and her glasses hang around her neck on a long black cord.

"It's just her father," I tell her. I open a brown bag and hold the box of spaghetti so the woman can see the price. She rings it on the machine and pushes the other groceries slowly down the rubber mat.

Barbara lived across the street from me when we were in grade school. We were exactly the same age. She didn't have a mother and her father let me sleep over every weekend night. My mother thought two nights in a row was too much, but she let me do it because she felt sorry for Barbara, being without a mother. Barbara and I would listen to her father's Harry Nilsson albums and would drink Coca-Cola out of wine glasses filled with ice cubes. She knew the words to the songs on all his records by heart and I would read them off the back of the album cover to sing along with her. Barbara loved to bake things—anything with sugar in it. One time we stayed up all night, waiting for a cake to cool so we could frost it with caramel frosting that Barbara had made by melting a bag of old Halloween caramels. I remember the only time she talked about not having a mother.

"My father would love to find a new mother for me," she said. "But I don't want one."

"Maybe he's looking for a mother for himself," I said. I had overheard my mother telling someone that Barbara's father was out to get a new wife.

"No," she said. "He doesn't care about things like that. He worries about me. He can take care of me, but he won't. He thinks I should be a part of a family."

"But don't you want to have a mother?"

"Not really. I don't need one," Barbara said. "I'd like to have a mother for only one reason. If I had a mother then she could braid my hair. I'd grow my hair as long as yours is."

My hair in grade school was long and straight. It was thin and wouldn't hold a curl even if I slept in curlers all night. I usually wore it braided on the sides and tied the ends with kitchen rubber bands that snagged and knotted when I pulled them out to wash my hair.

"It's not so great having long hair," I said. "You have to spend a lot of time washing it. My mom makes me come straight home from school to wash it at four o'clock so it will be dry by the time I go to bed."

"But my father won't even let me have long hair. He says it's too much trouble and he doesn't know how to take care of it."

"I braid my own hair now," I said. "My mother just yells about my hair. She says she finds it all over the house."

"At least you know how to braid it. I don't even know how to do that. I never learned."

"I can teach you. You just have to practice getting the rubber bands in without knotting your hair."

We pulled strands of yarn out of an afghan Barbara was making for a Christmas gift. I showed her how to braid the thick pieces into one strand. I showed her how to turn the right section over the left and then start to intertwine the middle section. She practiced on the yarn, then I untied my own hair and she braided a straight plait down my back. I had to put the rubber bands on the end.

I WALK HOME DOWN THE CENTER OF THE STREET, HUGGING THE BAG of groceries in both arms. The muscles above my elbows ache and I shift the weight of the bag down my arms, but it doesn't relieve the pressure. The streets are empty. I keep my head tucked into the collar of my jacket listening for the sound of a car. When I get home, my husband is sitting on the couch, not doing anything.

"Cold out?" he asks.

"It's freezing."

"You shouldn't go out so much. We have enough to eat right here. You're going to get sick if you keep going out in this weather."

"I thought you were going to get someone to help you jump-start the car." I rest the bag of groceries on the coffee table, while I take off my boots. The snow melts quickly, wetting the carpet. "I'd like to have at least one car running by the weekend."

"Why do you need a car this week?"

"It'd be nice to have one to run some errands. I don't like to go out at night without a car." His car is sitting in the driveway, out of gas. He says he doesn't need one, but last week my car died just as I was turning the corner of our block. Two kids from the junior high helped me push it in front of the house and it's been there ever since.

He won't talk about it. "Anything new happening out there?"

"Not much." I give him the newspaper. He tucks a corner of it under his leg without looking at it, which bothers me. I wanted him to read it. I take my boots into the bedroom, where I have compositions to correct. The principal at the school doesn't like us to use the public library because there might be students around. During the spring break, when the high school is closed, I set up a desk in the bedroom. It's really a card table with a dining room chair pulled up to it and one of the lamps brought in from the living room. I work for a half an hour before my husband comes in and sits on the edge of the bed. He watches me correct the papers.

"Do you want me to help?"

"No. That's okay."

"I did compositions in high school. I know what teachers look for in them. Read them aloud. I'll tell you what grade I would give them."

The high school counselor talked to a group of miners' wives in January. She told us how important it is to have patience. She said the worst thing you can do is to argue all the time.

"You'll get bored," I tell him. "It's not a very interesting topic."

"Do you have any football players in this class?" he asks.

"Two."

"Read those first."

"That's not fair, if you know they're guys," I say. But I always look at the name at the top of the composition before I read or grade the paper. "Besides, you don't want to hear compositions. They're just as boring as they were when you were in high school. Why don't you go down to Vinnie's? I saw some of the guys down there."

"I know what they're talking about," he says. "It'll be boring to be with them."

"I think they're watching the hockey game."

"But they're talking about the same things. I can hear their conversation from here."

"You don't know that." I stop pretending to read the paper in front of me.

"Can't you hear it? The whole town is buzzing. Drano and closing. Don't you listen when you go out? Can't you hear what everyone's saying?"

"It's not true. The town is not that small."

"Bullshit."

Without noticing, I have been writing on my hand with the red marker—tiny lines across my knuckles when I thought the cap was on.

"You know what I was thinking this morning?" my husband asks me. "I was wondering if all the color around the mines would fade."

"Color?" I am thinking about my hands and the pen marks. My husband is looking at my fingers too. But I know what he is talking about. The iron ore produces red particles which float in the air around the mines. The particles land on flat surfaces and dye them light pink. All the houses in the area are light pink—even the whitewall tires of the cars. My husband tells me the old guys who work at the security gate have pink teeth.

"No one said the mines are closing," I tell him. "You're just making that up. You're driving yourself crazy."

"Do you think I should call Lansing?" My husband stretches out on the bed. He pushes the pillow on the floor with his feet and stares up at the ceiling. He doesn't need sleep. He slept the whole month of January. He reminded me of a black bear. But not now. He has lost so much weight that his face has changed. His skin is tight across his cheek bones. He told me how much he weighs and it is just three pounds more than I weigh.

"Why would you call Lansing?"

"I want to talk to the governor about the mines. I have a right to know if I still have a job."

"No one's going to tell you anything you don't already know," I say.

"The mines are supposed to open on April 1. If they're not going to open, I have a right to know that now so I can start doing something about it." He talks to me with his eyes closed, his body flat on the bed.

"Last year you didn't start until April 14 and you were just as nervous about starting."

"There was a snowstorm. We couldn't work till then."

"You worry like this every year. The mines always open even after a winter of everyone believing that they won't."

His breathing has changed and I can tell he's sleeping. I stare at the papers in front of me, but the words disappear as I focus on the green petal of the flower in the bedspread. Someone told me that the ambulance driver thought Barbara had cut herself on glass, there had been so much blood. But the blood didn't have anything to do with the Drano. It was from her earlobe. She had pulled a tiny gold earring straight through her skin. They think it got caught in her sweater when she ripped it off her body.

I leave the compositions spread on the card table. I will do them later when he is not in the room. It makes me feel guilty to have things to do when he is around. I take my coffee mug from the drain board and bring it to the basement steps where there's a new jug of wine. I keep a gallon of rosé on the last step. My husband thinks it is the same bottle sitting there since Christmas but I have replaced it twice. I drink a glass of wine at dinner in front of him, but I want to have more. I think I could drink a whole bottle of wine and not feel anything. I sit on the bottom step, listening to the sounds of my house. Through my sweater I can feel the cold steel rim where the next step hits my back.

My husband and I argued the night before about money. He is getting nervous about spending money on food. He wants to start freezing meat so we will have something to eat in the summer months. He said it upsets him to see me spending so much money on groceries.

"We should start living on your salary," he told me last night.

"What about your unemployment check?" I asked him. "You're still collecting unemployment. You're getting your money every two weeks."

"I'm not going to cash those anymore. I'm going to open up another savings account."

"Why? We have enough money."

"Now. But we don't know about the future."

"You don't know that the mines are going to stay closed," I said. "You're just getting paranoid. Don't they always threaten to close?"

"To strike. Not to close. This is the first year they've really threatened to close for good," he said. "I just want to prepare for it."

"I remember last year. You were worried then that they were going to shut down. I remember because you started reading the classifieds in the Detroit newspaper. You told me you were thinking about moving downstate last year."

"This year I can feel it. Everyone's out of work this year. If I lose my job, we are going to move. I won't find anything here in town."

"How come you're the only guy in town who's dead sure they're closing?" I asked.

"I wish you could see things the same way I do," he said. And then he shut up. He refused to say anything else.

I fill the coffee mug again. The wine is bitter at first taste, but smooth as I drink more. I drink two refills and go upstairs when I hear my husband moving around. I have a head rush from drinking so fast. The sun's late shadows fall across the kitchen table to my ski jacket hanging on the back of the chair. My husband is in the bathroom. I can hear the pipes in the walls moan as he turns the faucets on and off. He has started taking long showers, sometimes up to an hour. Afterward his fingertips are wrinkled and swollen to a soft pink. He says they hurt because they are so tender. I don't want to be in the house anymore. I am tired of the day, the same as it was yesterday.

NANCY IS SURPRISED WHEN SHE OPENS THE DOOR. "I'M SO GLAD YOU stopped by."

"I was just up at the drugstore and thought you might want a little company," I say.

"You're getting stir crazy too?" she guesses. She smiles and tugs at the end of her shirt, which rides up over her belly. "If I watch any more afternoon television, I'll kill myself." Her voice trails off.

I turn to the door, but she has already seen that I am crying. I cover my face with my hands to hide the tears. I can't keep quiet.

"Please don't," she says. "It was stupid of me. I wasn't thinking."

I shake my head and try to swallow so I can speak, but there is too much in the way. I want to leave without saying anything else. Nancy takes my hands away from my face and holds them in her own.

She stands in front of me, rubbing my fingers, which are so numb I can barely feel her warmth. I catch my breath. "I'm sorry."

"I said it without thinking," Nancy says. "Please forget it." Her arms are swollen. The elastic arm bands of her shirt are too tight and there are red lines in the skin above her wrists.

We go into the kitchen and Nancy pours two cups of tea. She sits down and lights a cigarette. "I know I'm too far along to be smoking," she says. "I found a pack under the cushions in the couch. I just smoked a couple this afternoon."

I sip the hot drink and swallow the last of the tears in my throat. The overhead light fills the room with false brightness. I know I am overreacting because of the wine, but I feel calmer listening to Nancy.

"My mother always told me not to get pregnant in the winter. She said nothing could drive you crazier."

"Is Bob away?" My voice is thick. I cough, trying to clear it.

"Till Thursday."

Nancy's husband drives a truck for a beer distributor. He drives down to Chicago for the pickup and then into Milwaukee for the first delivery. He goes northwest for stops near Green Bay and then north into the Upper Peninsula. It takes him three days to make the deliveries.

"Does it bother you when he's away so much?" I ask. My throat is raspy and my head heavy from crying.

"Sometimes I'm afraid I'll have the baby when he's on the road," Nancy says. She taps the side of her cup with manicured nails. "He's going to take some time off when I'm due, but I don't know about that. I'm worried about having him around all day waiting. He'll probably make me so nervous that I'll never have this baby."

"No. You'll be fine."

"How's your husband?" Nancy asks. "I heard the winter's not treating him so good this year."

"Who told you that?" I ask. My heart quickens. "Where did you hear that?"

"You know how it is." Nancy looks away from me. "He really won't leave the house?"

I stare down at my half-filled cup. I didn't know anyone knew about my husband. It makes him sound weak, as if he doesn't have the same strength the others have. I feel guilty that I can't confide in Nancy, but I don't want to talk about him.

"It's a bad winter all around," Nancy says. Her voice is smooth. She sounds neither surprised nor upset, but accepting. "Barbara's death really scared me. She was always such a quiet person. Remember how quiet she was?"

"Not really," I say. "She talked all the time."

"Maybe she was just shy."

I don't know if I am telling the truth, but I continue to argue with Nancy. "I don't know why you said that. Barbara was normal. She was just like everyone else."

"I didn't say she was different," Nancy says. Her skin is transparent under her eyes—I can see the dark veins right underneath her skin. She looks tired.

"Everyone wants to make Barbara out to be weird. She wasn't. She was just like everyone else." I feel strong with my words and my voice gets louder. "The only difference between Barbara and everyone else is that Barbara didn't have a mother."

"What?"

"Barbara didn't have a mother."

Nancy watches me drink the last of my tea. When I finish, I get up and put my coat back on. I lean over and kiss Nancy on the cheek, where the skin is swollen. "I'll stop by and see how you're doing next week. I promise. Have you thought about what you're going to name the baby?"

"I have some names in mind, but nothing for sure." Nancy doesn't get up from the chair.

ALREADY AT EIGHT O'CLOCK THE STREETS ARE QUIET. THE INSIDE lights of the houses are enclosed by the frost in the windows. Hidden, everyone is protected from the night. As I turn the corner on Third Street, the wind pushes me forward and I stop to keep my balance. Ahead, Lake Superior is a black hole in the darkness surrounding me. I see the untwining of a braid of hair, the right piece loosening from the left and the middle strand unwinding, letting it hang free.

Evacuations

Manda Frederick

1.

In rape defense training, they make you practice screaming; it is unnatural
to your kind, so you must learn to vocalize fear, open the throat

and do it. It must not rise before you as a squeal or a song; it must advance
full-mouthed, stronger than any sound you've ever made. It must

strip oxygen from cells, darken your skin blue as you shape your voice
into an obstruction between you and the last sound you will ever make.

2.

This mid-December chill, a hundred degrees colder than the core
temperature of your body—labored air to strengthen your breathing.

Gather outside with the others despite the storm to practice:
wend your elbows backward into banks, drive knuckles into drifts,

feign escaping on the ice—white scramble falling, chests under pressure.
You must practice fear—the crucial sensation that tempers lungs feral, strips

control, conscious choice to hold the breath that would trap
your voices quiet; you must breathe because fear requires air.

Fear asks the heart to urge the limbs toward motion, to circulate
a bone-deep need toward flight; without breath: air hunger, lungs cannot

offer sound, cannot compel muscles strong—they will soften, made tender
with contraction, that familiar sensation of shivering or falling asleep.

3.

Later, the dark soft sizzle of propane, space heater at your feet,
an occasional flash of light from outside, a low crunch of sound

spreading through Marquette, a dense noisy fog. Get out of bed
and push aside the gauze that lazes over your window—you love

to watch the plows, blades and teeth, their disregard for the deference
expected of the night, their symmetry of sound carving exits

in the streets. Imagine tomorrow, all the buried people will use their shoulders
against their doors, force away the snow that traps them in their homes.

Some of you will climb out your windows, cut down the drifts
with ice picks and brooms. Greet your neighbors as you walk to school

but keep your scarf-strangled mouth down, do not stop to tell them
what occupies your mind: Blake's *Visions of the Daughters Albion*—

you obsess over Oothoon, a woman who is raped by Bromion
who Blake tells us overcomes her like a great storm as she flies

across a cold expanse to greet her Lover; her Lover, self-sick
with envy that she has shared a bed with someone else, he curses her,

binds Oothoon and Bromion back to back forever—though she cries
to him, he does not listen because he will not hear her.

4.

Having rape on the mind is like having fever in the limbs,
its ache reckless through the skin. Leave your window and draw a bath

to clear your mind. Strip down, stand naked in the steam,
drag your palms up your legs and wonder where they were that night—

wedged between the floorboards of this house so old the radiators
double as soup can phones; this is where you learned to keep

your voice low. You must forget this, now. You must wipe the wet
from the mirror, study the vocal reflection of your neck, confront

the superstitions that soak this room, acknowledge the deaf weight
that is your body: make it listen to you as you say your name three times.

The Solutions to Brian's Problem

Bonnie Jo Campbell

Solution #1

Connie said she was going out to the store to buy formula and diapers. While she's gone, load up the truck with the surround-sound home-entertainment system and your excellent collection of power tools, put the baby girl in the car seat, and drive away from this home you built with your own hands. Expect that after you leave, Connie will break all the windows in this living room, including the big picture window, as well as the big mirror over the fireplace, which you've already replaced twice. The furnace will run and run.

Solution #2

Wait until Connie comes back from the "store," distract her with the baby, and then cut her meth with Drano, so that when she shoots it up, she dies.

Solution #3

Put the baby to bed in her crib, and sit on the living room couch until Connie comes home. Before she has a chance to lie about where she's been, grab her hair and knock her head hard into the fireplace that you built from granite blocks that came from the old chimney of the house your great-grandfather built when your family first came to this country from Finland. Don't look at the wedding photos on the mantle. Don't let the blood stop you from hitting her one final time to make sure you have cracked her skull. Put her meth and her bag of syringes and blood-smeared needles in her hand so the cops find them when they arrive.

Solution #4

Just go. Head south where it's warm. Contact the union about getting a job with another local. Pretend not to have a wife and baby. When put to the test, Connie might well rise to the occasion of motherhood. Resist taking any photographs along with you, especially the photographs of your baby at every age. Wipe your mind clear of memories, especially the memory of your wife first telling you she was pregnant and how that pregnancy and her promise to stay clean made everything seem possible. The two of you kept holding hands that night—you couldn't stop reaching for each other, even in your sleep. She lost that baby, and the next one, and although you suspected the reason, you kept on trying.

Solution #5

Blow your own head off with the twelve-gauge you keep behind the seat of your truck. Load the shotgun with shells, put the butt against the floor, rest your chin on the barrel, and pull the trigger. Let your wife find your bloody corpse in the living room; let her scrape your brain off the walls. Maybe that will shock her into straightening up her act. Let her figure out how to pay the mortgage and the power bill.

Solution #6

Call a help line, talk to a counselor, explain that last week your wife stabbed you in the chest while you were sleeping, that she punches you, too, giving you black eyes that you have to explain to the guys at work. Explain to the counselor that you're in danger of losing your job, your house, your baby. Tell her Connie has sold your mountain bike and some of your excellent power tools already. Try to be patient when the counselor seems awkward in her responses, when she inadvertently expresses surprise at the nature of your distress, especially when you admit that Connie's only five foot one. Expect the counselor to be even less supportive when you say, hell yes, you hit her back. Then realize that the counselor probably has caller ID. Hope that the counselor doesn't call Social Services, because a baby girl needs her momma. Assure the counselor that Connie is a good momma, that she's good with the baby, that the baby is in no danger.

Solution #7

Make dinner for yourself and your wife with the hamburger in the fridge. Sloppy joes, maybe, or goulash with the stewed tomatoes your mother canned, your mother who, like the rest of your family, thinks your wife is just moody. You haven't told them the truth, because it's too much to explain, and it's too much even to say that, yes, you knew she had this history when you married her, but you thought you could kick it together, you thought that love could mend all broken things—wasn't that the whole business of love? Mix up some bottles of formula for later tonight, when you will be sitting in the living room feeding the baby, watching the door of the bathroom, behind which your wife will be searching for a place in her vein that has not hardened or collapsed. When she finally comes out, brush her hair back from her face, and try to get her to eat something.

Absent In Its Arrival

Manda Frederick

I.

At the Smithsonian, what strikes me most
about Lincoln's hat is not that he'd been wearing it
the night he was assassinated,

or that I imagine how it tumbled when his head hung
suddenly in his wife's lap—the dress she wore
at his inauguration hanging, now,

bodiless, on a dress form somewhere at my back—but the black
ribbon the father had draped about the brim
in mourning for his son, the one who died before him.

Seemingly everywhere: bronze casts of Lincoln's face
made posthumously—each feature motionless in its death
except the eyes: smeared as though hot metal brimmed

the skull, spilled about the brow, the last meaningful movement
within his head, the second-to-last: a play, the third-to-last:
a nightmare: three days before he'd told his wife

he'd descended stairs to death, disembodied cries,
    no living person in sight, the President assassinated—
    later, a funeral line through Illinois in April.

2.

April in D.C. is unlike April, here, northern Michigan,
    shoveling snow, dense, crushed under its own weight,
    I clear the walkway; the mail hasn't been coming.

I can feel my feet through boots, awkward as wearing rubber buckets.
    April throbs under tulip head muck, bulbous faces shaking free,
    flimsy lips are humming, eating upward through sod.

I turn to see clouds billow and dwindle like hoary pores on a sunless face.

Tomorrow I will make the Arctic plunge, toss myself fifteen feet
    off volcanic cliff, four degrees, vodka-thin blood, momentary stay
    of pain, dive into space where ice breaks and sways against rock,
    maybe hope the shock of cold doesn't kill me. Three months before:

3.

the night after the night I am raped, I sit bundled in a snow bank
    at Lower Harbor, watch the barges crush the ice
    through Lake Superior without hesitation.

I look out at ore docks—those multi-story boxes, steel shoots
    holding rust-red pellets and, once, a man who'd walked the tracks
    above and fell some fifty feet, broke his leg and died there.

I take off my snow boots, both pairs of wool socks, push my feet

into the snow. With blood slowing to my heart,
I now have clarity to leave the harbor, walk back into town,

back to my apartment where it happened, get thirty-five cents
so I can call my boyfriend in Chicago.

4.

Instead of going back there, I use driftwood to knock sand-ice
from the hinges of a trash can, dislodge four
frozen pop cans to return to the store for dimes.

The AT&T logo is as blue as the lake pushing through ice.
Outside Kim's Liquor store, I use a bobby pin to dig the snow
out of the coin slot, push the buttons a few times to get them working—

these are small details. In drama, they call these pick-up shots—
they aren't important to the plot, but supplement the scene.

Shot: Girl sways forward and back as if preparing to jump.
Shot: Girl bites down, hard, on each finger to test for feeling.
Shot: Girl pushes from her face red-blond hair, so long now it could smother her.
Shot: Girl dials his number—847, Illinois area code. He picks up, is at the bar.

Girl: "This is what happened."
Boyfriend from Chicago: "Well, what were you wearing, anyway?"

5.

I can't remember but realize Lincoln probably was not wearing
this hat when Booth—who knew the play well,
a farce called *Our American Cousin*—waited for laughter

to muffle his approach, a moment in the play when the American
cousin threatens a woman that he'll throw her into the cold
for being a man trap—it is very funny, and when the President laughs,

Booth fires his Derringer pistol, famously leaps, breaks his leg, escapes;
for the first time I think to leave Michigan.

6.

I want solid—mountains, maybe, West or South,
warm, where there's no need to escape the sub-zero air
after leaving that harbor-side bar, the house band wailing "Lola"

as it does every night, the c-o-l-a Cola open-shutting
with the doors, lyrics warning all those suddenly couples
that sometimes muscle knows no sex, instead a vision of confusion,

only ice and water and that museum burnt-out old-growth forest
near your home where those giant Herons build
their nests high, eerily resistant to gravity—

those prehistoric birds, thunder-head gray, their frightening grace,
unnatural circles about those stripped Jack Pines
as thin and pale as a dead person's throat—yes, leave

the threat of cold, the need to invite someone to come inside
this farce: mistaken identity, improbable situations, sexual
innuendo; tolerant transgressive behavior, no poetic justice;

later that week he pulls his Mazda 3000 into my drive,
knocks at the door to collect the sweatshirt he'd left
in the apartment, asks me out to lunch.

7.

The initial ascent West creates pressure in my skull,
fluid swelling behind the eyes, the seams
of my soda bottle squealing as air attempts escape.

I open my mouth, wide, to let it all out, not knowing
the pen I grasp has busted until the ink
is already in the creases of my hands,

black as the thread of dark horizon draped as far as I can see.

8.

But before I make my way from the docks to the pay phone,
I stay a bit longer, watch the Northern Lights—
light as sensual motion, the kind of touch absent in its arrival;

I am startled how it hangs there, solar flares stripped of their terrible heat
somewhere between there and now, bronze, aquamarine smears
drug—like everything else—down, indistinguishable from the water.

Winter Wind

Ellen Airgood

The wind wants nothing. This thing made by hot meeting cold and the earth spinning around, this moving air, is full of power and without desire. It is disappearing every moment and replacing itself. It seems to come from every direction and from nowhere. I want to stop it long enough to write it down.

This wind has made the winter bitter. It is a winter that only briefly lets you out of the house. The house, almost abandoned in the summer for the porch and the garden and the beach, is now the beginning and the end, a haven and a cage, all there is to life. The house is the only ship we have to sail across this Lake Superior winter. Inside I sit at the old oak table we bid $50 for at a summertime auction, writing in bad light, wrapped up in a wool blanket, cold on the left side and warm on the right. When I look out the picture window I see again, still, nothing but snow in the wind.

The snow rushes up the street in flurried gusts, acting as if it had somewhere important to go and were late getting there. It gives me the harrowed feeling of crowds pushing off the subway and swarming up the stairways to busy streets, hurrying to get to work on time. But it is only going to the drift at the base of the hill, until another gust carries it up and over the top. The wind worries the snow like a dog with a small, broken-necked animal in its mouth; it shakes the snow and will not let it alone.

The storm never sleeps. How many feet of snow have fallen, how many miles of wind have blown over the lake? How many hours have I listened to the wind whistling down the chimney? I begin to understand how an immigrant on an endless, arduous ocean journey from her old world to an unknown new one might have felt. I am marooned on a boat rocking in crashing waves, on a sea that looks the same in every direction. And what direction is there? I am surrounded by a tempest of white; snow on the ground, snow in the air, the view across the bay obscured by curtains of snow, and every day on the radio a prediction of "snow, blowing snow, and drifting snow." Are they serious, or is this simply dry, northern humor? Everyone can see that it's still snowing.

The streetlight a block away is only a dim blob of yellow. It could be the sun, shrunken and cold, for all I know. There is not a house, a human, a tree, or bush, or creature anywhere in the world. Or so you could think. In fact, there are houses close by on either side of this one, lost in their own private oceans of snow, blowing snow, and drifting snow. The wind has continued strong for weeks, and how can it? Where does it find its strength? I cannot look at the wind, but see it working; cannot touch it, but always feel it; can't grab or push or pull it, yet am inevitably propelled by its force. I would like to have that impressive power for myself, but it is not within my reach.

A week ago Sunday the sun shone, the wind died down, and I rushed outside to breathe, to take my snowshoes into the woods and look at rabbit tracks, to make avalanches out of trees with drifts of snow perched on their branches. The sun has not looked at us since then. Tonight for the first time since the storm began I could see the moon. It hung low and full out over the bay, a summertime moon, dim behind the thick falling snow. It was like seeing the sun shine during a rainstorm, an unexpected pleasure.

I wonder how it is out on the point, across the bay I cannot see. Rounding the corner to the point you enter a fiercer world, a world on the big lake, unprotected by any sheltering arm of land, undaunted by the large, quiet bay, the Grand Marais. In that world the wind has no second thought about lifting you off your feet and setting you down wherever it pleases, if you are foolish enough to tempt it. And the wind, when it is blowing down trees and lifting up roofs, can brush children off the land's shoulders into the lake, and not care at all. While all the people in this tiny town stood and watched, and hoped, and waited, they knew that despite the boats, the searchers, the helicopter with its spotlight against the dark, the lake would not give these children back. It would not return these sons to their mothers, would not allow us to rewind the tape and stop them from being fearless, reckless, life-filled boys daring the lake during a September storm. The night they died we could only lie in the dark and listen to the house cry in the wind for those boys, lost to the indifferent power of air and water.

But away from the memory of that day, I sit here at my table, surrounded by wind and snow and bitter cold, a virtual I-max of arctic breezes, and I know that I cannot stop the wind. I cannot entice the sun down beneath the clouds to warm us. I cannot make the snow lie down and rest. I can't even get in my car and drive away to a stretch of sunny Georgia highway; the car hasn't run in weeks, and the snow has erased the edges between the road and the swamps and the trees. The weather mocks the powerful inventions of the century. Cars, lights, plumbing; all are jokes the weather enjoys immoderately. On Christmas Day at five in the morning the thermometer in the kitchen read 41 degrees, the wind was blowing harder than ever, the temperature outside was below zero, and the wind-chill was some insane factor below that. The pipes were frozen and the electric lines were misbehaving, blowing out the lights and killing the blowers on the fireplace and woodstove, and I realized I had the flu. I lit the kerosene lamp, drew nearer to the fire, and was able to smile a little through my shivering teeth at our canniness in not relying too completely on modern things.

I am 25 miles from anywhere. That small, 25-miles-from-here place is only another little town that time forgot, with one grocery, a bar, a gas station, and a restaurant. What would be the point in going there? It's just like here, without the lake out the front window. So, 100 miles from anywhere, and the only highway going there closed for the last four days. How can 50 miles of highway be closed for days? What can there be that those humongous giants of equipment, the snowplows and graders and front-end loaders that chug so capably around town, can't conquer? Something, apparently. Something along that stretch of road where I saw a bald eagle fly over low just before Christmas. In town the snowplows roll by on tires as large as my old apartment. I know from flying in airplanes that the sun is shining up above all these clouds. I know it, but I don't believe it. Down here it is dark almost all the time, the same way in the summer it is light. If the day is a circle, one-third is light, all the rest dark, and dark sometimes a long walk back to the light again.

I never thought the storm could last so long. Now it dawns on me that it might go on forever. Only now do I begin to understand that there's no end to it. Not ever. It is a roller coaster ride that I have had enough of, only they aren't letting me off, they're making it go faster. It is getting, just beginning to start to be, scary. A little panic is setting up shop. I can hear the breath of the windigo whistling down the chimney, whispering to me. I never understood before how the windigo can make you do terrible things. Crazy things. Before it was an idea, but now it has the flickering edges of something real. The dog seems unaffected by any of it, panting in front of the fire and itching her nose with her paw, but I have to go out before the walls close in.

Outside, the wind makes a lonesome noise in the trees. The spindly maples, grown thick together on the untended corner lot, rattle and creak like a group of cantankerous old men, warning the younger generation of its waywardness. It is midnight-quiet, no one about, no sound except the cold, creaking trees. I have forgotten in the moment of listening to their eerie conversation to breathe into my scarf, and the wind reaches down my throat to my startled lungs in an icy rush. I cannot breathe, and I am afraid, a little. I wonder if I will make it home. I have walked three blocks downtown for eggs and milk and struggled back home into the east wind, and here in sight of the house maybe I will not make it. Panic is the mother of disaster. I give myself instructions: turn your back on the wind, bury your face in your scarf, relax and breathe, and go home; carry the eggs and milk and yourself to safety. On the kitchen radio they tell me not to go out if I can help it, the wind-chill is 50 below. I know, I say, I know.

The wind makes a lonesome noise at my bedroom window, too. It made that same lonesome noise at me all day long. It has been sighing outside the door for all these weeks, whistling down the chimney, breathing into the walls. It has found an easy way in upstairs, where all the windows are old and loose in their frames. We've been out on the ocean of winter so long, we'd not know how to walk on spring, at first. We'd be drunk on sunshine and warmth, if there were any. We'd push up the windows in their rattly frames, let a Chinook wind wave the curtains gently. We'd breathe deeply in and out and laugh, not being able to help ourselves. We'd shoo the windigo spirit back up the chimney with a whoosh; we'd send it back north across the lake and far, far up Hudson's Bay, to wait for another hard, crazy-making winter. If only the wind would be quiet for a while.

Jane's Christmas Gift 25 Dec 1841

Bame-wa-wa-ge-zhik-aquay
Translated by **Amélie Jumel** *and* **Ronald Riekki**

LE RENNE EST UN ANIMAL DE L'ESPÈCE DU CERF, ON LE TROUVE DANS LE pays du nord. Cet quadrupède est le principal bétail de les Lapon. Il à la figure d'un cerf, mais est plus grand, et plus ramasse, et les membres sont encore plus délié. La renne donne les Lapons leur lait, et fromage. Les rennes sont plus engraisser dans l'automne et dans l'été. La chair du renne est excellent. La peau du renne—est aussi très utile. La renne est plus égal nécessaire aux Lapons, que la vache est à nous.

JEANNE L. J. SCHOOLCRAFT
Decembre vingt-quatre.

THE REINDEER IS AN ANIMAL OF THE DEER SPECIES, THAT WE FIND IN the north country. This quadruped is the Lapland's main livestock. It has the figure of a deer, but it's larger, and stockier, and its limbs are even more slender. The reindeer of the Lapland give milk and cheese. The reindeer are more fattened in the autumn and in the summer. The meat of reindeer is excellent. The skin of the reindeer—is also very useful. The reindeer is very necessary to the Lapps, even more than the cow is to us.

JEANNE L. J. SCHOOLCRAFT
December twenty-fourth.

Dandelion Cottage excerpt

Carroll Watson Rankin

"THERE'S NO USE TALKING," SAID JEAN, ONE DAY, AS THE GIRLS SAT AT their dining-room table eating very smoky toast and drinking the weakest of cocoa, "we'll have to get some provisions of our own before long if we're going to invite Mr. Black to dinner as we promised. The cupboard's perfectly empty and Bridget says I can't take another scrap of bread or one more potato out of the house this week."

"Aunty Jane says there'll be trouble," said Marjory, "if I don't keep out of her ice box, so I guess I can't bring any more milk. When she says there'll be trouble, there usually is, if I'm not pretty careful. But dear me, it *is* such fun to cook our own meals on that dear little box-stove, even if most of the things do taste pretty awful."

"I wish," said Mabel, mournfully, "that somebody would give us a hen, so we could make omelets."

"Who ever made omelets out of a hen?" asked Jean, laughing.

"I meant out of the eggs, of course," said Mabel, with dignity. "Hens lay eggs, don't they? If we count on five or six eggs a day—"

"The goose that laid the golden egg laid only one a day," said Marjory. "It seems to me that six is a good many."

"I wasn't talking about geese," said Mabel, "but about just plain everyday hens."

"Six-every-day hens, you mean, don't you?" asked Marjory, teasingly. "You'd better wish for a cow, too, while you're about it."

"Yes," said Bettie, "we certainly need one, for I'm not to ask for butter more than twice a week. Mother says she'll be in the poorhouse before summer's over if she has to provide butter for *two* families."

"I just tell you what it is, girls," said Jean, nibbling her cindery crust, "we'll just have to earn some money if we're to give Mr. Black any kind of a dinner."

Mabel, who always accepted new ideas with enthusiasm, slipped quietly into the kitchen, took a solitary lemon from the cupboard, cut it in half, and squeezed the juice into a broken-nosed pitcher. This done, she added a little sugar and a great deal of water to the lemon juice, slipped quietly out of the back door, ran around the house and in at the front door, taking a small table from the front room. This she carried out of doors to the corner of the lot facing the street, where she established her lemonade stand.

She was almost immediately successful, for the day was warm, and Mrs. Bartholomew Crane, who was entertaining two visitors on her front porch, was glad of an opportunity to offer her guests something in the way of refreshment. The cottage boasted only one glass that did not leak, but Mabel cheerfully made three trips across the street with it—it did not occur to any of them until too late it would have been easier to carry the pitcher across in the first place. The lemonade was decidedly weak, but the visitors were too polite to say so. On her return, a thirsty small boy offered Mabel a nickel for all that was left in the pitcher, and Mabel, after a moment's hesitation, accepted the offer.

"You're getting a bargain," said Mabel. "There's as much as a glass and three quarters there, besides all the lemon."

"Did you get a whole pitcherful out of one lemon?" asked the boy. "You'd be able to make circus lemonade all right."

Before the other girls had had time to discover what had become of her, the proprietor of the lemonade stand marched into the cottage and proudly displayed four shining nickels and the empty pitcher.

"Why, where in the world did you get all that?" cried Marjory. "Surely you never earned it by being on time for meals—you've been late three times a day ever since we got the cottage."

"Sold lemonade," said Mabel. "Our troubles are over, girls. I'm going to buy *two* lemons tomorrow and sell twice as much."

"Good!" cried Bettie, "I'll help. The boys have promised to bring me a lot of arbutus tonight—they went to the woods this morning. I'll tie it in bunches and perhaps we can sell that, too."

"Wouldn't it be splendid if we could have Mr. Black here to dinner next Saturday?" said Jean. "I'll never be satisfied until we've kept that promise, but I don't suppose we could possibly get enough things together by that time."

"I have a sample can of baking powder," offered Marjory, hopefully. "I'll bring it over next time I come."

"What's the good?" asked matter-of-fact Mabel. "We can't feed Mr. Black on just plain baking powder, and we haven't any biscuits to raise with it."

"Dear me," said Jean, "I wish we hadn't been so extravagant at first. If we hadn't had so many tea parties last week, we might get enough flour and things at home. Mother says it's too expensive having all her groceries carried off."

"Never mind," consoled Mabel, confidently. "We'll be buying our own groceries by this time tomorrow with the money we make selling lemonade. A boy said my lemonade was quite as good as you can buy at the circus."

Unfortunately, however, it rained the next day and the next, so lemonade was out of the question. By the time it cleared, Bettie's neat little bunches of arbutus were no longer fresh, and careless Mabel had forgotten where she had put the money. She mentioned no fewer than twenty-two places where the four precious nickels might be, but none of them happened to be the right one.

"Mercy me," said Bettie, "it's dreadful to be so poor! I'm afraid we'll have to invite Mr. Black to one of our bread-and-sugar tea-parties, after all."

"No," said Jean, firmly. "We've just got to give him a regular seven-course dinner—he has 'em every day at home. We'll have to put it off until we can do it in style."

"By and by," said Mabel, "we'll have beans and radishes and things in our own garden, and we can go to the woods for berries."

"Perhaps," said Bettie, hopefully, "one of the boys might catch a fish—Rob *almost* did, once."

"I suppose I could ask Aunty Jane for a potato once in a while," said Marjory, "but I'll have to give her time to forget about last month's grocery bill—she says we never before used so many eggs in one month and I guess Maggie *did* give me a good many. Potatoes will keep, you know. We can save 'em until we have enough for a meal."

"While we're about it," said Bettie, "I think we'd better have Mrs. Crane to dinner, too. She's such a nice old lady and she's been awfully good to us."

"She's not very well off," agreed Mabel, "and probably a real, first-class dinner would taste good to her."

"But," pleaded Bettie, "don't let's ask her until we're sure of the date. As it is, I can't sleep nights for thinking of how Mr. Black must feel. He'll think we don't want him."

"You'd better explain to him," suggested Jean, "that it isn't convenient to have him just yet, but that we're going to just as soon as ever we can. We mustn't tell him why, because it would be just like him to send the provisions here himself, and then it wouldn't really be *our* party."

In spite of all the girls' plans, however, by the end of the week the cottage larder was still distressingly empty. Marjory had, indeed, industriously collected potatoes, only to have them carried off by an equally industrious rat; and Mabel's four nickels still remained missing. Things in the vegetable garden seemed singularly backward, possibly because the four eager gardeners kept digging them up to see if they were growing. Their parents and Marjory's Aunty Jane were firmer than ever in their refusal to part with any more staple groceries.

Perhaps if the girls had explained why they wanted the things, their relatives would have been more generous; but girllike, the four poverty-stricken young housekeepers made a deep mystery of their dinner plan. It was their most cherished secret, and when they met each morning they always said, mysteriously, "Good morning—remember M. B. D.," which meant, of course, "Mr. Black's Dinner."

Mr. Black, indeed, never went by without referring to the girls' promise.

"When," he would ask, "is that dinner party coming off? It's a long time since I've been invited to a first-class dinner, cooked by four accomplished young ladies, and I'm getting hungrier every minute. When I get up in the morning I always say: 'Now I won't eat much breakfast because I've got to save room for that dinner'—and then, after all, I don't get invited."

The situation was growing really embarrassing. The girls began to feel that keeping house, not to mention giving dinner parties, with no income whatever, was anything but a joke.

How to Draw a Crow

Anne Ohman Youngs

AHEAD ARE FROZEN FIELDS AND A CAR PARKED AT THE ROADSIDE, ITS trunk gaping and rust puncturing a wired door. The driver shuffles over crusty snow toward a deer hit by some earlier car or truck. He slips on steaming entrails and breaks the snow as he bends to lift and examine the hind legs.

Beside a gravel road, his three children wait for a school bus. They never play parcheesi or fold origami, and when the blowing snow speaks, they don't hear it above their voices choked with wood smoke. In the house behind them, their mother, wearing long gray socks with holes, brushes crumbs and carries chipped plates to the kitchen sink. Her mornings match her afternoons and evenings perfectly.

Bobbing his head up and down, the man follows his footsteps back to the car, removes an axe and tests its edge with his thumb. Now do you understand the crow? Can you draw it with your pencil? Fill it in with that kind of happiness?

Imprinting

Janeen Rastall

> You were aimed from birth.
>
> —William Stafford

I. Migration

For long hours
it is only roofs,
    a backlit yard flickering
    or a basketball net
reaching to snare the night.
    Streets meet, cross,
thin to single grey threads.
    Trees take over,
swell to canopies.
A pool has been calling since birth,
    its coordinates tattooed on DNA.
Even though a road draws a noose around the shore,
houses perch on the water's lip,
the gander knows this lake,
lands feet first, calls to the flock,
    beacons them home.

II. RACINE

The town has
collapsed in the center,
strip malls spreading north and south.
Once you see the scarred Piggly Wiggly,
you know your way.
You follow the old bus route,
wind past the park and cemetery,
recreate the rides of summer:
your grandmother close beside you,
her purse between her feet,
in crimped hands, she holds a paper sack—
apples, Wonder Bread, a waxed envelope of lunch meat.
You drive without hesitation
to the house on the cul-de-sac,
look for the window
where you pressed
your nose against the glass
to watch your grandfather,
lunch pail in hand,
walk to the tannery down the street.

III. LAKESTRUCK

An accident led you here.
You went to see another frozen lake,
to walk among the ice volcanoes,
listen to the floes bump and crack.
You did not know
Superior waited
deep-hearted,
battering its song

against black rocks.
You have been pulled in
like trout
    from the Au Train
or the Chocolay,
    drawn to deeper waters.
Your breath syncs to the sound of the surf.

The Lost Lie

Anne Sexton

There is rust in my mouth,
the stain of an old kiss.
and my eyes are turning purple,
my mouth is glue
and my hands are two stones
and the heart,
is still there,
that place where love dwelt
but it is nailed into place.
Still I feel no pity for these oddities,
in fact the feeling is one of hatred.
For it is only the child in me bursting out
and I keep plotting how to kill her.

Once there was a woman,
full as a theater of moon
and love begot love
and the child, when she peeked out,
did not hate herself back then.
Funny, funny, love what you do.
But today I roam a dead house,

a frozen kitchen, a bedroom
like a gas chamber.
The bed itself is an operating table
where my dreams slice me into pieces.

Oh, love,
the terror,
the fright wig,
that your dear curly head
was, was, was, was.

The Break Away

Anne Sexton

Your daisies have come
on the day of my divorce:
the courtroom a cement box,
a gas chamber for the infectious Jew in me
and a perhaps land, a possibly promised land
for the Jew in me,
but still a betrayal room for the till-death-do-us—
and yet a death, as in the unlocking of scissors
that makes the now separate parts useless,
even to cut each other up as we did yearly
under the crayoned-in sun.
The courtroom keeps squashing our lives as they break
into two cans ready for recycling,
flattened tin humans
and a tin law,
even for my twenty-five years of hanging on
by my teeth as I once saw at Ringling Brothers.
The gray room:
Judge, lawyer, witness
and me and invisible Skeezix,
and all the other torn

enduring the bewilderments
of their division.

Your daisies have come
on the day of my divorce.
They arrive like round yellow fish,
sucking with love at the coral of our love.
Yet they wait,
in their short time,
like little utero half-borns,
half killed, thin and bone soft.
They know they are about to die,
but breathe like premies, in and out,
upon my kitchen table.
They breathe the air that stands
for twenty-five illicit days,
the sun crawling inside the sheets,
the moon spinning like a tornado
in the washbowl,
and we orchestrated them both,
calling ourselves TWO CAMP DIRECTORS.
There was a song, our song on your cassette,
that played over and over
and baptised the prodigals.
It spoke the unspeakable,
as the rain will on an attic roof,
letting the animal join its soul
as we kneeled before a miracle—
forgetting its knife.

The daisies confer
in the old-married kitchen

papered with blue and green chefs
who call out *pies*, *cookies*, *yummy*,
at the charcoal and cigarette smoke
they wear like a yellowy salve.
The daisies absorb it all—
the twenty-five-year-old sanctioned love
(If one could call such handfuls of fists
and immobile arms *that*!)
and on this day my world rips itself up
while the country unfastens along
with its perjuring king and his court.
It unfastens into an abortion of belief,
as in me—
the legal rift—
as one *might* do with the daisies
but does not
for they stand for a love
undergoing open heart surgery
that might take
if one prayed tough enough.
And yet I demand,
even in prayer,
that I am not a thief,
a mugger of need,
and that your heart survive
on its own,
belonging only to itself,
whole, entirely whole,
and workable
in its dark cavern under your ribs.

I pray it will know truth,

if truth catches in its cup
and yet I pray, as a child would,
that the surgery take.

I dream it is taking.
Next I dream the love is swallowing itself.
Next I dream the love is made of glass,
glass coming through the telephone
that is breaking slowly,
day by day, into my ear.
Next I dream that I put on the love
like a lifejacket and we float,
jacket and I,
we bounce on that priest-blue.
We are as light as a cat's ear
and it is safe,
safe far too long!
And I awaken quickly and go to the opposite window
and peer down at the moon in the pond
and know that beauty has walked over my head,
into this bedroom and out,
flowing out through the window screen,
dropping deep into the water
to hide.

I will observe the daisies
fade and dry up
until they become flour,
snowing themselves onto the table
beside the drone of the refrigerator,
beside the radio playing Frankie
(as often as FM will allow)

snowing lightly, a tremor sinking from the ceiling—
as twenty-five years split from my side
like a growth that I sliced off like a melanoma.

It is six P.M. as I water these tiny weeds
and their little half-life,
their numbered days
that raged like a secret radio,
recalling love that I picked up innocently,
yet guiltily,
as my five-year-old daughter
picked gum off the sidewalk
and it became suddenly an elastic miracle.

For me it was love found
like a diamond
where carrots grow—
the glint of diamond on a plane wing,
meaning: DANGER! THICK ICE!
but the good crunch of that orange,
the diamond, the carrot,
both with four million years of resurrecting dirt,
and the love,
although Adam did not know the word,
the love of Adam
obeying his sudden gift.

You, who sought me for nine years,
in stories made up in front of your naked mirror
or walking through rooms of fog women,
you trying to forget the mother
who built guilt with the lumber of a locked door

as she sobbed her soured milk and fed you loss
through the keyhole,
you who wrote out your own birth
and built it with your own poems,
your own lumber, your own keyhole,
into the trunk and leaves of your manhood,
you, who fell into my words, years
before you fell into me (the other,
both the Camp Director and the camper),
you who baited your hook with wide-awake dreams,
and calls and letters and once a luncheon,
and twice a reading by me for you.
But I wouldn't!

Yet this year,
yanking off all past years,
I took the bait
and was pulled upward, upward,
into the sky and was held by the sun—
the quick wonder of its yellow lap—
and became a woman who learned her own skin
and dug into her soul and found it full,
and you became a man who learned his own skin
and dug into his manhood, his humanhood
and found you were as real as a baker
or a seer
and we became a home,
up into the elbows of each other's soul,
without knowing—
an invisible purchase—
that inhabits our house forever.

We were
blessed by the House-Die
by the altar of the color T.V.
and somehow managed to make a tiny marriage,
a tiny marriage
called belief,
as in the child's belief in the tooth fairy,
so close to absolute,
so daft within a year or two.
The daisies have come
for the last time.
And I who have,
each year of my life,
spoken to the tooth fairy,
believing in her,
even when I *was* her,
am helpless to stop your daisies from dying,
although your voice cries into the telephone:
Marry me! Marry me!
and my voice speaks onto these keys tonight:
The love is in dark trouble!
The love is starting to die,
right now—
we are in the process of it.
The empty process of it.

I see two deaths,
and the two men plod toward the mortuary of my heart,
and though I willed one away in court today
and I whisper dreams and birthdays into the other,
they both die like waves breaking over me
and I am drowning a little,

but always swimming
among the pillows and stones of the breakwater.
And though your daisies are an unwanted death,
I wade through the smell of their cancer
and recognize the prognosis,
its cartful of loss . . .

I say now,
you gave what you could.
It was quite a ferris wheel to spin on!
and the dead city of my marriage
seems less important
than the fact that the daisies came weekly,
over and over,
likes kisses that can't stop themselves.

There sit two deaths on November 5th, 1973.
Let one be forgotten—
Bury it! Wall it up!
But let me not forget the man
of my child-like flowers
though he sinks into the fog of Lake Superior,
he remains, his fingers the marvel
of fourth of July sparklers,
his furious ice cream cones of licking,
remains to cool my forehead with a washcloth
when I sweat into the bathtub of his being.

For the rest that is left:
name it gentle,
as gentle as radishes inhabiting
their short life in the earth,

name it gentle,
gentle as old friends waving *so long* at the window,
or in the drive,
name it gentle as maple wings singing
themselves upon the pond outside,
as sensuous as the mother-yellow in the pond,
that night that it was ours,
when our bodies floated and bumped
in moon water and the cicadas
called out like tongues.

Let such as this
be resurrected in all men
wherever they mold their days and nights
as when for twenty-five days and nights you molded mine
and planted the seed that dives into my God
and will do so forever
no matter how often I sweep the floor.

The Inventory of Goodbye

Anne Sexton

I have a pack of letters.
I have a pack of memories.
I could cut out the eyes of both.
I could wear them like a patchwork apron.
I could stick them in the washer, the drier,
and maybe some of the pain would float off like dirt?
Perhaps down the disposal I could grind up the loss.
Besides—what a bargain—no expensive phone calls.
No lengthy trips on planes in the fog.
No manicky laughter or blessings from an odd-lot priest.
That priest is probably still floating on a fog pillow.
Blessing us. Blessing us.

Am I to bless the lost you,
sitting here with my clumsy soul?
Propaganda time is over.
I sit here on the spike of truth.
No one to hate except the slim fish of memory
that slides in and out of my brain.
No one to hate except the acute feel of my nightgown
brushing my body like a light that has gone out.

It recalls the kiss we invented, tongues like poems,
meeting, returning, inviting, causing a fever of need.
Laughter, maps, cassettes, touch singing its path—
all to be broken and laid away in a tight strongbox.
The monotonous dead clog me up and there is only
black done in black that oozes from the strongbox.
I must disembowel it and then set the heart, the legs,
of two who were one upon a large woodpile
and ignite, as I was once ignited, and let it whirl
into flame, reaching the sky
making it dangerous with its red.

Eighteen Maple Trees

Jane Piirto

I call the city manager
to ask who cut down
18 maple trees
on our street,
the oldest street in town
the one with the stone wall

she says, "What trees?
No one has called to miss
18 maple trees
except you and you don't
live here anymore.
You say they were cut down
the end of last summer?
The City of Ishpeming
only cut down 14 trees.
Only one was on Jasper Street.
They had to be cut by
The Cleveland Cliffs Iron Company.
They own all the land."

I call the company, C.C.I.
"Who cut down the trees?"

"What trees?" the P.R. man says.
Don was in high school
2 years ahead of me.
Head of the Chamber of Commerce.
Certainly he cares about
18 maple trees.
"It wasn't C.C.I.
that I'm aware of."
I ask the neighbors
"When were the maples cut down?"

No one seems to remember.
Maybe last summer maybe not.

Neighbor Paulie says he heard
Arvo requested they be cut down.
With all the skiers coming up
to the new ski trail,
the branches fell on the street
after snowstorms.
"It was dangerous."

Why can Arvo request such a thing
and they would just do it?
"Don't the neighbors
need to know?"
We can't ask Arvo.
Arvo fell off his roof
cleaning ice.

He died last year.
Paulie says he'll ask
the city crew if they did it.

I check the stumps,
count the rings,
stop at 90,
dense and not diseased.
I ask Paulette,
a neighbor who's a teacher
in the health food co-op
with my mother.
"They were just gone

one day at the end
of last summer."

There have always been
changes in the woods
where The Company
mines iron in open pits
we hear heavy machinery
boom through the forests
blasts like earthquakes
echo in the sky

but we, blithe
pick blueberries
we go tobogganing
celebrate family fests
hunt and orienteer

ski cross-country hills
we swim in fresh spring-fed lakes
we forget—forgive the rampage
of necessary commerce:
The Company

just behind Lake Ogden
a gaping mine in the earth
miles wide and very deep
the red earth yields low-grade iron
for pellets for steel
only seen by nonminers
from commuter planes
when the weather is good
now The Company has blocked off
Cliff's Drive; all gashing is hidden

Ogden flows into Lake Sally
the town's water supply
they changed the water supply
to Teal Lake and then to wells last year.
Sally and Ogden
drop in levels month by month
the mine is two miles
from our home.
The Company
owns the land.

I ask my mother
"Why didn't you complain
about the missing trees?"

"I assumed
they had a reason," she says.
"I feel
like a collaborator
with the Nazis," she says.

I Am a Knife

Roxane Gay

My husband is a hunter.

I am a knife.

Last deer season, he took me on a hunt with him. At four in the morning, he shook me awake. He made love to me. He always makes love to me before the hunt. There is a quality to his efforts that is different, more intense. There is a rawness to how he touches me, as if he is preparing himself for what he is about to do. He takes me. He uses me. He marks me. I allow him. I revel in it. When my husband took me hunting with him, he told me not to shower after he lay on top of me heavy, sweaty, his lips pressed against the dark curve of my neck. As we dressed, I still felt him inside me, sticking to my thighs. It was cold outside. In the cab of his truck, I leaned against his arm, my eyes closed. He drank coffee from a thermos that used to belong to his father, who is dead from black lung. My husband's beard smelled like coffee for the rest of the day.

We spent hours in the deer blind, doused in deer piss, waiting. I grew bored but stayed silent. Several does passed before us but my husband held one finger to his lips. We were waiting for a buck. "I want to kill something majestic today," my husband said earlier that morning. He believes killing brings him closer to God. He is always looking for God even though he has little faith left. More time passed. Our bodies grew stiff. My stomach felt hollow. I hungered. His shoulders slumped as his hope faded but then a massive buck galloped into our sights. The creature was indeed majestic—its musculature pronounced, body thick, standing tall. My husband raised his rifle, inhaled deeply, held his finger against the trigger. He waited. The buck turned his head and looked at us with black, glassy eyes. I held my breath too. We waited. My husband pulled the trigger and exhaled slowly. We waited. The bullet hit the deer in his neck, making a neat black hole from which a thin stream of blood began to flow. My husband nodded his head once, set his rifle down. He is a gun.

The buck was still alive when we got to him, breathing shallow. I pressed my hand to the matted fur, felt the animal's warmth, the strength of the muscles beneath his coat and the bones beneath the muscle and the blood holding the muscle and bone together. My husband reached for his knife, preparing to slit the buck's throat. I grabbed his arm, shook my head. I placed my hand over the buck's heart, waited for it to stop beating. We waited. We waited for quite some time. My husband prayed, offering acts of contrition into the still air around us. When the buck was finally dead, I used one fingernail, cutting the creature open from his neck to his rear. His flesh fell open slowly, warm innards steaming out into the cold air. The air became sharp and humid with the stench of death.

My husband reached into the dead animal then stared at his hand covered in dark red, almost black blood. He ran his thumb across my lower lip, then slid his thumb into my mouth. I sucked slowly, tasting the deer's blood, salty and thick. I moaned. My husband rubbed his bloody hand over my face and as the blood dried, my skin felt thin and taut. I lay back on the ground, now soaked with the deer's blood. My husband undressed me slowly, then stood and stared at me naked, shivering next to the animal he killed. I wondered if he could tell us apart. The woods around us were so silent I felt a certain terror rumbling beneath my rib cage. When he lay on top of me, I spread my thighs, sank my teeth into his shoulder. My husband smelled like an animal and took me like an animal. Together, we were animals. I left my mark on the broad expanse of his back.

Later, my husband field dressed the animal, removing all the internal organs. We bound the deer's forelegs and hind legs, and my husband carried the open, bloody animal across his shoulders. I carried our guns and followed in his footsteps. When we got home, he took his kill to the work shed behind our home and began to butcher. It is a long, bloody affair, butchering an animal. There are things that need to be done in order for the kill to provide—the carcass needs to be broken down, the meat stored properly. For the next several months, we would bring our friends all manner of venison wrapped carefully in brown butcher paper, tied with strong twine. My husband would make jerky and sausage to share with the men he plays poker with, his brother, strangers at the bar. I would eat none of it. I do not care for the taste of venison. It tastes too much like the flesh of an animal.

We live in a large home that is beautiful and empty. We never talk about the emptiness or the failed attempts to fill the void. It is a sorrow we share but do not share. Sometimes, I sit in one of our empty rooms, perfectly decorated, frozen in time. I sit on the floor and stare at the pink wallpaper and the wooden letters on the wall spelling a name and the linens my mother made for a perfect, tiny bed. I rock back and forth until I cannot breathe and then I crawl into the hallway and gasp for air.

My husband's family is religious. They believe in God. Their God is angry and unkind. Their God has made them in his image. Every Sunday, my husband and I go to church with his family—brother, mother, stepfather. This is the only time I spend with them. My husband's faith is weak. I have none left. We sit in church on the hard pews pretending we believe, pretending we belong. Sometimes, I feel his mother staring at me with her pursed lips and narrow eyes. When I feel her staring, I dig my fingernails into a hymnal or the pew or my husband's thigh. After church, we go to my in-laws for a meal. They do not trust me because I don't eat venison. His mother resents having to accommodate my culinary peculiarities, but each week she prepares me a dry breast of chicken, carelessly broiled, unseasoned, and I eat the rubbery meat and smile while doing so. This makes her even angrier. I help wash the dishes while my husband and his stepfather work in the barn and then, mercifully, we can leave. His mother always stands on the porch and watches as we drive away. I make sure to sit so close to my husband in the cab of his truck, it looks like I'm sitting on his lap. I make him kiss me, and I kiss him back so hard it's like I'm devouring his face. I want her to know what her son and I hold between us.

My family lives far away in the heavy heat of South Florida. They rarely visit, don't know how to deal with the cold. They can't understand why my husband and I stay in the North Country. When we visit my family, my husband is overwhelmed by the humidity and constantly being surrounded by people who look so different from him, few who speak English. He always grips my hand tightly when we're in Florida. He looks so scared, so young. It is only when we leave our home I realize it's not that he won't live anywhere else but that he cannot. My sister, my twin, comes to visit often because she understands why I stay with my man in a place I do not love. She understands he loves me so good I would live anywhere with him. They get along well because he loves me right.

My sister never stays with one man too long, says she lives vicariously through me as I do through her. She doesn't need to get married. I don't miss being single. She's always calling me to tell me about a man she met in a bar or at a bookstore or in line at a coffee shop and how that man ended up in her bed but rarely in her heart. When she visits, she fools around with my husband's best friend, a guy named Grant, a powder monkey on my husband's logging crew who thinks he and my sister share something so special it keeps her coming back. The four of us like to go bowling. We drink and bowl and drink and bowl and then we go down by the lake with a case of beer and make out on wooden park benches like teenagers with nowhere else to go. When I shiver after my husband slides his big hands beneath my shirt, she moans and when she spreads her legs and pulls Grant's hand into her pants, I clench my thighs. People ask us if we have some kind of special connection. We lie when we answer their questions.

The wives of loggers tell stories about men broken by falling limbs or treetops or wild chainsaws—they call these things widow makers. I listen to these stories and think, if something happened to my man, I would cut down every tree I ever saw for the rest of my life. When my husband is late coming home from work, I feel uneasy. I imagine our empty home even emptier than it already is. I make sure the phone is working, that I haven't missed any calls and when he does get home, I beat his chest with my fists. I damn him for making me worry. Most nights, he comes home smelling of sweat and sap, sometimes sawdust if he's been in the mill. He takes his dirty work boots off and undresses in the mudroom. I watch, leaning in the doorway, holding a cold beer. He always smiles at me, no matter how his day has been. He takes a long sip of his drink, kisses me, his breath warm and yeasty. I tell him how lonely my body has been without him all day. He presses his lips against my neck, pulls at my skin with his teeth.

My sister calls and I hear in her breathing something is wrong before she says a word. I sit at the kitchen table and hold my chest, try to ignore the slow, spreading ache. My husband is in the family room watching a documentary on helicopter loggers, complaining loudly about how they're doing everything wrong. "What is it?" I ask. I try to sound calm. My skin hurts. My sister says, "I'm pregnant," and I exhale slowly. I say, "It's going to be okay." That is the only thing there is to say. I swallow something hard and mournful. I dig my fingernails into the palms of my hand. I am a knife. She says, "I understand," and I smile and hold my stomach, running my fingers along the slightly raised scar that refuses to disappear even though it has been some time since I was cut open. "Can I come stay with you while I figure out what I'm going to do?" she asks, even though she doesn't need to ask. We talk a while longer, then I join my husband. I sit on his lap and bury my head against his chest. I tell him my sister is coming and why and he holds me so tight that even hours later, when we're in bed and he's asleep, I feel him holding me together.

My sister and I were once in a car accident. We were sideswiped by a drunk driver on a backcountry road, the only kind of roads up here. There were high stalks of corn lining either side of the road and bugs were everywhere, their high-pitched humming making the night thick. My sister was unconscious, her pulse weak. The drunk driver was passed out, an angry cut pulsing along his hairline. He reeked of cheap wine. The stench of him made me throw up. My sister was dying so I was dying. I pulled him toward our car. He was so heavy it felt like my shoulders might separate from my body as I pulled and pulled and pulled. Sweat pooled between my breasts and trickled down my spine. When I reached my sister, I fell to the ground, sweaty and out of breath. I pressed two fingers to my sister's neck. She was born seven minutes after me. She could not die before me. Her pulse was even weaker. Her heart was dying. My heart was dying. I cut the drunk driver's chest open, gutted him from the base of his throat to his navel, then ripped his ribcage open, the bones separating neatly. I reached into that careless man's body, wet and warm, and I pulled out the heart he did not deserve. I felt no sadness or mercy for him as the slick organ throbbed in the palm of my hand. I cut my sister's chest open, carefully this time, with a neat incision. I put that man's heart into her chest next to her heart. The two hearts nestled together and began beating as one. My sister stopped dying so I stopped dying. I pulled the flaps of skin back over her open chest and said a silent prayer as her skin fell back in place. I held my sister in my arms until help came. I kissed her forehead and whispered acts of contrition into the night air so she would know she was not alone. I kept her warm and safe.

My sister fits easily into our lives. The house is less empty. She makes a small home for herself in one of our empty rooms. Her stomach swells and her skin glows. I often catch her walking around our property, along the tree line, humming to herself, holding her belly. She is changing and growing a new life. I am not. Sometimes, I catch my husband staring at her. When he notices me watching him watching her, he blushes, looks away guiltily. One night, we are lying in bed. We have just made love and he is still lying on top of me. He is still inside me. He brushes my hair out of my face and kisses me hard and I kiss him back and we bruise each other with our mouths. He says, "I wish we could take the child growing in her and put it inside you where it belongs." I hate him for saying this. I love him for saying this. He rests his head against my breasts and I run my fingers through his hair. I whisper, "If only that could be." He doesn't respond and soon he is snoring lightly, his breath tickling my chest, leaving me cold.

Grant stops by almost every evening to check on my sister. He is convinced the child is his. He brings her clothes for the baby, soft blankets, the food she craves, an expensive stroller. When she is in a good mood, she lets him stay the night. She says he is a comfort. She loves his hands and his voice and the thick matte of hair on his chest. She says she doesn't know if that is enough. I tell her it could be. When I hear them laugh, when I see how he looks at her, there is a loud, painful ringing in my ears that does not go away until I punch myself in the stomach. When her baby kicks, I feel a flutter just below my navel. I imagine reaching into my own belly, cutting away all the damage there.

My sister's belly grows and grows and grows. Her whole body becomes full. Her ankles swell. She walks slower and slower, holding her lower back. Her skin still glows. Her lips are constantly spread in a genuine smile. Toward the end of March, we sit on the porch. It won't be long before she gives birth. She says, "I love this thing inside of me but I want it out." She stretches her legs and groans, then leans against my shoulder. She takes my hand and holds it over her stomach, covering my hand with hers. We are silent but she is asking me something. Her belly is firm and warm and I feel the baby moving around in its amniotic sac. The child is a boy or a girl. The child is strong. Its mother has two hearts. She asks, "What is it like, giving birth?" My own heart throbs dully and all the air from my chest escapes. I close my eyes. I say, "It feels like something wild is tearing your body from the inside out." She closes her eyes, squeezes my hand harder. The scar across my belly splits open and blood dampens my shirt but I sit still, I sit with my sister. She needs this from me.

A piercing scream in the loneliest part of the night wakes me up. My husband leaps out of bed, his hair standing on end, his boxers hanging loosely around his waist. He looks around the room, his fingers balled tightly into fists. His eyes are bright white. We hear another scream. I get out of bed. The floor is cold. I go to my sister's room. She is sitting up in bed, sweating heavily, her long hair clinging to her face. She looks at me, her eyes clouded with fear. Grant is holding his phone. He says, "I called for the ambulance but it will be hours before they can come to." This is how life is in the North Country. There is never the kind of help you need when you need it. My husband and I know all too well what happens when the only ambulance in four counties is hours away. You end up bleeding in the cab of a pickup while your child dies inside of you, while your husband speeds to the hospital, an hour away, over icy, winding backcountry roads, crying because he knows he cannot get you there in time. I place my hand on Grant's arm. I say, "Leave us," and my husband pulls Grant out of the room.

I kneel on the bed next to my sister. I think about how I am holding her life in my very hands. I say, "Close your eyes," and she does. She trusts she is safe. I press the palm of my hand to her forehead and whisper sweet words so she will feel no pain. I drag my fingernail across her lower abdomen and her skin parts easily. There is so much blood. I cut through the layers of dermis, the fat, yellow, soft globes that fall away loosely. I am careful. I am sharp. When I reach the uterus, I am gentle and neat, making another horizontal cut. There is still so much blood. I see the dark head of a child covered in thick fluids. I pull the child free, it is a boy, and he is followed by a long cord of slick membrane. I cut the boy free from the cord, hold the dirty little creature against me as my sister lies quietly, cut open, there is so much blood. My sister waits, she trusts me. Her boy is hot in my arms. When he opens the slits of his eyes, I bite my tongue until I taste blood. I look at this boy, his tiny fingers curled, his limbs narrow and long, and it hurts to think of all the moments he will have. I am angry. I want to carve the anger out of my body the way I cut everything else. My sister holds her arms open. She trusts me. Our eyes lock.

That night, in the cab of his truck, the heat wouldn't work so every breath made my chest ache. I bled all over the seat and held my husband's thigh and shivered and forgot what warmth felt like. He refused to look at me but over and over he said, "I will get you there." The wild thing inside me was trying to get out. The pain was clear and constant and exceptional. I leaned forward, moaning softly. I spoke the last prayer I would ever pray. I told my husband I loved him. I told him, "Do not let this happen to me." I begged the silence around us for mercy. At the hospital, my husband carried me inside, grunting with every step. He explained to the doctor I was due any day. He said, "Everything's going to be okay, right?" The doctor nodded. The doctor cut me open and hollowed me out and left an ugly scar, country medicine. He pulled a frail, bloody girl from my womb who could not breathe on her own, could not cry. Her head was strangely large, her skin almost translucent, as if we could see right through her. She was a wild thing but did not live long. We gave her a name. We held her and held her and held her until we could no longer hold her and then I did not speak for a very long time.

The night after my nephew is born, after I cut my sister open and hold her life in my hands and close the wounds I made to save her child, my husband fucks me in our bed while my sister and a man and a baby boy sleep in her bed. They are at peace. My husband and I are loud and violent with each other. When I bite him, I draw blood. He touches me like he's trying to fix everything broken inside me, like he's trying to break me even more, like he is trying, through will alone, to create another life inside of what is left of my womb. I believe through him all things are possible. I wrap my arms around his back. I press my knees against his ribs. We do not look away from each other. His every thrust hurts more, hurts everywhere, but I spread my legs wider, open myself more to him. He is a gun. I am a knife.

Skin on Skin

Sally Brunk

five little girls
Kiowa, Pawnee, Ojibwa, Choctaw, Crow
we were babies out of our teens
hundreds, a thousand miles
separating us from loved ones
Haskell Indian Junior College
was our home

a simple walk to the 24-hour grocery store
"Strength in numbers," Montana said
this statement was true, but not for us
Dillon's, hangout to the skinheads
they were present
as reliable as the locusts that claimed
everything in Kansas that summer

it started with taunts through the store
down one aisle then another
continued into the muggy heat
that took one's breath away
hearts racing,
we turned toward our version of home

we kept close to one another
"Stay near the houses,
they wouldn't want witnesses," Jocelyn whispered
we could see the rooftops of our dorm,
when they made their move
then we made ours

run! Is what instinct told us
what Mother said to do in that situation
I could feel ancestors next to me
felt long black hair brushing against my sweaty face,
was it my own, or someone else's?

we were caught in the tall dry grass
bordering campus
I felt dead dry stalks pushing through my t-shirt
realizing nothing thrives in this state
except the hate which was delivering
blows to my face and head

I swallowed blood, smelled the fear
coming off the skinhead
who was kicking me in the ribs
I heard cries, screams
and above anything else . . . rage

I remember a flash of black boots
I remember the words
"Dirty, stupid squaws, get out of our state!"
"All you stupid squaws need haircuts!"
then I saw the flash of a switchblade
gleaming in the hot September sun

I heard my Grandmother's voice screaming
"Move, Makoose, move!"
I felt the strength & love of my family with me
as I began to kick, scream and rage
against my attacker
my friends did the same,
I believe our helpers were with us

soon we heard screaming brakes on asphalt
I saw a flurry of Indian boys
friends on the football team
just getting out of practice

my last image of my attacker
is his black T-shirt gleaming in the sun
as he ran with his fellow skinheads
for the high ground, like a war party
was on their trail

I felt strong arms lifting me up
holding me, trying to stop
the bleeding from my nose, lip and eye
the wound near my ribs
these scars I still carry

they never found our attackers
I guess all skinheads look the same right?

I didn't tell my parents for two years
when I finally did, we had a healing ceremony
for the whole family

sometimes, late at night, nightmares still haunt me
I wake up sweating, shaking & clutching my ribs
where your knife made contact

someday you, like my scars
will fade away

My Grandmother tells me this.

The Rocky Islands

Janet Loxley Lewis

There are wolves
Cracking dry bones
On ledges
Among sweet gale bushes.

And at night
I climb to meet them
Over the light
Still flakes of rock.

Incomer

Gloria Whelan

In all of his imaginings Luke Klein had not imagined himself in jail. As in most things in his Detroit suburb, his cell, scrubbed clean, was upscale. There were even a few thumbed copies of *Vanity Fair*. Some preppy with time on his hands and no little talent had painted a pink-and-green crocodile on one of the cell walls. After a drunken teenager had been returned, penitent and tearful to his parents, Luke was the jail's only resident. His wife, Miranda, was with her father, who was posting bail and who was furious with Luke. Luke's foolishness would reflect on his father-in-law and his father-in-law's business. Luke's own partners would not be happy. What was a doctor doing with a gun? He wondered if his rifle would be returned to him or confiscated. It was his dad's and he wanted it back.

Luke and Miranda had argued because Luke put out food at night for the coyote. Articles in the local paper said not to do that. A couple of little dogs had been attacked, and Luke and Miranda had a Bichon named Sip. The Bichon had belonged to Miranda before they were married, and it snarled and nipped at Luke when he got close to Miranda. It wasn't a breed Luke would have chosen. When he was growing up in Michigan's upper peninsula, his family had a series of German Shepherds with names like Blitz and Rebel.

Most of the homes in the suburb were comfortable three- and four-bedroom colonials with a few Tudors left over from the twenties. Their own place was located on one of a handful of streets of small spruced-up cottages.

Mansions had once lined the suburb's lakeshore, and the cottages had been homes for the servants who worked in the mansions. Living in the suburb was Miranda's idea. It was where she had always lived, and where all of her friends had settled. Luke disliked living in a servant's cottage. He had grown up in one. But he was just finishing his oncology residency and it had been all they could afford.

He was as much an alien in the suburb as the coyote. When he went for a walk he found handprints on everything, a landscape of plan and order instead of chance and scatter. Only the suburb's trees appeared transcendent, their height and breadth making them too formidable to tamper with. The nearby lake was placid and no substitute for his boyhood Lake Superior, whose storms swallowed freighters. He had to make do with rabbits and squirrels instead of wolves and moose. He ignored the tame world around him and walked with the images of the wilder world in which he had grown up. Somewhere he had read that you could imagine only what was absent.

Luke and Miranda met because Miranda's parents came each summer to a private club, Arcadia, in Michigan's Upper Peninsula. Luke's father, Ed, was the club's caretaker, and Luke and his parents lived in a cabin on the club grounds. Luke would trail around after his dad as he repaired screens or primed a well. When he was little he had the idea the whole club would fall apart were it not for his father. The club members were polite to Luke, calling him by name and teasing him about his skill as a fisherman. That was a double-edged compliment because the brookie he had caught when he was just twelve, one for the record books, had been caught in a stream that ran though the club and was for members only. Luke shouldn't have been fishing there.

He hadn't had much to do with Miranda in those years. She was three years younger than he was, practically a baby. All the children of the club's members had to have Minders. The Minders were full-time baby sitters, taking the kids on hikes, supervising their swimming in the club pool, and doing whatever it took to keep them out of their parents' way. Luke's mother hadn't thought much of the arrangement. "What's the point of having children if you're not the one to bring them up? It isn't as if those ladies had something else to do." A couple of local women did the housework in the cabins of club members. Dinners were taken in the big lodge.

His dad didn't like to hear criticism of the club. "As long as I'm living on their land and taking their money, I owe them some respect." Although a couple of times he had nearly resigned, like the time the club acquired several hundred acres of land that years ago had been lumbered and then abandoned for taxes. Locals had always hunted there, but the club told Luke's dad to put up "No Hunting" signs. His dad complained to Luke, "I'm not going to do it. I've got to live here in this township and I won't be able to look my friends in the eye."

Ed Klein simmered for a day or two and then marched over to tell the club president, who happened to be Douglas Raynart, Miranda's father, "Either you let the locals hunt there or you'll have to look for a new caretaker."

Raynart had laughed. "I had no idea. Not a problem."

Ed took the whole thing seriously and hadn't liked being laughed at.

Luke received an academic scholarship to University of Michigan. After his graduation he entered the university's medical school. When the members at Arcadia heard, they quietly took up a collection. Every year of the four years they handed over an envelope in the fall. His dad always checked to be sure Luke had written a thank-you note. Luke didn't need prompting. Without the help of the club, he would have ended up with a lifetime of loans.

Luke stayed on to intern at the university hospital. His medical fraternity gave a party, and Miranda had been there with a date. He wouldn't have recognized her but when he heard the familiar last name, he asked. He was always looking for a way to bring his northern home into his life. She ditched her date, and the two of them headed out to walk in the nearby university arboretum. Luke ran there in the mornings, and even with no moon the paths were familiar to him. A couple of student beer parties were going on, but they were in the distance. It was early September. The nights were still warm. Cicadas sung in the trees. The grass was damp, and Miranda held on to his arm as she took off her shoes. She was so slight he hardly felt her weight. Once in

Florida on a spring break he had smelled real orange blossoms, and that was what she smelled like.

"These woods are so dark and mysterious," she said.

"Not very mysterious. In the daytime you'd be able to see signs identifying every bush and tree."

"When I was little I was terrified of going on those hikes in the woods with our Minders. I was sure we'd run into a tiger or a lion. Do you get back often?"

"No. I haven't had the time or the money. Dad died a couple of years ago and Mom's living in Florida with her sister. I dream about it a lot." He hadn't meant to tell her about the dreams. "How about you?"

"The family goes back each summer, but I usually stay in town."

That should have been a warning, but Luke was lost in the wonder of being with someone who had spent her childhood summers where he had. They talked about how nearly impossible it was to swim in the freezing waters of Lake Superior; how deer browsed on the flowers the club members planted; the summer the bears, driven away by a new fence around the town dump, had begun scrounging the club's garbage cans. She even knew the bog where there were sundews and pitcher plants that digested flies. He believed she had discovered it as he had, wandering in the woods, only learning later that she had been on an "ecology walk" the club put on for the kids.

They began dating and Luke survived the awkwardness of meeting her parents. "Of course," Mr. Raynart said, "Ed's son. I remember when you were a little fellow giving your dad a hand. I was sorry to hear you lost him. We had a little dust-up once over some hunting rights, but Ed was the best caretaker we ever had. Well, we have a lot to talk about. I hope we see more of you. All the members were proud when you went off to medical school."

The transition had been made from caretaker's son to Miranda's young man about to be a doctor. When he traveled to spend a week with Miranda and her parents at Arcadia, the club welcomed him. Because of his knowledge of the best fishing spots, he was much in demand among the club's fly fishermen. Miranda complained she never got to see him. The truth was, he spent every minute he could steal revisiting his favorite trails or hiking the shore of Superior, scrambling over logs and boulders. At first he tried to take Miranda with him, but she said, "You're behaving like one of the Minders." She worked on her tan and played bridge with her mother's friends.

In the evenings he sat with the family on the Raynarts' big porch sipping drinks, waiting for the moment when the sun slipped down behind the trees and the cool breeze that had been waiting swept in from the big lake. There was talk about past events at the club and a special effort was made to bring Luke into the talk. He was ecstatic about being back. He imagined his summer vacations there with Miranda, bringing their children to all the places he loved. Sometimes, if he didn't push it quickly from his mind, he wondered if it wasn't Miranda's gift of Arcadia, rather than Miranda herself, that attracted him.

They were married at the beginning of the second year of his residency. He had hoped Miranda would want a wedding at Arcadia. He saw them exchanging vows on the shore of Superior. His relationship with the wild lake was religious, and the marriage needed its blessing.

Miranda protested, "You mean a destination wedding? Arcadia isn't the Bahamas. It's not an attraction. Where would everyone stay? In one of those Upper Peninsula motels? They probably have bedbugs. And who would we get to cater it? The cooks at the club aren't up to much more than fried chicken and apple pie. Anyhow, months ago when she saw where we were headed Mom snagged a Saturday afternoon date at our church and at the country club." He didn't object, but he hadn't appreciated being anticipated.

The wedding was a big affair. The Raynarts had so many friends no one noticed that, apart from Luke's fellow residents and their dates, his mother and aunt were his only guests. He was afraid all the airs and graces might overwhelm his mother, but to her the Raynarts and their friends were still the people who rented out their kids all summer and were too lazy to cook their own meals. She was polite but contained. His aunt Mary, though, could hardly get enough. Her digital camera kept winking as if it had something it its eye.

When his residency was ending and it was time to consider his future,

Luke asked Miranda, "What would you think about my practicing up north? There's a large hospital only a couple of hours from Arcadia. We could live in town, and summer weekends we'd stay at the club."

"I could never live there. I don't know a soul. What would I do? I was bored up there even in the summer, and it snows from September to June."

"That's an exaggeration." Though he knew it wasn't, having seen snow in both of those months. "Anyhow, it's a college town, not the end of the world. You'd make friends, and in the winter we could snowshoe and cross-country ski in the woods." He was thinking of his own silent journeys when he had scared up a fox or sent a grouse exploding out of its snow bank cover. Once in a snowstorm he had come upon a rare white-coated moose. He could close his eyes and see it still, the great white moose walking through white snow, its appearance a convergence with another world.

When he brought up practicing in the Upper Peninsula for the second time, Miranda went to her father, and Mr. Raynart introduced Luke to a friend of his, the head of a local internal medicine group looking for an oncologist. Luke was offered a position. He took it, and Miranda and her mother began working with a realtor to find a larger home in the suburb.

Around that time, the local paper published the first picture of a coyote. "Spotted on Lake View Drive," the headline said. That was only two blocks from their home. The coyote had wandered from the country club's golf course, thought to be its home ground. Luke studied the grainy picture of the coyote in the newspaper, happy to see a bit of wilderness in all that tamed landscape. Miranda, seeing the picture, stopped letting Sip out in the back yard. When she took the little Bichon for a walk on its leash, in addition to the usual plastic bag, she carried a can of pepper spray.

The coyote entered Luke's dreams, an elusive shape slinking into shadows and loping down darkened pathways. Luke considered writing a letter to the editor of the paper in support of the coyote. "We should be pleased," he wanted to write, "that a wild creature has chosen to live among us. We should welcome the coyote." Or perhaps less compassionately, "If you're worried get a *big* dog." When he ran in the mornings he headed for the trails on the golf course where the Raynarts were members. It was early November and the course was deserted, the ghosts of summer's players implicit in the occasional golf ball. The bare branches of the trees cut into gray skies. There were a few blue jays and some undecided robins, and once he had seen a red-shouldered hawk, but no coyote, and then on a Saturday morning he found tracks at the edge of a water hazard.

That night he left some of Sip's dog food out on their patio. Later when he turned on the porch light he found the dish was empty, the coyote's tracks still visible in the snow. Luke was thrilled. After that, without saying anything to Miranda, he put out food every night and then got up early in the mornings to remove the dish. Sometimes the coyote had been there; sometimes he hadn't. Luke was surprised at how happy the coyote's appearance made him, how it transformed his day. He thought about trapping the animal and driving north with it. They would both escape.

The coyote was discussed during Thanksgiving dinner at Miranda's parents'. Mrs. Raynart told what had happened to a friend of hers. "Jeanie's miniature poodle was out playing in their yard and Jeanie heard these horrible squeals. She ran out and scared the creature off with a broom. The poor little poodle had to have stitches."

"Coyotes are varmints," Mr. Raynart said. "The police ought to hunt the animal down and shoot it."

Miranda gave Luke a satisfied, superior look, but didn't betray him. The evening before she had discovered the dish of dog food Luke was leaving out for the coyote. "You're feeding a killer," she accused. "You're encouraging it. It's like leaving the phone numbers of little boys for perverts."

"That's an absurd comparison. If the coyote has enough food, it'll leave dogs alone."

There was talk at the Thanksgiving table of summer plans. Mr. Raynart had retired, and the Raynarts now spent the entire season at Arcadia. "I suppose you won't have too much vacation your first year," Mr. Raynart said to Luke, "but I hope you'll manage a week or two with us."

Before Luke could give his eager assent, Miranda said, "Dad, I've spent half my life up there. I want to see a little of the rest of the world. Mary Lee and John bought a place in the Dordogne. They want us to visit."

Luke hadn't heard a word of the Dordogne, wasn't even sure where it was. He considered sending Miranda off to this Dordogne place and going up to Arcadia by himself, but the Raynarts would not welcome that. Even if they did, without Miranda he would once again be the caretaker's son.

He felt betrayed, and when they returned home after the dinner he made a point of letting her see him empty another can of dog food into an aluminum dish and put it outside. Miranda marched upstairs, gathered her down pillow, and slept in the guest room with Sip.

Luke felt the emptiness in the bed. He regretted what he had done. His dream of returning to the woods was slipping away. Recently he and Miranda had gone to a concert. The choral group sang Juris Karlsons's *Mans Ezers*, My Lake. "How the sun shines, my lake glitters; but in the depth itself lies my heart, and throbs, and throbs, and throbs." Even if they made occasional visits to Arcadia, Miranda's reluctance would be everywhere, in the woods, along the shore of the lake, spoiling it for him. Minders, not he, would be the ones to teach the lake and the woods to his children. He had to win Miranda over.

Luke hurriedly dressed and went downstairs. It had started to snow. By now there would be twelve-foot high drifts up north. The eerie ice volcanoes would be building out on Lake Superior. His father's hunting rifle was in the basement. Like some Neanderthal huntsman, he would kill the wild animal and bring it like a trophy to his woman, who would praise his prowess. She would love him again. She would forgo this Dordogne place.

Neighbors reported the sound of the gunshots. A squad car pulled into their driveway. When the policeman shone his flashlight on the dead coyote, Luke was shaken by the slightness of the animal he had lured to its death. The policeman appeared pleased. "We've been after that bastard for a couple of weeks. We get calls all the time from ladies with little dogs. Actually I think we got one from around here. I should thank you for doing our job for us, but laws are laws, and we're the ones who can use a gun, not you."

All his life Luke had been scrupulous in his relationship with his prey. It was catch and release with trout, deer were taken in the proper season, he had never treed a bear with a dog. He was overcome by the enormity of his betrayal.

Miranda, who had thrown on a coat and hurried out to see what was happening, had been disgusted, and embarrassed for Luke. The rifle was confiscated, and Luke sentenced to community service at a senior citizen health clinic, his medical education saving him from picking up trash in the local park or giving lectures in the schools on gun safety. When the local paper came out there were quotes from the police and the judge. It was against the law to discharge a firearm in the suburb. A rifle shot could travel a couple of miles and might ricochet into someone's home.

In the article, a professor of animal behavior was quoted, "You get rid of one coyote, and another one moves right in." It was reassuring to Luke that in this place he would not be alone.

Here

Jane Piirto

Where is the wanderer's home?
—Runo 34, *Kalevala*

at our grandmother's birthplace,
in her very front yard,
here, my mother, sisters, and I
walk the very path.

Here, very here, this very river
in Vimpeli, Finland,
here this yellow round church,
here, this brown swift river.

Did she swim in it?
Here we, her American children
come to see, to feel, to touch.
No, the river runs fast and deep.

Here, the very view she saw here
her whole young life.

Part of her myth is
she was a very good swimmer.

Here, this very old church steeple,
the one in the old photograph.
Here, these new green reeds.
She would swim out to the middle of the lake.

She would float for hours out there
at camp in the Upper Peninsula.
Here, we are in her dream time.
After she left at 19, she never returned.

Authority Figure

Sally Brunk

I sit in class watching, observing
fellow students trying to outdo each other,
being "esoteric" using every big word they just learned
I shake my head, every class the same.
I think, "This is not my version of knowledge,
this is not how one earns respect."
Every day my worlds collide, that
30-minute ride from the rez to campus
alters my perceptions,
flips my world as a shutter closes and
gray area moves in
like a fog or thief in the night
my parents never finished high school
never went to college,
but are two of the most intelligent people I know
respected Elders of the tribe
wise beyond 90% of the people
walking on this campus,
than the so-called intellectuals I
have to spar with every day
walking this fine line between academia and

rez life can wear one down
there is a delicate balance to be maintained.
My family understands the necessity of classes, essays, and stories
but in my mind, I think, "This doesn't put food on the table."
. . . not yet anyway
Is all this practical?
I laugh & question that every day I cross that
invisible line, that boundary drawn in the sand
the intellectuals think it's fascinating, interesting
to be "Indigenous."
I'm looked at as a specimen, a rarity, lab rat,
THE authority on Native issues, sovereignty, treaty rights,
Mascots, language, trickster stories, traditions
of EVERY tribe in the country
yeah . . . that's me,
I got it all in my back pocket.
but . . . come to the rez, find it for yourself.
Know where it is? In every pair of Native eyes you see.
Ask them all, every question that fills your book.
you may learn, but will you
UNDERSTAND?

Waiting on Bats at Dusk

Manda Frederick

It was their space I needed,
away from Lake Superior's effect
of persistent exposure. I waited

to make my way through the mouth
by touch, from sand at my back,
the way blank drifts into blank,

to this water-dug cave, half-sleeping
shelter, dank arches weighted
with those quiet shadows swinging,

slow hearts sleeping, inverted rows
of lust-black lashes batting at no one,
any moment to become sharp eddies

swarming, 10,000 hot-beating stones
all falling at once, no two, touching—
their purpose shapeless as smoke rising

out of the sand. I waited: for that tangle
of air, momentary instinct toward change,
that indiscernible motion of trust in the dark.

Winter in Gold River

Catie Rosemurgy

Pretty girl. The weather has knocked her down again
and given her to the lake to wear as a skin.

Why am I always being the weather?
There were days in the winter
when her smile was so lovely I felt
the breathing of my own goodness,

though it remained fetal and separate.
I was a scavenger who survives

with a sling and stones, but whose god
nonetheless invents the first small bright bird.
And it was like flight to bring food to her lips

with a skeletal hand. But now she will always
be naked and sad. She will be what happens

to lake water that is loved and is also
shallow enough. The thickening, the slowing,

the black blood of it, the chest opened
to reveal the inevitable heart attack.

God, the silence of the chamber
we watch from. What happens to water
that isn't loved? It undergoes processes.

It freezes beside traffic.
But the reaching out to all sides at once,
the wet closing of what was open?
That is a beautiful woman.

So of course I stand and stare, never able
to pinpoint the exact moment I killed her.

New Year's Eve

Catie Rosemurgy

The lake wouldn't let us in. We had to walk on it
like a family of children talking to a mother's grave.

The snow lifted from the ice like a face
breaking apart. Our own skin held tight
but smelled crushed

like mint. The wind had licked the sky clean,
but then we showed up with our pulses

tucked in gloves. We stood out
against the blankness like creatures
that needed to be studied. Even the color
of my cousin's jacket was portentous.

If it were summer, we would've sunk,
and we would've done it anyway.

What had crawled into our hearts?
We were losing track of one another
and the shore. My aunt appeared briefly

and touched my cheek. The night had hardened
and gotten heavier. The stars dropped it.

We were sent to witness our inability to pick it up.
We were our true selves briefly.

Billy Recalls It Differently

Catie Rosemurgy

The rattle of my tin shed where I kept
my crocus bulbs was like the rattle
of my teeth as I slid into bed. Packed blooms.
Sweet fists. I liked to be able to look at
the delicate things I would never say.
My house rose up through pine needles and dust.
My house reared up in its white paint and cobwebs.
I shivered as I slipped from its belly
into the snow at quarter to seven
every morning. I blinked to strut my stuff.
Every morning there was a second
of darkness. Every morning it calmed
me down. Every morning cold wind for blood.
Every morning was not like this one.
A girl-shaped leaf had fallen onto my bed.

Persephone

Andrea Scarpino

She sent spectres, ruled the ghosts, and carried into effect the curses of men.

—1911 *Encyclopedia Britannica*

So it's you, all along, to whom I should have prayed,

ruler of ghosts, curses. I dreamed of my father night after night,

wished when I opened my eyes he would be sitting on my bed,

waking me to eat. Each turn down a grocery aisle,

I looked for his cart filled with fruit, coffee. Driving his car,

I held my hand across the passenger seat, waited to feel

his fingertips. Nothing. Persephone, I know you

didn't choose Hades, know you make the best of it,

loving the beautiful dead, touring the Underworld with kings,

using the harvest moonlight to carry out your whims.

I know you don't give up your dead. But what about

the weakest version of all they used to be, slightest glint

of their eyes, maybe, scent of their hair on a pillow, sheet.

If I offer you gifts of colored glass, fresh evergreen,

silk robes, berries, if I offer to take your place two months

of every year, if I sing at your knees. . . . Iron Queen,

I will pay any price. Just send me my father's ghost.

Bones: *Okaniman*

Echoe Deibert

(*Okanbiinde Onji-Kitche Minising niin-inaabandan bangishimog*)
(From Grand Island, I see something in the West as in a dream)

Asleep, awake? I do not know.
I see a mountain standing
on a verdant plain.

The mountain rises, comes to me;
stark white, mist shrouded,
floating . . . over endless grass.

Nothing moves, breathes . . .
except this mountain. Lightnings
sizzle, explode in thunder claps.

The mountain rests before me,
exhales a cloud of whiteness rising . . .
like the great bird, Migizi.

And I see bones . . .
a mountain of desiccated bones:
bones from blankets of disease,

bones from all the Wounded Knees,
and underneath the human bones,
the bones, bones, bones of Pte.

NOTES

Migizi is the Ojibwe word for the Bald Eagle.

Pte is the Lakota word for a female bison, or for the herd.

[What horror to awake at night]

Lorine Niedecker

What horror to awake at night
and in the dimness see the light.
        Time is white
        mosquitoes bite
I've spent my life on nothing.

The thought that stings. How are you, Nothing,
sitting around with Something's wife.
        Buzz and burn
        is all I learn
I've spent my life on nothing.

I'm pillowed and padded, pale and puffing
lifting household stuffing—
        carpets, dishes
        benches, fishes
I've spent my life in nothing.

Paradoxical Undressing

Emily Walter

A girl walking home through blizzard
can sometimes hear her blood's rhythm.
She counts the beats with her hands spread open
in the chord of C. Her fingers scissor
each note as she lifts the bodice
of dress over head, her face flushed pink
in the heat of the numb sun. She wets her lips
shut, unties the knot at her neck, stands naked
in a chemise. When she's found with only
her bonnet in a bank of snow, her eyes
are all smiles. Her last tracks outline a waltz.
Her body, no longer a pulse counted
but pearled in the field. Not a snow globe shaken
with bone and rice. Not something trapped under glass.

Errata

Lisa Fay Coutley

As the story goes, the raven's wings
aren't black. They're waves, capping
dark omens. Crows with curtained throats.
Who knows what falls from the shelf
inside us. Even gods skin their knees
to bleed. The man at the end of the aisle
is pocketing two-for-one toothbrushes.
The cashier is hand-perking her breasts
and picking her teeth with a receipt.
I'm sorry you won't see your son, his skin
peeling its white scarf through blizzards.
I haven't sanded the road, won't
strut across town in my ballet slippers.
Your shape in this bed is my shape.
Erase my whole notes from your page.
Two stoplights ago, the wind
off a pickup pulled us further from home.
When I said the moonlight made graves
to square off the night, I meant to say
pull over. Listen: my heart's a gutter
of ravens tugging at the firmament.

Mishosha, or the Magician of the Lakes

Bame-wa-wa-ge-zhik-aquay

In an early age of the world, when there were fewer inhabitants than there are now, there lived an Indian, in a remote place, who had a wife and two children. They seldom saw any one out of the circle of their own lodge. Animals were abundant in so secluded a situation, and the man found no difficulty in supplying his family with food.

In this way they lived in peace and happiness, which might have continued if the hunter had not found cause to suspect his wife. She secretly cherished an attachment for a young man whom she accidentally met one day in the woods. She even planned the death of her husband for his sake, for she knew if she did not kill her husband, her husband, the moment he detected her crime, would kill her.

The husband, however, eluded her project by his readiness and decision. He narrowly watched her movements. One day he secretly followed her footsteps into the forest, and having concealed himself behind a tree, he soon beheld a tall young man approach and lead away his wife. His arrows were in his hands, but he did not use them. He thought he would kill her the moment she returned.

Meantime, he went home and sat down to think. At last he came to the determination of quitting her for ever, thinking that her own conscience would punish her sufficiently, and relying on her maternal feelings to take care of the two children, who were boys, he immediately took up his arms and departed.

When the wife returned she was disappointed in not finding her husband, for she had now concerted her plan, and intended to have despatched him. She waited several days, thinking he might have been led away by the chase, but finding he did not return, she suspected the true cause. Leaving her two children in the lodge, she told them she was going a short distance and would return. She then fled to her paramour and came back no more.

The children thus abandoned, soon made way with the food left in the lodge, and were compelled to quit it in search of more. The eldest boy, who was of an intrepid temper, was strongly attached to his brother, frequently carrying him when he became weary, and gathering all the wild fruit he saw. They wandered deeper and deeper into the forest, losing all traces of their former habitation, until they were completely lost in its mazes.

The eldest boy had a knife, with which he made a bow and arrows, and was thus enabled to kill a few birds for himself and brother. In this manner they continued to pass on, from one piece of forest to another, not knowing whither they were going. At length they saw an opening through the woods, and were shortly afterward delighted to find themselves on the borders of a large lake. Here the elder brother busied himself in picking the seed pods of the wild rose, which he preserved as food. In the meantime, the younger brother amused himself by shooting arrows in the sand, one of which happened to fall into the lake. PANIGWUN, the elder brother, not willing to lose the arrow, waded in the water to reach it. Just as he was about to grasp the arrow, a canoe passed up to him with great rapidity. An old man, sitting in the centre, seized the affrighted youth and placed him in the canoe. In vain the boy addressed him—"My grandfather (a term of respect for old people), pray take my little brother also. Alone, I cannot go with you; he will starve if I leave him." Mishosha (the old man) only laughed at him. Then uttering the charm, CHEMAUN POLL, and giving his canoe a slap, it glided through the water with inconceivable swiftness. In a few moments they reached the habitation of the magician, standing on an island in the centre of the lake. Here he lived with his two daughters, who managed the affairs of his household. Leading the young man up to the lodge, he addressed his eldest daughter. "Here," said he, "my daughter, I have brought a young man to be your husband." Husband! thought the young woman; rather another victim of your bad arts, and your insatiate enmity to the human race. But she made no reply, seeming thereby to acquiesce in her father's will.

The young man thought he saw surprise depicted in the eyes of the daughter, during the scene of this introduction, and determined to watch events narrowly. In the evening he overheard the two daughters in conversation. "There," said the eldest daughter, "I told you he would not be satisfied with his last sacrifice. He has brought another victim, under the pretence of providing me a husband. Husband, indeed! the poor youth will be in some horrible predicament before another sun has set. When shall we be spared the scenes of vice and wickedness which are daily taking place before our eyes."

Panigwun took the first opportunity of acquainting the daughters how he had been carried off, and been compelled to leave his little brother on the shore. They told him to wait until their father was asleep, then to get up and take his canoe, and using the charm he had obtained, it would carry him quickly to his brother. That he would carry him food, prepare a lodge for him, and be back before daybreak. He did, in every respect, as he had been directed—the canoe obeyed the charm, and carried him safely over, and after providing for the subsistence of his brother, told him that in a short time he should come for him. Then returning to the enchanted island, he resumed his place in the lodge, before the magician awoke. Once, during the night, Mishosha awoke, and not seeing his destined son-in-law, asked his daughter what had become of him. She replied that he had merely stepped out, and would be back soon. This satisfied him. In the morning, finding the young man in the lodge, his suspicions were completely lulled. "I see, my daughter," said he, "you have told the truth."

As soon as the sun arose, Mishosha thus addressed the young man, "Come, my son, I have a mind to gather gulls' eggs. I know an island where there are great quantities, and I wish your aid in getting them." The young man saw no reasonable excuse; and getting into the canoe, the magician gave it a slap, and uttering a command, they were in an instant at the island. They found the shores strewn with gulls' eggs, and the island full of birds of this species. "Go, my son," said the old man, "and gather the eggs, while I remain in the canoe."

But Panigwun had no sooner got ashore, than Mishosha pushed his canoe a little from the land, and exclaimed—"Listen, ye gulls! you have long expected an offering from me. I now give you a victim. Fly down and devour him." Then striking his canoe, he left the young man to his fate.

The birds immediately came in clouds around their victim, darkening the air with their numbers. But the youth seizing the first that came near him, and drawing his knife, cut off its head. He immediately skinned the bird, and hung the feathers as a trophy on his breast. "Thus," he exclaimed, "will I treat every one of you who approaches me. Forbear, therefore, and listen to my words. It is not for you to eat human flesh. You have been given by the Great Spirit as food for man. Neither is it in the power of that old magician to do you any good. Take me on your backs and carry me to his lodge, and you shall see that I am not ungrateful." The gulls obeyed; collecting in a cloud for him to rest upon, and quickly flew to the lodge, where they arrived before the magician. The daughters were surprised at his return, but Mishosha, on entering the lodge, conducted himself as if nothing extraordinary had taken place.

The next day he again addressed the youth—"Come, my son," said he, "I will take you to an island covered with the most beautiful stones and pebbles, looking like silver. I wish you to assist me in gathering some of them. They will make handsome ornaments, and possess great medicinal virtues." Entering the canoe, the magician made use of his charm, and they were carried in a few moments to a solitary bay in an island, where there was a smooth sandy beach. The young man went ashore as usual, and began to search. "A little farther, a little farther," cried the old man. "Upon that rock you will get some fine ones." Then pushing his canoe from land—"Come, thou great king of fishes," cried the old man; "you have long expected an offering from me. Come, and eat the stranger whom I have just put ashore on your island." So saying, he commanded his canoe to return, and it was soon out of sight.

Immediately, a monstrous fish thrust his long snout from the water, crawling partially on the beach, and opening wide his jaws to receive his victim. "When!" exclaimed the young man, drawing his knife and putting himself in a threatening attitude, "when did you ever taste human flesh? Have a care of yourself. You were given by the Great Spirit to man, and if you, or any of your tribe eat human flesh, you will fall sick and die. Listen not to the words of that wicked man, but carry me back to his island, in return for which I will present you a piece of red cloth." The fish complied, raising his back out of the water, to allow the young man to get on. Then taking his way through the lake, he landed his charge safely on the island before the return of the magician. The daughters were still more surprised to see that he had escaped the arts of their father the second time. But the old man on his return maintained his taciturnity and self-composure. He could not, however, help saying to himself—"What manner of boy is this, who is ever escaping from my power. But his spirit shall not save him. I will entrap him to-morrow. Ha, ha, ha!"

Next day the magician addressed the young man as follows: "Come, my son," said he, "you must go with me to procure some young eagles. I wish to tame them. I have discovered an island where they are in great abundance." When they had reached the island, Mishosha led him inland until they came to the foot of a tall pine, upon which the nests were. "Now, my son," said he, "climb up this tree and bring down the birds." The young man obeyed. When he had with great difficulty got near the nest, "Now," exclaimed the magician, addressing the tree, "stretch yourself up and be very tall." The tree rose up at the command. "Listen, ye eagles," continued the old man, "you have long expected a gift from me. I now present you this boy, who has had the presumption to molest your young. Stretch forth your claws and seize him." So saying he left the young man to his fate, and returned.

But the intrepid youth drawing his knife, and cutting off the head of the first eagle that menaced him, raised his voice and exclaimed, "Thus will I deal with all who come near me. What right have you, ye ravenous birds, who were made to feed on beasts, to eat human flesh? Is it because that cowardly old canoe-man has bid you do so? He is an old woman. He can neither do you good nor harm. See, I have already slain one of your number. Respect my bravery, and carry me back that I may show you how I shall treat you."

The eagles, pleased with his spirit, assented, and clustering thick around him formed a seat with their backs, and flew toward the enchanted island. As they crossed the water they passed over the magician, lying half asleep in his canoe.

The return of the young man was hailed with joy by the daughters, who now plainly saw that he was under the guidance of a strong spirit. But the ire of the old man was excited, although he kept his temper under subjection. He taxed his wits for some new mode of ridding himself of the youth, who had so successfully baffled his skill. He next invited him to go a-hunting.

Taking his canoe, they proceeded to an island and built a lodge to shelter themselves during the night. In the mean while the magician caused a deep fall of snow, with a storm of wind and severe cold. According to custom, the young man pulled off his moccasins and leggings and hung them before the fire to dry. After he had gone to sleep the magician, watching his opportunity, got up, and taking one moccasin and one legging, threw them into the fire. He then went to sleep. In the morning, stretching himself as he arose and uttering an exclamation of surprise, "My son," said he, "what has become of your moccasin and legging? I believe this is the moon in which fire attracts, and I fear they have been drawn in." The young man suspected the true cause of his loss, and rightly attributed it to a design of the magician to freeze him to death on the march. But he maintained the strictest silence, and drawing his conaus over his head thus communed with himself: "I have full faith in the Manito who has preserved me thus far, I do not fear that he will forsake me in this cruel emergency. Great is his power, and I invoke it now that he may enable me to prevail over this wicked enemy of mankind."

He then drew on the remaining moccasin and legging, and taking a dead coal from the fireplace, invoked his spirit to give it efficacy, and blackened his foot and leg as far as the lost garment usually reached. He then got up and announced himself ready for the march. In vain Mishosha led him through snows and over morasses, hoping to see the lad sink at every moment. But in this he was disappointed, and for the first time they returned home together.

Taking courage from this success, the young man now determined to try his own power, having previously consulted with the daughters. They all agreed that the life the old man led was detestable, and that whoever would rid the world of him, would entitle himself to the thanks of the human race.

On the following day the young man thus addressed his hoary captor. "My grandfather, I have often gone with you on perilous excursion and never murmured. I must now request that you will accompany me. I wish to visit my little brother, and to bring him home with me." They accordingly went on a visit to the main land, and found the little lad in the spot where he had been left. After taking him into the canoe, the young man again addressed the magician: "My grandfather, will you go and cut me a few of those red willows on the bank, I wish to prepare some smoking mixture." "Certainly, my son," replied the old man, "what you wish is not very hard. Ha, ha, ha! do you think me too old to get up there?" No sooner was Mishosha ashore, than the young man, placing himself in the proper position struck the canoe with his hand, and pronouncing the charm, N'CHIMAUN POLL, the canoe immediately flew through the water on its return to the island. It was evening when the two brothers arrived, and carried the canoe ashore. But the elder daughter informed the young man that unless he sat up and watched the canoe, and kept his hand upon it, such was the power of their father, it would slip off and return to him. Panigwun watched faithfully till near the dawn of day, when he could no longer resist the drowsiness which oppressed him, and he fell into a short doze. In the meantime the canoe slipped off and sought its master, who soon returned in high glee. "Ha, ha, ha! my son," said he, "you thought to play me a trick. It was very clever. But you see I am too old for you."

A short time after, the youth again addressed the magician. "My grandfather, I wish to try my skill in hunting. It is said there is plenty of game on an island not far off, and I have to request that you will take me there in your canoe." They accordingly went to the island and spent the day in hunting. Night coming on they put up a temporary lodge. When the magician had sunk into a profound sleep, the young man got up, and taking one of Mishosha's leggings and moccasins from the place where they hung, threw them into the fire, thus retaliating the artifice before played upon himself. He had discovered that the foot and leg were the only vulnerable parts of the magician's body. Having committed these articles to the fire, he besought his Manito that he would raise a great storm of snow, wind, and hail, and then laid himself down beside the old man. Consternation was depicted on the countenance of the latter, when he awoke in the morning and found his moccasin and legging missing. "I believe, my grandfather," said the young man, "that this is the moon in which fire attracts, and I fear your foot and leg garments have been drawn in." Then rising and bidding the old man follow him, he began the morning's hunt, frequently turning to see how Mishosha kept up. He saw him faltering at every step, and almost benumbed with cold, but encouraged him to follow, saying, we shall soon get through and reach the shore; although he took pains, at the same time, to lead him in roundabout ways, so as to let the frost take complete effect. At length the old man reached the brink of the island where the woods are succeeded by a border of smooth sand. But he could go no farther; his legs became stiff and refused motion, and he found himself fixed to the spot. But he still kept stretching out his arms and swinging his body to and fro. Every moment he found the numbness creeping higher. He felt his legs growing downward like roots, the feathers of his head turned to leaves, and in a few seconds he stood a tall and stiff sycamore, leaning toward the water.

Panigwun leaped into the canoe, and pronouncing the charm, was soon transported to the island, where he related his victory to the daughters. They applauded the deed, agreed to put on mortal shapes, become wives to the two young men, and for ever quit the enchanted island. And passing immediately over to the main land, they lived lives of happiness and peace.

Spring

Primavera

Lines Written Under Severe Pain and Sickness

Bame-wa-wa-ge-zhik-aquay

Ah! why should I at fortune's lot repine,
Or fret myself against the will divine?
All men must go to death's deform'd embrace,
When here below they've run their destin'd race;
Oh! then on Thee, my Savior, I will trust,
For thou art good, as merciful and just,
In Thee, with my whole heart I will confide,
And hope with Thee, forever to abide.
To Thee, my God, my heart and soul I raise,
And still thy holy, holy name I'll praise!
O! deign to give me wisdom, virtue, grace,
That I thy heavenly will may ever trace;
Teach me each duty always to fulfill,
And grant me resignation to Thy will,
And when Thy goodness wills that I should die,
This dream of life I'll leave without a sigh.

The Sleep

Caitlin Horrocks

THE SNOW CAME EARLY THAT FIRST YEAR, AND SO HEAVY THAT WHEN Albert Rasmussen invited the whole town over, we had to park around the corner from his unplowed street. We staggered through the drifts, across the lawns, down the neat stretches of sidewalk where a few of Al's neighbors owned snowblowers. Mr. Kajaamaki and the Lutven boys were still out huffing and puffing with shovels. We waved as we passed, and they nodded.

Al stood that November in his family room, arms outstretched, knee-deep in a nest of mattresses and bedding: flannels and florals mixed with Bobby Rasmussen's NASCAR pillowcases, Dee's Disney Princess comforter. The sideboard had a hot plate and an electric kettle plugged into a power strip. Al opened drawers filled with crackers, tinned soup, bags of pink-frosted animal cookies, vitamin C pills and canned juice to prevent scurvy. "Hibernation," he announced. "Human hibernation."

This was before the cameras, before the sleep, before the outsiders, and the plan sounded as strange to us then as it would to anybody. Our town had always wintered the way towns do: gas bills and window plastic, blankets and boots. We bought cream for our cracked skin and socks for our numb feet. We knew how we felt when our extremities faded temporarily away, and we knew how much we hurt when they prickled back to life.

Al showed off a heater he'd built that ran on used grease, and the filter that sieved out the hash browns and hamburger. Al had always been handy.

He'd been the smartest kid in school, back when Bounty still had its own high school. He was the senior everyone called "college material" until he decided to stay, and then we called him "ours." Our Albert, Albert and his girl Jeannie, who were confident that everything they could want in the world was right here in Bounty. We went to their wedding, the Saturday after graduation, and then stood by, helpless, when Albert's parents lost their farm three years later. Maybe the family should have gotten out then, moved away and never looked back. Al might have found a job that paid better than invisible fencing, and Jeannie might not have been killed by Reggie Lapham, seventeen years old and driving drunk eight months before Al's November invitation. Al might never have struck on hibernation, and we might all have gone along the way we'd been going, for better or for worse.

But they had stayed, and Jeannie had died, and Reggie had been sent to a juvenile detention facility downstate. The accident happened in early spring, when patches of ice were still dissolving on the roads, and what no one would say within Al's earshot was that the weather had killed her as much as Reggie had. Al needed something small enough to blame, and Reggie, skinny as a weed and driving his father's truck, served as well as anything could. Al had always seemed older than he was, had transitioned easily from high school basketball star to assistant coach. Now, in his thirties, he looked twenty years older, bent and exhausted. We wondered if the weight on his shoulders was truly Jeannie, or if he'd been carrying, for more years than we'd realized, some piece of Bounty, and he'd invited us over to make sure we understood that he was putting it down.

We'd all stayed in Bounty the way Al had stayed, had carried it as best we could. When our high school shut down, we sent our children to the next town over, then to the county consolidated when that one closed, too. They came home with their history textbooks about the fur trade, the timber trade, the copper rush, the iron rush, the silver, the nickel, the tourists. About land that gave until it couldn't give, and the chumps who kept trying to live on it. Our children came home and told us that we were the suckers of the last century.

"But what if you love it here?" we asked them. "What if you don't want to leave?"

"What's to love?" our children asked, in surly disbelief: What kind of morons hustle for jobs that don't even pay for cable television? What kind of people spend twenty years buying beer at the Hop-In and drinking in the quarry, the next thirty drinking at The Pointes, the last sodden ten at the Elks Lodge?

Our kind of people, we thought.

"SLEEP," AL SAID, THERE IN HIS LIVING ROOM, AND EXPLAINED HOW in the old days in Russia people sacked out around a stove when the snows came, waking to munch a piece of rye bread, feed the fire, slump back into sleep. Only so much food could be laid in, and the thinking went that unless a man could come up with something to do in the cold and the dark that justified the calories he'd expend doing it, he was better off doing nothing. Those villages would wake up skinny and hungry, but they'd wake up alive.

We worried that maybe the Rasmussens were harder up than we had thought. Times were tough for everybody, but others weren't shutting down their houses and lives and planning to warm their kids with burger grease. "What do we do all winter?" Al asked, the kind of question we knew he considered rhetorical. "Why work like dogs all summer to keep the television on, the furnace cranked, noodles on the stove? Why scrape off the car to burn fuel to go to the store to buy more noodles? That's pointless."

Mrs. Pekola, of Pekola Downtown Antiques, opened her mouth for a moment, as if she were going to point out that that routine wasn't much different from plenty of people's autumns and springs and maybe summers, in which case Al was saying that we might as well all blow our brains out and have done with it. But she stayed silent, probably because she thought of many things we didn't need to hear.

"What about Christmas?" Mrs. Drausmann, the librarian, offered.

"We're staying awake for it. Just doing a two-month trial run this year, January and February," Al explained.

"School," Bill and Valeer Simmons said. "Your kids."

Al shrugged. Both his kids were bright and ahead of their classes. At seven, Dee read at a sixth grade level. Bobby was nine and the best speller at Bounty Elementary. Al had picked up copies of the upcoming curriculum: long division, suffixes, photosynthesis, cursive.

"We're having a sleepover instead," Dee said.

"You know what Mrs. Fiske has planned for February? *Fractions!*" Bobby yelled, and the kids bopped around the room until Al chased them upstairs.

"They'll get caught up in spring," Al said. "I don't think they'll have difficulty."

He looked around at us, his old compatriots, the parents of the handful of children still enrolled at the school, and apologized. "I didn't mean anything by that," he said. "I don't think they're special. But they probably won't miss much."

We nodded. Being the children of a dying town had taught us that none of us were special. Whatever our various talents, we'd all ended up here, in the Rasmussens' family room.

"Don't try to convince me anything worthwhile happens in this town during January and February. I've lived here as long as you have," Al said. We could tell he meant to joke, but nobody laughed. "I'm not crazy. NASA studies this stuff. They're planning for astronauts to hibernate through long voyages. So they don't go stir-crazy and kill each other, bust out the shuttle walls." Al's fingers twitched a bit, and we looked at his walls: scuffed beige paint, three china plates with pictures of Holsteins, a family portrait taken at the JCPenney in Kingsford when Jeannie was still alive, and a single round hole at the height of a man's fist-height, sloppily covered with paint and plaster. Their walls looked a lot like our walls, and all of a sudden we were tempted to jam our fists in and pull them down.

"You think we're like that?" Nils Andersen asked from the back of the crowd, all the way in the front foyer, and people parted to let him come closer. He'd been a point guard to Al's shooting guard on the old high school basketball team. The two still sometimes took practice shots into the hoop on Al's garage.

"Like what?"

"Russians and astronauts. You think we've got two options, asleep or dead?"

Al started to shake his head, because we're not a town that likes to offend. Then he paused, ran his big hands through his hair, and let them drop to his sides. Fair and broad and tall, like his parents and grandparents and Norwegian great-grandparents, like a lot of the rest of us, he looked suddenly large and unwieldy. As if he could only ever fit in this little room curled up asleep, and we'd all been crazy to hope otherwise. He hunched his shoulders and looked down at the floor. "Maybe," he said. "This is about my family. I never meant any of you had to be involved. But maybe."

We'd thought our town's silence had been stoic; we glimpsed now how much we simply hadn't wanted to say. We rustled in the blankets but kept our mouths shut, put on our shoes, and drifted out into the snow. Some of us drove straight home. Others took longer routes down Main Street, past First Lutheran, The Pointes, the Elks Lodge, Mrs. Pekola's antique store, the single-screen movie theater with the marquee still announcing CLOSED, as if the closing were news. The public library was housed in the old pharmacy; we checked out our books at the prescriptions counter and bought our prescriptions thirty miles down the road. We looked at all the shuttered stores and tried to remember what each one had sold.

We cruised back and forth like bored teenagers on Saturday nights, watching the road run quickly from empty storefronts to houses and trailers. We turned around at the Hop-In on the west end of town, near the park with its silent gray bandstand. We drove east until we passed the elementary school and empty high school, then turned into the parking lot of the mill, the beams of its collapsed roof poking skyward and its windows like eyes. Bounty had never been a pretty town, but we'd tried to be proud of it. Now we examined it carefully, looking for new reasons to stay awake. One by one we gave up, peeled off, and drove home. We turned into our shoveled driveways in the tiny grid of residential streets, or took spokes of blacktop and gravel out to scattered houses in the woods. Bounty was an assertion, an act of faith. It looked best left unexamined.

A few of us met back at The Pointes that night for beer and darts. The hours went by, but no one said a thing about Al Rasmussen and we were all waiting for it. "Fucking *grease*," Nils finally said. "Like fucking *Russians*." We were able to laugh then and walk out to the parking lot, slapping each other's backs and leaving trails of footprints in the snow. We felt better about ourselves, sitting side by side in our idling cars, waiting for the engines to warm.

ON NEW YEAR'S DAY THE RASMUSSENS MADE NEIGHBORHOOD ROUNDS, dropping off house keys and perishables: a gallon of milk and some apples for the Lutven boys; carrots for Valeer Simmons; a bag of shredded cheese and half a loaf of bread for Mr. Kajaamaki. We wished them luck and hung the keys on pegs. We could have robbed them blind while they slept, but we knew they didn't have anything worth taking. We tiptoed in ones and twos to watch the family sleep, to see how this hibernation thing was working out. The kids looked peaceful. The food disappeared in barely perceptible increments. The room was stuffy by late February, smelling of night-sweat and canned soup, but the Rasmussens didn't seem to mind. Mrs. Pekola lit a lavender-scented candle on the sideboard and found it blown out the next day. All in all, they looked cozy.

IN MARCH THE CHILDREN WOKE FIRST, BOUNDING OUT THE FRONT door in their pajamas. Spring hadn't started yet, the snow gray and dirty. But the fiercest part of winter was over. Al looked rested for the first time since Jeannie's death, the terrible tension gone from his shoulders. His body looked more like that of the man most of us had known for years, but his eyes looked like a stranger's. No one could place the expression except those of us whose children or grandchildren had left Bounty, gone off for college or work. When the children came back, we said, their eyes looked like that, like departure. *Imagine,* we thought: *Albert had found that look in his sleep.*

He asked for all the updates. A blizzard in early February had blown the roof off the old hardware store. Mr. Fiske had had a heart attack on his snowmobile. The license agent at the DNR field office died of cirrhosis, and half the town had applied for his job. The youngest Lehto boy had tried to hitch home from work at the power plant one evening, but nobody stopped. He decided to walk and disappeared into the snow. We drove poles down, walking in formation, bracing ourselves to strike flesh. We never found him; now that spring had come, we probably would.

"Anything good?" Al asked.

We struggled. We hadn't thought about how dark the winter had been when we were in its midst. "One of the Thao girls had a baby," we said.

Al smiled, although half of the town thought the Thaos belonged to us, and half wanted nothing to do with them. "That's something."

"What did *you* do?" we asked, and before he could say "I slept," we specified: "What was it like? How did it feel?"

"I had these long dreams," he said. "Unfolding over days. I dreamed I was in Eden, but it was mine. My land. I picked pineapples every day."

Al Rasmussen had wintered in Eden, we thought. We started to feel a little like suckers.

Bobby and Dee had boundless energy, and spent a lot of it recounting dreams to their schoolmates. Soon many of the children were planning for their own long sleep, and the ones who weren't were calculating how scary empty classrooms might get, how the forest of raised hands would thin and they'd get called on over and over, expected to know the right answers. They pictured how lonely the playground would be, all lopsided seesaws and unpushed swings, and soon all the children of Bounty were begging to spend the next winter asleep.

Quite a few of them got their way. The Lutven boys were happy not to catch the bus in the dark, standing around in twenty below. The pudgy Sanderson girl, all bushy hair and braces, woke up with her teeth straighter and her belly flat. She showed off her new smile for Lucy Simmons, and Lucy confessed that her period had started sometime in early February. How easily, they thought, so much of the hard work of growing up had happened while they were asleep, while no one could make fun of them for it.

Mrs. Sanderson fit into clothes she hadn't worn since high school. The styles had changed, but she paraded around in her high-waisted, acid-washed jeans just so we could admire what sleep had done for her. Mr. Sanderson had started off awake, reporting to the outdoor supply store north of town at nine every morning, the way he'd done for years. But suddenly he saw the unfairness, his creaking out of bed while his wife rolled over with a slack, content smile. "Our food costs were way down," he said at The Pointes one night the next spring. "The heat bills. Gas. For once my daughter wasn't pestering for a new pair of jeans. I asked for a temporary leave. They said sales were down so far I'd be doing them a favor."

A lot of us lived in houses our parents or grandparents had owned; mortgages weren't usually our problem. Just the daily costs of living, and the closer those got to zero, the less we needed to work. The outdoor supply store lost three more before the winter was over. Other folks didn't have any employers to apologize to. The families that still kept animals thought we were all a bunch of pansies, at least according to Nils, but then we imagined him slogging to the barn every morning at five, his fingers stiff and snot frozen in his mustache, and we mostly just felt smart.

Mrs. Drausmann, the town librarian, hated the sleep even more than Nils. She cornered Bobby and Dee after story time, near the shelves that once held skin creams and now held paperbacks, and threatened: "This will be like Narnia under the White Witch. Always winter and never Christmas."

"After Christmas," Dee asked her, "What's there to like? What do *you* do?"

"I keep the library open," she said. "So everyone has books. They come and use the computers and get their music and their movies."

"If you're dreaming, you have your own movies," Dee said gravely, and Mrs. Drausmann sighed. We tried to make it up to her, registered for her summer reading program, and attended fall story time. But Dee was right. Sleeping folk needed almost nothing—a little food, a little water, air, and warmth. They definitely didn't need DVDs.

THAT SECOND WINTER, THE ROAD CREWS NOTICED LESS TRAFFIC, AND some of the plow drivers' hours were cut. Several decided to screw it and just sleep, and by the time the county and the drivers were done sniping at each other the budget for next year's salting and plowing was half what it had been. The harder leaving your driveway was, the easier the choice to stay home.

THE THIRD YEAR, A FAMILY DIED OF CARBON MONOXIDE POISONING from an unventilated gas heater. An electric space heater started a fire at the Simmons'. They got out, but the house was a loss. Al staggered into the snow bleary-eyed, called his neighbors dumbasses, and then invited them to pile on into his family room. When he woke up for real in March, he announced that if we were all going to do this thing, we should do it right. He didn't have enough old grease for everyone, so he charged hourly for consultations about different compact heating systems, then for assembly and installation, and soon he was doing well enough to quit invisible fencing.

We were glad Al had the new business, because that October Reggie Lapham came home. He'd been seventeen when he hit Jeannie three and a half years earlier, and as young as that was, as much as we remembered the ice on the road and the evenings we'd gotten behind the wheel when we shouldn't have, we weren't sure how to forgive him. Our hearts went out to Reggie and then to Jeannie and then to Al and Bobby and Dee and then back to Reggie until we couldn't keep our hearts straight and peaceful in our own chests. They were all ours, and we were too much like all of them. We needed men like Al to lead us and we needed young people like Reggie to stay. We looked to Al for permission to take Reggie back.

But Reggie seemed to know Al wasn't going to give it, at least not that autumn, because he walked from his parents' van into his house and wouldn't come out again. We spoke to Mrs. Lapham at the Hop-In. "He's looking forward to the sleep," she said. "That's really all he wants to do. I don't think he would have come back if he had to—"

She broke off and we wondered, *Had to what? Leave the house? Talk to people? Get a job?* The family went to bed a few days after Thanksgiving. Mrs. Lapham said that seemed like the easiest way to get through what had to be gotten through. Then we heard that Al had put his kids to bed early too, without Christmas, and then some of us started calculating the money we could save not buying presents. Those of us without small children, or without extended families, had to admit that the holidays were a downer as often as not. We knew that the Laphams and Rasmussens weren't sleeping for the healthiest of reasons, but we understood the urge.

Mrs. Drausmann called into a radio psychologist when everyone woke up the next spring, about whether sleeping through four months of strife was sanity or just denial. She talked her way past the producers, but Dr. Joe wouldn't believe her. "Sure, excessive sleeping is a sign of depression," he said. "But no one hibernates." Then he hung up.

Several of us heard the call and it prompted some soul searching, both about why so many of us were listening to *The Dr. Joe Show* and about what our town might look like to outsiders. We started to wonder if Reggie Lapham should maybe be talking to somebody. If Al and Reggie needed help, we weren't giving it to them, because sleeping was easier for us, too.

A woman from the *Escanaba Daily Press* heard *The Dr. Joe Show* that night and came to ask Mrs. Drausmann some questions. We braced ourselves for the story, but the reporter apparently couldn't figure out whom to believe or what the heck was going on, and before she hit on the answer, the Ogden company laid her off. We saw Nils Andersen and Al having a beer at The Pointes a few weeks later, the first time they'd been social together in years. "She came to interview me," Nils said. "I told her the hibernation business was bullshit."

"I know you think the sleeping's bullshit," Al said. "You don't need to tell me."

"I told her Drausmann was bullshit. I told her nothing was going on in this town that was any of Dr. Joe's business or the *Escanaba Daily*'s. I told her to leave you alone." Nils shook his head and clinked the neck of his bottle against Al's. "I figured you've always known what you needed. Crazy fucker."

A few weeks later we watched the grease heater leave the Rasmussen house in parts, the foam-taped exhaust pipe, the burger filter. The mattresses came out, Bobby and Dee's sheets, graduated now from NASCAR and Disney to plain solids, navy and lavender. We worried Al was abandoning the cause until we found out he'd reassembled it all at the Andersen place. With more people to share shifts taking care of the animals, Al explained, everyone could get some sleep.

More people economized like this, throwing in their lots with friends, neighbors. The Simmonses rebuilt their burnt house with a single large room on the ground floor, an energy efficient heat stove in the center, with nonflammable tile around the base. They went to ask Al's permission and then invited the Laphams to spend the next winter. They knew what a chill felt like, they said, as well as to be given shelter when nothing but cold was all around you.

Mrs. Drausmann stayed awake. She had her books; she had her own kind of dreaming. She and Mrs. Pekola would walk up and down the streets, Mrs. Drausmann's snowboots and Mrs. Pekola's orthopedics the only prints for miles. Mrs. Pekola's faith wouldn't let her sleep. She walked to the Lutheran church every December 24th to light the Christ candle. "I'm sorry," she whispered to God. "They don't mean anything by it. They don't mean to disrespect you." She tried to tell us in spring how lonely our church looked, a single candle alight in the empty sanctuary.

In the first years, the reverend turned the electricity back on whenever the temperature hit forty-five, but then someone hit on the idea of Easter. We flipped the switch on the day that Christ rose. "Alleluia, alleluia," we sang, uttering the word we had denied ourselves for Lent, one of the first words to pass our lips since waking. The Rasmussens and the Laphams stood in their old pews, just across the aisle from each other. They didn't embrace at the greeting-neighbors part of the service, didn't say "Peace be with you" or "And also with you," but they didn't flee. Al stood between his children, with an arm draped over each of them, and we realized with surprise that Bobby was fourteen now and nearly as tall as his father. He would have been good at basketball too, if he'd been awake for the season. Dee's pale hair had darkened to a dirty blonde, and her face was spotted with acne. The kids leaned into their father, facing forward, until Dee looked to her right and nodded at Mrs. Lapham. Just then, Reggie turned his head to peer anxiously over his mother, and we saw Dee freeze and then slowly nod at him, too. We all nodded our pale faces at each other, and that seemed like enough.

In the end the Hop-In is what brought the outsiders. Corporate couldn't understand why winter-quarter sales were down 95 percent from five years earlier. A regional manager came out, and then his supervisors, and finally news crews from Green Bay. The satellite vans were hard to miss, and we stayed up that night for the eleven o'clock news. We hadn't expected the story they chose to tell: it wasn't a human-interest piece about ingenuity or survival. Our hibernation practice was horrible, the anchors announced, from up and down the state, then across the country. Horrifying. Another product of the recession. A new economic indicator: in addition to tumbling home prices and soaring unemployment, a town was going to sleep. A blond reporter asked the Sandersons if they were making a statement.

"We get tired," they said. "Is that a statement?"

We were annoyed at how they filmed the shabbiest parts of our town, until we flipped through the newscasts and realized that together they'd filmed nearly all of our town and that it all looked equally shabby. We were used to our potholes and tumbledown barns, and now alongside those were cracked sidewalks and collapsing houses. The gray bandstand in the park leaned heavily to one side; the flat roof of the old high school had caved in under last year's snow. Raccoons and groundhogs hibernated in some of the downtown buildings and chased each other up and down Main Street in their spring excitement. A few had gotten into Mrs. Pekola's antiques store, either for burrow bedding or just to be troublesome, and we were plagued by a video clip of skinny raccoons bursting out the store's front door, trailing gnawed-up christening dresses and crib quilts. A badger birthed a spring litter in the church basement on a pile of old Sunday school workbooks. We told ourselves that none of this mattered. We weren't using the buildings anyway: the bandstand, the high school, most of downtown. We reminded ourselves that Bounty had never been a pretty place. It was built for function, not ornament, and as long as it functioned the way we wanted, we shouldn't be ashamed. We had never had any great architecture in Bounty, and the certainty that we never would didn't seem a sacrifice.

We might have become a tourist attraction except that getting to us when we were sleeping was so hard. The snow accumulated in giant drifts. We put a big stick out by the WELCOME TO BOUNTY sign and let it measure how deeply we were buried. People could come in on the highway, as far as the county plowed it, and then see a wall of snow taller than their car greeting them at the entrance.

THAT WAS THE ESTABLISHING SHOT, A TINY CAR NEXT TO A WALL OF snow, when the documentary was released. On the tenth anniversary of the sleep, Detroit Public Television contacted us and said they planned to take a more balanced approach than the news crews. We liked that they promised to hold the premiere in Bounty, projected after dark onto the wall of the old mill, since the movie theater had been condemned.

They interviewed Bobby in his dorm room in the last weeks of the fall semester. Michigan State University had offered him a small baseball scholarship. He was a one-sport kid. "I'm not sure where I'll go for Christmas break," he said. "I haven't had Christmas in years. My dad and my sister won't even be awake." He was broad like his father, a young man there in his cramped college room, and we wondered if Jeannie would even have recognized him.

The Lutven boys had already finished college, worked for a year in St. Paul, and then come home. They liked the pace of life here, they said. They liked the way winter gave you a chance to catch your breath. One of them married the Sanderson girl, who'd taken over the antiques store and chased the raccoons out. Even after two Lutven babies, ten-pound Scandinavian boys, she fit into the shop's old clothes, the slim, fitted dresses. She liked the quiet way her boys were growing up, she said, polite and calm and curled for five months like warm puppies at her side.

Mrs. Pekola had passed away, which we knew, but we hadn't known her family blamed us. Her eldest daughter was living in Florida, and the filmmakers had gone down to interview her about how her mother had died alone in a church pew, frozen to death in a wool coat and orthopedic shoes. "No one found her 'til spring," the woman said, her anger fresh and righteous.

Mrs. Fiske had taught all the Pekola girls over the years. "Fractions," she whispered in the audience. "That girl just hated fractions."

Dee had never left Bounty, never expressed any interest in going anywhere else. She was *ours*, like her father before her, despite her faraway look most days, her eyes the color of the ice that froze over the flooded quarry. Her dirty-blond hair had darkened to brown, and her teenage acne had faded into a nearly translucent paleness. She volunteered at the library with Mrs. Drausmann and took over story time. The film showed her sitting in a rocking chair with books far too advanced for the children gathered cross-legged around her. "He heard the snow falling faintly through the universe and faintly falling, like the descent of their last end, upon all the living and the dead," she read, as the children squirmed. She wasn't very good at story time, but Mrs. Drausmann had grown hoarse and weary over the years.

One by one we tried to explain for the cameras. Why stay? What is Bounty worth? Three months? Four? Half your life, spent asleep? Our people had moved to Bounty because the land was there and it was empty, and now all we had was the emptiness and each other. We had the lakes and tall trees and a sun that felt good when you'd waited for it half the year. We had our children, the ones we'd feared for, feared their boredom and their recklessness and their hunger for somewhere else. We'd feared becoming Jeannie Rasmussen, and we'd feared becoming Reggie Lapham. We'd feared wanting too much and ending up with less than what we already had. Now Al and Nils dreamt the sound of a basketball bouncing off the warped, snow-soaked floor of the high school gymnasium. Al dreamt of nights asleep in Jeannie's arms. Reg Lapham probably dreamt his life differently too, but he seemed content with what he had: he was interviewed with his son on his lap, a boy who had never made a snowman, never opened a Christmas present. He spoke about that first year back, about how the sleep had saved him, and when his voice foundered his wife, Nkauj Thao-Lapham, reached over to squeeze his hand.

Dr. Joe, interviewed, said that the sleep was profoundly unhealthy, that legislation should be passed before the custom could spread. The documentary included interviews with American history professors at the University of Michigan, experts on what had happened to our county over the past two centuries. Someone in a bowtie said he was dismayed by what had happened to our immigrant spirit, to our desire to press on and out to something better. Our congressman pointed out that the immigrant spirit might have pushed us all the way on out of the state, further west or back east or south. Instead, we'd found a way to stay, and the census didn't ask if you were awake or asleep. It just asked where you lived, and, now more than ever, we were proud to say we lived in Bounty.

"*Sisu*," old Mr. Kajaamaki grunted for the camera, with his hand held in front of his mouth; his teeth had fallen out, but he'd never bothered with dentures, and we felt a bit guilty that no one had insisted on driving him to Escanaba to get some fitted. Our people were shabby, like our houses, our streets, our ancient coats and boots. But our ancestors had come, and they had stopped, and we persisted. Persistence, Mr. Kajaamaki's Old World word for it. The endurance of a people who had once starved and eaten bark and come across an ocean to another sea of snow, to make new ways of life when the old ones seemed insufficient.

"But do you regret their decision? Your father's?" the interviewer, off camera, prodded. The film cut back to Dee and Al standing together. They were outside, walking down the shuttered main street of our town, the sky blue and endlessly wide. Dee squinted in the light, and Al squinted at his daughter. He'd been quiet in front of the cameras, tentative to the point of taciturn, and as we watched the movie from lawn chairs in the mill parking lot, we could see him fidgeting, turning his head to check the expression on his children's faces, turning around in his seat to look at the people he'd led into sleep.

"I barely remember what our life was like before. I remember being cold."

"And now?"

Dee looked baffled, not able to find words sufficient to explain half her life, the happier, more perfect half. The camera turned to Al, but his face was unreadable. "Now?" Dee said. "Now I guess we're not."

Now we are the people of Bounty, the miners of dust and cold, the harvesters of dreams. After the lumber, after the copper, after the railroad, after the crops, after the cows, after the jobs. We're better neighbors in warm beds than we ever were awake. The suckers of the last century, but not of this one.

Censors

Stellanova Osborn

When I carry
The woes of the world
    Into the woods
    Branches reach out
And brush them gently off.

Spring

Beverly Matherne

I hear you hissing
In the distance.
Soon, you'll come
Round the bend,
Roaring and rifting.

Pound on me,
Sun-frothed spring,
I am smooth
Creek-bed rock.

Sleeping in Spirit's Room

Diane Sautter

Something just came here.
We feel it like a caress,
and open our eyes
to find the night has prepared a play,
our personal bedroom window light show.

We look out at the beginning of the word.
I've never seen anything like this, you say,
as torrents of painted lights sweep over the lake
to settle in our own dark pines.

We watch with tears of awe.
Yet there is not need to praise
when the sky is doing it for you.

The Grandmother Remembers

Janet Loxley Lewis

Ah, the cold, cold days
When we lived
On wintergreen berries and nuts,
On caraway seeds.

The deer went over the grass
With wet hooves
To the river to drink.

Their shadows passed
Our tent.

The Village

Janet Loxley Lewis

Among grey cones
Odour of sweet grass
And warm bodies;

Burnt fish, about
The lukewarm stones,
And ash.

And the night, like ice,
Cuts color and odor
Like flowers under a sickle.

These bodies, so still
In the deluge
Of fine air.

The Baby Discovers

Julie Brooks Barbour

Her mouth is a cavern that begins the longing
of her human life. My breast, a ball,

and the orange nose of her doll all warrant a search
by the finely tuned buds of her tongue.

Nothing escapes: bits of torn paper and a cat's whisker
are pulled from her mouth, turned over by fingers,

investigated by eyes, tried again by taste.
Her tongue will never want for these small things

so eagerly again. Once her fingertips learn
the odd tingle of sensation, once her mouth learns

certain textures it touches have no taste, no smell,
then she will yearn for the candies,

the soft creams melting in her mouth.
One day, she will seek softness and warmth

beyond my breast—the smoothness of someone else's skin
against her lips—and every inch of her body will learn

what now her tongue only knows,
what now her mouth opens itself toward.

The Poet's Vision

Beverly Matherne

And a sword shall pierce your heart.

—Luke 2:35

1.

The poet in a coma, the Virgin Mary dresses her in a white robe. She whispers in her ear.

The poet is to found a chapel in honor of the Virgin, at the highest point in the attic of her Victorian home. Fully Gothic, its cathedral ceiling assures the upward gaze of eyes.

That evening, Christ descends, joins His Mother at the poet's bedside, blood glistening from His wounds. The poet drinks from the gash in His side. Christ slides a band onto her finger. When dawn filters through summer lace, Blessed Mother and Son ascend, seraphim chanting, the scent of roses filling the room.

2.

The poet stops eating meat, takes mostly broth and kale she grows at her bay window, wears coarse burlap beneath her garments. In winter, she snowshoes in bare feet, from ache to exquisite agony, loss of the senses, *durée*. Oh, ecstasy!

Before long, the poet hires an auctioneer. Quickly go her oak bed, its sturdy hand-carved posts and headboard; her tall armoire; the Bombay chest, its floral inlay and marble top. Equally go the fainting couch, Limoges plates, Lunt silver. Soon, she has all she needs for the chapel.

3.

In Christmas season, the bishop schedules an appointment with the poet. He wants to see for himself that woman, that place. On his way, he thinks of her addled mind, her foolish claim that she has seen, multiple times, visions of the Virgin in a grotto of chandeliers.

When the poet opens her wrought iron door, the scent of magnolia fills the hall. Intoxicated by the perfume, beauty and purity of the woman, the bishop loses his composure, falls into plush folds of a Louis XIV couch. He bangs his head on its frame, of fruit wood from France, probably pear.

Soon, the bishop takes his leave. He sinks into the seat of his car, clings to his steering wheel, sobs. Beads of sweat form on his brow. His heart beats wildly. Finally, he quiets, collects himself but unsettles again, for before him, at the foot of an arbor, blue clematis pushes up from the snow.

4.

Soon, the poet hires a carpenter. For the chapel, he builds a large Gothic arch. He carves bas-reliefs of *fleur-de-lis*, acanthus leaves, liana.

At Butler Antique Mall, the poet finds a stained glass window. In its lower panel, a pelican feeds her three young. Beaks having punctured her tender abdomen, they draw blood. Drops, big and swollen, fall from her wounds.

The poet places the stained glass before two vertical windows at the back of the chapel. To the right, she stands her large statue of the Virgin clad in white gown, blue cloak, slender girdle at her small breasts.

Light filters through royal blue and red. Prisms play over the tender lips of the Virgin.

5.

Across the Upper Peninsula, from Copper Harbor to Whitefish Point to Sault Ste. Marie, from Big Bay to Marquette to Ishpeming, believers and non-believers, come to the chapel, inspired by rumor or fervor. In light of votives and stained glass, amidst the scent of wild rose and hardwood maple, crystal rosaries fracture light.

Women of Italian descent come, of Cornish descent, of Irish origin, of Greek origin, come. Ojibwa of Catholic persuasion, and not, come. Lutheran women—from the Finnish church, the Norwegian church, the German church—also come to the Virgin. Jews come. Muslims come. Shamans, priests, pastors come. Rabbis, imams come. They petition for the safe return of daughters, of sons, of spouses—serving or captured—in Afghanistan, Iran, Iraq. In Jordan, Egypt, Libya. In Tunisia. In Yemen.

6.

Since the opening of Our Lady's Chapel, scores have come home from military tours, from embassies, haunted by visions of entranced freedom fighters, mothers raped and killed, infants crying for them. Etched in memories forever is the blood of innumerable bodies, sacrifice that will resurrect cities, harvest wheat for bread, tap waters sweet as wine.

In the chapel, sudden revelations enthrall many. Prayers, and sometimes wailing, fill the evening, the night.

7.

Since the dedication of the chapel, the poet has written a thousand psalms in honor of the Virgin, a thousand villanelles, in her honor, five hundred pantoums, scores of sonnets, in her honor, Fibonaccis, ghazals, haiku, and more, all in her honor. Hundreds the Virgin has cured of heart disease, nervous disorders, depression.

8.

At age 99, the poet dies peacefully in her sleep. At her autopsy, the pathologist notes the uncommon swell of her heart, the way it fills her chest cavity, how, when he tries to slice it, blood falls in swollen drops. With ease, the undertaker removes the poet's entrails. He cannot dislodge her heart.

9.

The funeral takes place at St. John's in Ishpeming in May. When the priest sprinkles holy water on the poet's coffin, a strange sound, almost inaudible, emanates from within. Unnerved, the priest raises the volume of his voice. The heart persists. A sigh. A wave. Drumbeat in the distance.

10.

When the coffin is lowered into earth, sun emerges from gray clouds, with uncommon brilliance. Lilies of the Valley reach from the poet's heart, through satin, through the bronze of her casket. Lilies of the Valley spring from soil at her grave, spill into streets of the town, across cities, across seas, atop mountains, into deserts. Everywhere, Lilies of the Valley bloom. Lilies of the Valley bloom. Lilies bloom.

Postscript

Stellanova Osborn

As jewelweed to the shore
and fireweed to the clearing
I will come back forever,
In spirit,
Dear island.

For the Chinese People, Who See the Same Stars

Elinor Benedict

Lake Michigan
lies flat in the dark
a black pool wide as a prairie.

The sky stands perpendicular
over the water's body.

Its tall onyx multiplies
the harbor lights
into a millennium of seeing

the clockless house of the hunter
the queen in her jeweled chair
the two bears eating
drinking, pouring

the everlasting cup.

In a Far City

Elinor Benedict

Sampans toss and groan under our hotel window.
At two A.M. my daughter and I cannot sleep
together in this bed so many worlds
from home: our snow-hushed rooms, warm
and separate, changed to this stiff
intimacy under silk. Neither of us knows
the other's skin. Hers is smooth, blue as milk;
mine crinkled, scalded cream. We try

not to cough or sway the ancient mattress.
But I want to tell her how this dark
hotel's a buried city of women like us.
In this room we meet and part from our
mothers, children, lovers, breath.
This bed swings like a bridge
over all that divides us.

Lac Vieux Desert

Sally Brunk

This road fills my dreams
Mother says it is nine miles long
Full of twists and turns
I can close my eyes and remember every curve
Grandfather Frank Brunk Sr. walked this road every day
Father Al walked it with his siblings to get to school
This road connects Watersmeet to the old village
When I visit this place, I offer tobacco to the ancestors and
My relations who have passed on
This sacred place where Father was born and raised
Where my relations are buried and now rest
I dream of it when I miss Dad the most
I wonder what the village was like when he was young
This place is where the eagles dance and connect with the Anishinabe
This place is held close to our hearts
Generations have connected
Through the dances of old and
The powwows now held there
If you close your eyes and listen close,
You can hear the old songs mingle with the new
The dancers of the new powwows

Share these ancient grounds with the old ones
Whose dances now inspire them today
My Grandparents brought their children up in the old village
The foundation of their home is all that is left
I took a brick home, one of the last times I was there
It has a place of honor on my bookcase
When I see it as I rise for another day,
I am pulled back to Lac Vieux Desert
To the eagles, the voices held on the wind
The dreams of my Grandparents so long ago
That our blood would continue on
I think they would be proud to know
We as a family, are still here.

Summer

Niibin

If One Stands Next to Lake Superior

Amy McInnis

What's a cove but a way for water to be more fluid
than a lake. Some forethought,

then the words *Waves break*, mess with molecules,
like what happens in a rainstorm:

gravel and/or air wriggle(s) in, puddles and droplets
keep their shapes. We should know better.

It's not tension anymore, just stickiness, how a period
stays in a small black circle

at every major breathing point
and edge rocks are the tips of arrows, and arrows don't end

any more than anything does,
or if one believes in arcs, eventually curve back to themselves

and never really begin. A sudden lakewind
makes me wrap my arms around myself,

the integrity of a shore: needed badly.
A sandy slope into cold and depth: wanted.

The sweater that would've been nice to have:
too long a walk away.

Summer in Gold River

Catie Rosemurgy

Our town squishes like a pillow against our cheeks.
Its coolness is the best river. We have the best life,
the best wind, the best large birds. We cannot be bitten
by the teeth that are everywhere. We've built a roof
on each of our triumphs. We are also lucky in these ways:
radiance is the most lovely harbinger of death,
and it feels as if the clouds have been wrung from our hearts.
We have the best sense of compressing life
into simple greetings here. Some people have asked the question,
what is a bad sign? I'm considered a type of child
but I say it's when people you love go missing.
And yet, curled up each night at the end of our yard
is a faded lake sent as a gift from another world.
We swim in it once the work of watching the sun stay whole
is truly over. We've survived as a species
mainly because of the dripping. It's best if our skin
is alive and moving when we head through the trees,
when we stop on our path to sniff the air like dogs.
It's best that it's dark, and that we're no longer sure
if what we are bathed in is actually water.

Ironing

Judith Minty

The pattern flows. Leaves and flowers blend, a river spinning over the cotton. It is my daughter's blouse. Green ripples under my fingers. Pink and blue blossom under the iron's steam. Tiny buds. The cement floor presses its back against the soles of my feet. The pipes gather pearls of moisture. I am a tree. I rise from the earth. I shade the ironing board. My hand passes back and forth, a branch in the wind. One sleeve, then the other.

Summer, but this basement remembers winter and holds loam to its heart. The water in these pipes wants to go underground, back to the dark. It is June, and my daughter sleeps in the heart of her dream. She is far from my belly now, on her white bed, still as a breath in the hospital wing. I have washed the blood from her blouse. Now this iron passes over a sleeve, it curls around a button. Colors intertwine, tangle. The petals blur. They bleed into leaves on the vines.

The car was thick with glass, little beads of glass, blue and yellow in the sun. The lace of slivers of glass, glistening on her skirt, under her bare feet. Glass clinging to her blouse, her skin. Glass in the upholstery, on the carpet, the dashboard. Prisms in the sun. A clink and tinkle like wind chimes when she stirred. Her hands gliding to her face. Glass glinting in her hair. Blood shining on the glass. Glass flowing, separating, as she stirred on the seat of the car.

I pass this iron over her blouse. Steam hisses. I hear her voice as she is lifted from the car. Steam rises from the flowers, the petals. The leaves. I am a tree. Her long hair matted with blood, the cut open on her scalp. My feet curl like roots on the floor. Sweat gathers on the pipes. I rustle over her blouse. Her hair unfurls on the pillow. The flowers blend, the leaves blur. My hand glides over the pattern, a river spinning. Her dream flows without sound. Steam hisses from the iron. Petals and leaves mingle pink and blue. Green. I am ironing her blouse. Only this motion is left.

For the Healing of All Women

April Lindala

Sunday morning. Baraga pow wow 2004.

July winds blew against my face. The sun felt brilliant. Lisa and I hung our dresses on hooks from the ceiling of her open porch to catch the morning breeze. Lisa's white satin jingle dress was a bit dusty after a day of dancing, but it was still striking. Her hands brushed away the dust. Hundreds of silver cones swayed and sparkled from the sunlight. Her black velvet yoke also hung with her dress. Baby blue and yellow beads: an Ojibwa floral design.

My traditional dress is made with a deep blue velvet fabric. Numerous brilliant waterbirds are sewn all over; purple, pink, orange and yellow. A circle of eagle feathers are sewn on the front. This dress is snug around my bust, but overall a nice fit. I picked up this dress from my friend, Summer just before I left for Finland and just after my injury.

Two weeks earlier 2004. Sugar Island pow wow.

"How is your ankle, April? Still bothering you?" Robelle sat upright in her lawn chair, eager for my answer.

"Fine . . . as long as I dance traditional," I smiled at her, but the question poked at my emotions—it had been three years.

The sounds of the pow wow—drums, singing, bells, laughter, crackling fry bread oil—were in the distance. Robelle and I sat at her camping area where we could visit in private.

Robelle was not dancing either. She wore a white top with a skirt that went right to the ground. Robelle never wore a lot of makeup, but her lips had a hint of pink lipstick. Her dark eyes focused on me.

"I just can't dance jingle. Doctor's orders—no 'bouncing.'" I shifted in my lawn chair.

"Yup . . ." Robelle nodded. ". . . jingle dress dancing is right out." She brushed her hair away from her face. Her hair was much shorter now than when we first met. It hung just below her shoulders, a mix of black, charcoal, grey, and white strands.

"I can dance when my foot is wrapped." My hands air-wrap my foot as I spoke. "See, there is this way to wrap your ankle, kind of like they do for athletes when their Achilles is injured. Anyway, I can sort of dance, but then I can't walk. So that doesn't do me much good."

She shook her head. "No, I guess not." Robelle was attentive to my every word.

"I tried it a couple of times, but after a couple of hours, I'm in pain. So I end up taking the wrap off anyway."

My cheeks were warm. Tears started. I stared at my feet so I would not have to look Robelle in the face.

"I can't stand it," I continued. "I can't stand this—being sidelined. This sucks." My throat was starting to get scratchy. "Have . . . have I done something wrong?"

Robelle shook her head no.

"You are in mourning," Robelle said quietly after a moment. "You did nothing wrong. You are in mourning for that dress."

Summer. 1992.

"When you make a jingle dress, you have to be in the right frame of mind." Robelle's voice was soft but her tone was serious. Parental. "You have to be in a good place. Of course it's always a good idea to smudge. I try to keep smudge going the entire time I roll cones."

Robelle wasn't old enough to be my mom, but her voice was confident. Her long dark hair almost reached her waistline.

We sat across from each other at her large dining room table that had been converted to a temporary sewing center. A large abalone shell about the size of a soup bowl was placed between us. Grey sage leaves were made into small round bundles about the size of grapes. These tiny balls of leaves were burning steadily in the shell creating a thin line of smoke. The smell was bitter and gave the air a slightly harsh taste. But it was familiar and felt safe.

Robelle shared with me the responsibilities of a jingle dress dancer as I cut dozens and dozens of Copenhagen snuff can lids. Collecting lids was not an easy task: we often had to answer to looks of confusion upon asking for the lids.

Each lid carried a tart scent of tobacco and metal. My job was to trim the sides of the lid so that I was working with a flat, round piece of metal. Robelle was helping me. We used scissors that were not made for cutting metal. My twenty-three year old hands were tired and not as self-assured as Robelle's. The muscles between my right thumb and its index finger cramped. My palm throbbed but I continued without complaint.

I held the lid with my left hand and the scissors in my right. I trimmed it in a counterclockwise motion until a slender ringlet of metal was formed and the lid itself was flat. Over and over and over again I cut these lids: hundreds of them. Ringlet after discarded metal ringlet. Vaguely artistic. Prickly against my tender fingertips.

Robelle's method was quick and simple—take the scissors, cut into the lid lip with one turn of the lid. *Voilà*, flat metal.

Sunday 11:25 A.M. Baraga powwow 2004.
Grand entry in less than an hour.

As our dresses caught the summer air, Lisa and I sat on her dining room floor. The thick rug didn't cushion my bottom as I had hoped. Regardless, I sat and began inspecting my regalia accessories. Hair ties: blue, pink, lavender and white ribbons with a heart-shaped shell at the top. Bracelet: black, grey, and silver beads sewn onto dyed grey leather. The bracelet was already ten years old.

My fingers ran through the emerald fringe on my mint green shawl to clear out tangles from the day before. Various pieces of jewelry, large turquoise rings, bone earrings, and silver bracelets, hid in their respective places within a small, black bag next to me on the floor.

Lisa was sitting in front of a large mirror propped against the wall. She braided her long, black hair. Her hands moved rapidly, twisting and weaving; the tattoo on her wrist caught my eye. *Nemikigokwe.*

My brown eyes caught her brown eyes in a quick glimpse in the mirror. We giggled at nothing special. I wondered if this was what it was like growing up with a sister: trying on each other's clothes and brushing each other's hair.

My tired knee-high deer hide boots needed attention. Two inch fringe hangs from the top of the boots. Temptation hit me. I put the boot to my nose . . . and sniffed. The whiff of the soft deer hide did not hold its sweet smell from years prior.

I turned the boot over to look at the elk hide sole. "Damn!" The tape was coming off.

Lisa looked over. "A good blow-out this time, huh." We laughed. My right boot had a thin, but very apparent rip. The rip was right against the bottom edge of the right sole, just under my big toe. The tear was over two and half inches long. The soles had never torn like this before. I had made a makeshift bandage with white electrical tape the day before, but some of it was coming off already. I checked the clock. Grand entry was quickly approaching.

I pulled out a small roll of white electrical tape from my bag, not sacred, but definitely necessary. I ripped several small strips of white tape to cover the tear. I rubbed my thumb against the smooth tape and thought of my dad—an electrician by trade.

My dad is not Indian; however, he made me these pair of hide boots for dancing when I was very young. He made them just a bit too big. "So you can grow into them," he said. My feet never did "grow into" them. But they always feel the best.

Summer. 1992.

Tobacco stained my hands. My fingertips ached from the sharpness of the metal. A small cut on the inside of my index finger made me wince. I licked the cut immediately. My tongue recoiled: tobacco dust. I hung my tongue out for the taste of fresh air. Robelle took notice.

"Even as you cut yourself now, you are sacrificing yourself for your people. This is a dress of healing for others, not for you." Robelle stood up from the dining room table and went to the kitchen sink. Not missing a beat she handed me the moist paper towel, sat back down and went on with her teachings.

"This first dress is the only dress that I will help you with. After that, you are on your own. It will be your turn to pass these teachings on to someone else." Robelle continued helping me cut the lids. She was moving much quicker than I was and with what looked to be little effort.

"Each time you roll a cone it represents a prayer for someone." Robelle put more sage in the shell and lit it with a match. After it caught the flame, she waved her hand over the leaves to create smoke. "This is why you must first be in a good place yourself. Each cone may be dedicated to someone different or several cones may be for the same person; maybe one who is very sick."

After all of the lids were cut, I rolled each one with needle-nose pliers. Robelle could not help me with this. These were my prayers. The muscles in my palms and fingers loosened with each turn of the needle-nose pliers. I felt inadequate to be "praying for the people" so I kept these prayers in my head.

First, I prayed for my mom. Then I rolled a cone. Not an easy task. Robelle showed me a couple of times how to roll these lids into cones. Her hands moved so confidently that she made it look too easy. I fumbled with the pliers as I turned the metal. I tried to avoid the sharp edges. Pretty soon I got the hang of it and returned to my silent prayers. I prayed for my parents, family and friends. I prayed for my husband. I prayed for people I knew who were sick. I prayed for my friend's son who suffered from leukemia.

"What if you run out of people to pray for?" *Silly question.*

Robelle had been lining up patterns and cutting up fabric. She looked up for a moment to answer me. "Prayer is a personal thing. Just pray from your heart. It will come to you."

Hoping that I wasn't cheating, I started over with my mental list but this time I was more specific with everyone's problems. My dad's knees were bothering him again and mom was facing more hearing loss. This time the prayers were tougher but came easier. More and more faces began to appear through my closed eyelids. Some people needed more than one cone. Matt, my friend's son with leukemia, needed at least ten cones.

Sunday at noon. Baraga pow wow grand entry.

Veterans raised their flags: numerous eagle feather staffs, the American Flag, the Canadian Flag, a Vietnam Veteran flag and several tribal flags. Colors, sounds, and emotions ensued. A well-respected group of singers from northern Minnesota was host drum. Their beat was unified, solid, and purposeful. Over a dozen of them struck the drum assertively and with accuracy; their voices precise, high and melodic.

Beads of sweat formed against my back. Sunbeams peeked through the tall pine trees and struck me with a wave of heat as purposefully as the singers struck the drum. The timid breeze could not penetrate my velvet dress. My breastplate hung over my shoulders. My mint green shawl was placed carefully on my left arm. A slight headache snapped at my temples due to the tightness of my braids. No matter. My feet felt every little rock under them. My toes wiggled, ready to dance.

A buzz started in the grand entry line; dancers stood on their tiptoes to see who had entered the dance arena. Hundreds of women in bright outfits adorned with jewelry, beaded barrettes, and eagle plumes clipped in their hair. Our eagle feather fans circulated the air around us. Grand entry goosebumps.

In single file, we entered the arena by age. We stepped with gentle intention, bending each knee slightly. Each step with each drumbeat: the heartbeat of Mother Earth, the heartbeat of our nations.

The jingle dress dancers came in the dance arena behind us women traditional dancers. A more agile dance, these ladies jumped and bounced on the balls of their feet. The steps exact, their motions faithful to each beat. I recalled what it felt like, entering the arena with my jingle dress on, surrounded by other jingle dress dancers.

The grand entries where the hair on my arms stood straight up . . .

We entered the circle from the eastern direction and danced clockwise heading into the southern direction. Pride consumed me.

Where are the chills?

Probably sixty or more women traditional dancers were in front of me; some in hide dresses, many in cloth dresses. Another four or five traditional dancers were behind me and the jingle dress dancers immediately behind. My ears sought out the elegant resonance of the thousands of cones shaking the air with a metallic melody.

I followed the traditional ladies into the western direction and raised my fan to honor the eagle feather staffs held by the veterans who were dancing in place.

It felt like lightning cracking against the ground, yet still, I was light and free as a plume.

Gentle steps, knees bent slightly. My shawl swung and the fringe dangled. I moved forward now rounding the circle moving in the northern direction. Because of the July heat, the elder traditional women made the decision to dance in place. Even though I wanted to keep going forward, this was their right. I turned and faced inward. Our line of traditional women turned to dance shoulder to shoulder.

The jingle dress dancers kept going and danced in front of us; vivid dresses with the glistening reflection of sunlight from the cones. The tender crashing of the cones consoled me.

There were over 250 dancers for the afternoon grand entry.

Summer. 2000.

My jingle dress is difficult to wash. The fabric soaked up sweat, smoke, and summer dust. The organic smell really doesn't bother me. But I haven't washed her in at least three or four powwows. It is important to wait for a hot and windy day, not a forecast easily found in upper Michigan. I will not place her in the washing machine because of the cones and I don't trust any dry cleaners with her.

She is a sacred dress. So I hand wash her. It can be painful when the cones, formally Copenhagen lids, cut my skin. Because of her cones—365 of them—she is heavy.

I kneel down and twist the faucet on. My white antique tub fills slowly with warm water and my knees ache as they point down with all of my weight. I lean against the tub to pour a cap of Woolite into the water. I drop my fingers in the water to shake bubbles to life.

I smell (or perhaps imagine) fresh, cherry-flavored pipe tobacco as I undress the hanger. I carefully hold her with both arms. She hangs as if she has collapsed in sleep. I drop back down to my knees and place her into the tub, as if I am placing a dozing child into bed. The top of the dress lies back against the tub. She looks like she is sitting up, waiting for me to wash her back.

Temperate bathwater is soft over my hands. She shifts as if to move on her side. My hands must move fast because she cannot stay in the water long. I carefully select pieces of her, first the stiff arms, then the front of the skirt. I rub the fabric together furiously. I turn her over and wash the back of the skirt. I turn her back again to do the top part of the dress last. This area has painting on it and I am shy to really scrub this part for fear the paint will be altered or even ruined. I submerge her breast, collarbone and shoulders into the water.

Detergent bubbles have foamed and covered the entire dress as it is submerged. I lift her back up with one arm and drain the water. I, then, rinse the dress off with cold water. I squeeze bits of her here and there to ring out excess water. I hang her on a line outside to dry. She is beautiful.

She is my third and favorite jingle dress. It has been eight years since I started dancing jingle. I look at her for a while as she blows gently in the breeze. Mainly maroon fabric in color with green, maroon, and pink ribbon. The maroon color is purposeful. It represents the life blood that we, as women, give each month. Our moon time is sacred. It is considered ceremony.

The top of the dress, satin eggshell in color at one time, is now a bit worn and faded but still maintains a minor sheen. At the top of the dress are paintings of roses. The edges of each petal are dark pink and naturally fade into a white flower.

At each collarbone a matching pair of rose buds peeking out from their opening petals. This represents the stage of a girl's life: opening up to a new world around her, where she will face changes—her first moon, her first kiss, or perhaps her first fast.

The arms wear matching roses, one fully open, two smaller roses open a bit more than the front ones. One can see the inside petals more. This represents the young women who are not quite adults but no longer children; women who are not yet mothers, but are learning how to take care of young ones.

On the back of the dress, there is a full bouquet of roses in full open bloom. These roses represent the adult woman. This is where I am at in my life. I am not a mother, but I do have several children in my life and several women surrounding me on my path. This bouquet represents that collective of strong women at the full bloom of their lives. It helps me remember the women in my life; women who have helped me become who I am. Women who have taught me life lessons, women who have sung with me, sweat with me, danced with me, cried with me, sat silent with me. It reminds me of the women who have laughed with me, prayed with me, taught me, learned with me. These women know who they are. It is for these women and all women that I wear this dress. She is for the healing of all women.

Sugar Island 2004.

"You did nothing wrong. You are in mourning for that dress." Robelle said quietly.

"Yeah, I know." I sighed and concentrated: *No crying.* "It's really hard because I have been working on this hide dress and I feel as though I am having a slow time of it because I still feel like I should be a jingle dress dancer . . ." *Oh shit. I'm going to start crying.* ". . . and I can see her all the time. She is hanging right in my sewing room."

I stopped to think about this. *Was she watching me and wondering?*

"Perhaps you need that dress to heal you," Robelle suggested. I looked towards her for her wisdom but didn't make eye contact. "Do you remember when I carried Kristin's dress into the arena?" My head nodded. Kristin, Robelle's youngest daughter, was sick and facing many challenges in her young life.

Robelle continued, "Do you remember how I hung it over my arm and carried the dress like a shawl? Perhaps that is what you need to do. Let that dress heal you now. The people who know you, who love you . . . they will understand what you are doing."

I simply continued to nod in agreement and looked at the grass below my feet. Robelle and I talked more about our hopes for the future, our own healing. I heard the drums in the distance. The recognizable sound of the drum and Robelle's voice comforted me.

Baraga pow wow. Sunday sometime after 3:00 P.M.

The emcees announce the jingle dress exhibition. Drops of sunlight reflect off of the metal cones, beads, shells, and silver causing a glittery wave of lights in the dance arena. Many of us in the audience stand out of respect for the sacredness of these outfits and the sacrifice that these women make to dance for our people.

Lisa in her white dress appears confident, proud. Her cones move with each beat, her moccasins bounce upon the earth. She lifts her eagle feather fan for the honor beats. I watch her and all of the ladies in the arena with her. Cones crash together. It sounds like a healthy rain, a rain for cleansing and healing—it is the sound that I miss most.

I happen to look down at my feet. Unconsciously, my toes are tapping—specifically, the toes on my right foot. I don't feel the tear under my big toe. I pick my right foot up and check on the tape anyway. *Still holding—but not nearly as white as earlier in the morning.* I set my foot back down and secretly wish one of the dancers is praying for my injured ankle.

August 2010

Summer and I sit in her basement. Fabric pieces, ribbon pieces and bits of hairy threads seem to be growing out of the busy tables where we work. The buzz of the sewing machine zips along smoothly as Summer guides pieces of dark green and beige fabric. The two bits of fabric magically became one piece of art: a future arm of a new dress.

My fingers are not nearly as certain as hers as I work on her second sewing machine. This dress matches the colors of my rose dress. She is forest green and maroon with a beige material that contains a slight sheen. We cut out numerous black designs; each one requiring a skilled hand to sew them on the fabric. A hint of copper thread is sewn throughout.

After several sessions of sewing in her basement, Summer has sewn together my fourth jingle dress. Summer's craft is breathtaking.

September 2010. Sunday morning.

This dress is amazing; she fills a slight hole that has resided within my heart. I stand alone when I roll the cones. Lines of sweet grass smoke circle the lids and I hold the braid of medicine like a conductor holds and moves a baton.

My fingers then stumble as I begin to work the needle-nose pliers around the first lid. It has been years since I rolled lids. *Do I feel arthritis?* I cannot think of my own pain.

My prayers are for the women who are fighting breast cancer, the grandmothers who can no longer dance, the mothers who are fighting loneliness, their daughters who are fighting with their mothers . . . or those daughters fighting the silence—where their mother once spoke wise advice.

Even though I am not supposed to think this way about this dress, I believe it is as much for me as the women out there that I love.

Acknowledgments

This book is dedicated to Trevor Capogrossa.

I would like to give a very deep thank you to Michigan State University Press, Carolyn Stacey, Karen Riekki, Amy Lynn Hess, and especially Janeen Rastall, as their collective editorial suggestions were invaluable to finalizing which texts deserved inclusion in this anthology.

I would also like to thank Julie Loehr for believing in this book.

Thank you to all of the venues—bookstores, libraries, theaters, churches—that have hosted U.P. Book Tour events. A special thanks to the U.P. Book Tour headliners over the years, including Steven Wiig (2010), Steve Hamilton (2011), Don Hall (2012), and Bonnie Jo Campbell (2013); without their dedication to appearing for events, each year's tour would never have been such a success.

Lastly, thank you to those others who took time to give suggestions for whose work should be within these pages, especially people who gave top three lists of their favorite U.P. writing of all time—Marty Achatz, Randall R. Freisinger, Sue Harrison, J.D. Haske, L.E. Kimball, Janice Repka, Vincent Reusch, Jillena Rose, Cathy Seblonka, Cameron Witbeck, and many, many more whose input I so appreciate.

There are a lot more people I'm forgetting, so thank you to anyone I may have forgot to thank.

Please ensure your shelves include books by the authors included in these pages. Support U.P. literature. These names are some of the region's greats.

(The Permissions and Contributors sections are wonderful places to find names of books to read from the authors in these pages whose words you fall in love with. Please consider buying those books from U.P. bookstores.)

Permissions

South of Superior by Ellen Airgood, copyright © 2011 by Ellen Airgood. Used by permission of Riverhead Books, an imprint of Penguin Group (USA) LLC.

"Winter Wind" by Ellen Airgood was originally printed in *Sierra Magazine*, July/August 1994. Reprinted by permission of the author.

["Here in my native inland sea"] by Bame-wa-wa-ge-zhik-aquay; previously printed as "Lines written at Castle Island, Lake Superior" in *The Sound the Stars Make Rushing Through the Sky: The Writings of Jane Johnston Schoolcraft* (University of Pennsylvania Press, 2007, ed. Robert Dale Parker). Public domain (Library of Congress and Abraham Lincoln Presidential Library).

"Jane's Christmas Gift 25 Dec 1841" by Bame-wa-wa-ge-zhik-aquay, translated from the original French by Ronald Riekki and Amélie Jumel; previously printed as "La Renne" in *The Sound the Stars Make Rushing Through the Sky* (University of Pennsylvania Press, 2007, ed. Robert Dale Parker). Public domain (Library of Congress and Abraham Lincoln Presidential Library).

"Mishosha, or the Magician of the Lakes" by Bame-wa-wa-ge-zhik-aquay was published in *Algic Researches: Comprising Inquiries Respecting the Mental Characteristics of the North American Indians* (Harper & Brothers, 1839) by Henry Rowe Schoolcraft; previously printed as "Mishösha, or the Magician and his Daughters: A Chippewa Tale or Legend," *The Sound the Stars Make Rushing Through the Sky* (University of Pennsylvania Press, 2007, ed. Robert

Dale Parker). Public domain (Library of Congress and Abraham Lincoln Presidential Library).

"Lines Written Under Severe Pain and Sickness" by Bame-wa-wa-ge-zhik-aquay; previously printed in *The Sound the Stars Make Rushing Through the Sky* (University of Pennsylvania Press, 2007, ed. Robert Dale Parker). Public domain (Library of Congress and Abraham Lincoln Presidential Library).

[Because Bame-wa-wa-ge-zhik-aquay's writings can be in various forms with words and punctuation added or crossed out, there is—similar to Shakespeare—textual variation. My editorial decisions create versions that should not be treated as definitive, but rather as a mesh of sources. I encourage scholars to continue to unearth the materials within the Henry Rowe Schoolcraft papers at the Library of Congress' Manuscript Division; also see http://www.gutenberg.org/files/35175/35175-h/35175-h.htm#Page_91.]

"The Baby Discovers" by Julie Brooks Barbour appeared in the chapbook *Come to Me and Drink* (Finishing Line Press, 2012) and as "Eleanor Discovers" in *Taproot Literary Review*, 2008. Reprinted by permission of the author.

"Announcement" and "Sudden Calm at Maywood Shores" by Elinor Benedict appeared in *Late News from the Wilderness* (Main Street Rag, 2009), copyright by Elinor Benedict, 2009. Reprinted by permission of the author.

"In a Far City," "For Those Who Dream of Cranes," and "For the Chinese People, Who See the Same Stars" by Elinor Benedict appeared in *All that Divides Us* (Logan: Utah State University Press, 2000), copyright by Elinor Benedict. Reprinted by permission of the author.

"My Upper Peninsula" by Mary Biddinger was published in *La Fovea*. Reprinted by permission of the author.

"Copper Harbor" by Mary Biddinger was published in *The Bedside Guide to No Tell Motel* and, revised, in *Prairie Fever* (Steel Toe Books, 2007). (The version included is from *Prairie Fever*.) Reprinted by permission of the author.

"Skin on Skin" by Sally Brunk appeared in *Studies in American Indian Literatures*, vol. 14, no. 1, Spring 2002; *Sharing Our Stories of Survival: Native Women Surviving Violence* (AltaMira Press, 2008, and *Quiet Mountain Essays*, vol. 3, no. 3, Summer Issue, Aug 2010. Reprinted by permission of the author.

"Authority Figure" by Sally Brunk appeared in *Studies in American Indian Literatures,* vol. 14, no. 1, Spring 2002. Reprinted by permission of the author.

"Lac Vieux Desert" by Sally Brunk is from *The Way North: Collected Upper Peninsula New Works* [ed. Ron Riekki]. Copyright © 2013 Wayne State University Press, with the permission of Wayne State University Press.

"The Solutions to Brian's Problem" by Bonnie Jo Campbell is from *American Salvage*. Copyright © 2009 Wayne State University Press, with the permission of Wayne State University Press. [Note: The author has made some slight variations to the original text, with approval from Wayne State University Press.]

"Sweet Grass Spirit" by Clara Corbett was published in *Voice on the Water: Great Lakes Native America Now* (Northern Michigan University Press, 2011), eds. Grace Chaillier and Rebecca Tavernini. Reprinted by permission of the author.

"My Lake" by Lisa Fay Coutley appeared in *Cave Wall* no. 8, Summer/Fall 2010, and in *Best New Poets 2010: 50 Poems from Emerging Writers* (Samovar Press/Meridian, 2010, eds. Claudia Emerson and Jeb Livingood). It is included in *In the Carnival of Breathing* (Black Lawrence Press, 2011). Reprinted by permission of the author.

"Errata" by Lisa Fay Coutley appeared in *Linebreak*. It is included in *In the Carnival of Breathing* (Black Lawrence Press, 2011). Reprinted by permission of the author.

"Bones: *Okaniman*" by Echoe Deibert appeared in *Voice on the Water: Great Lakes Native America Now* (Northern Michigan University Press, 2011, eds. Grace Chaillier and Rebecca Tavernini). Reprinted by permission of the author.

"Mad Dog Queen" by Sharon Dilworth was published in *The Long White* (W.W. Norton & Company/University of Iowa Press, 1988) and in *Indiana Review* 11, no. 2, Spring 1988. Reprinted by permission of the author.

"Winter Mines" by Sharon Dilworth was published in *The Long White* (W.W. Norton & Company/University of Iowa Press, 1988). Reprinted by permission of the author.

"Evacuations" by Manda Frederick is from *The Way North: Collected*

Upper Peninsula New Works [ed. Ron Riekki]. Copyright © 2013 Wayne State University Press, with the permission of Wayne State University Press.

"Absent In Its Arrival" by Manda Frederick is from *Press 53 Open Awards Anthology*, ed. Kevin Morgan Watson (Press 53, 2011). Reprinted by permission of the author.

"Waiting on Bats at Dusk" by Manda Frederick is from *Press 53 Open Awards Anthology*, ed. Kevin Morgan Watson (Press 53, 2011). Reprinted by permission of the author.

"North Country" by Roxane Gay was published in *Hobart* (April 2011) and in *The Best American Short Stories 2012* (Mariner Books, 2012, eds. Tom Perrotta and Heidi Pitlor). (The published version here is a longer, unedited version.) Reprinted by permission of the author.

"I Am a Knife" by Roxane Gay was published in *The Literarian*, no. 4. Reprinted by permission of the author.

"Lopsided" by Barbara Henning was published in *Cities and Memory* (Chax Press, 2010). Reprinted by permission of the author.

A previous version of "The Sleep" (not originally set in the U.P.) by Caitlin Horrocks appeared in *The Atlantic* Fiction for Kindle series (July 2010), and in *The Best American Short Stories 2011* (Mariner Books, 2011, eds. Geraldine Brooks and Heidi Pitlor). Reprinted by permission of the author.

"Seney" by Charmi Keranen was published in *Passages North*, no. 31, and *The Afterlife Is a Dry County* (Big Wonderful Press, 2011). Reprinted by permission of the author.

"The Rocky Islands" by Janet Loxley Lewis was published in *The Indian in the Woods* (Monroe Wheeler, 1922). Public domain.

"The Grandmother Remembers" by Janet Loxley Lewis was published in *The Indian in the Woods* (Monroe Wheeler, 1922). Public domain.

"The Village" by Janet Loxley Lewis was published in *The Indian in the Woods* (Monroe Wheeler, 1922). Public domain.

"For the Healing of All Women" by April Lindala is from *The Way North: Collected Upper Peninsula New Works* [ed. Ron Riekki]. Copyright © 2013 Wayne State University Press, with the permission of Wayne State University Press.

"Spring" by Beverly Matherne was published in *Great River Review*, poetry ed. Orval Lund Jr., no. 22, April 1993. Reprinted by permission of the author.

"The Poet's Vision" by Beverly Matherne was published, as an earlier version, in *100 Thousand Poets for Change* (Libellula Edizioni, 2012, eds. Michael Rothenberg, Anny Ballardini, and Obododimma Oha). Reprinted by permission of the author.

"The Next Thing that Begins" by Amy McInnis was published in *Cut River*, Holland Prize Winner 2006 (Logan House Press, 2006) and in *CutBank*. Reprinted by permission of the author.

"If One Stands Next to Lake Superior" by Amy McInnis was published in *Cut River*, Holland Prize Winner 2006 (Logan House Press, 2006). Reprinted by permission of the author.

"Ironing" by Judith Minty is from *Dancing the Fault: Poems* (Gainesville: University Press of Florida, 1991, page 9). Reprinted by permission of the University Press of Florida. ["Ironing" was also published in *The Party Train: A Collection of North American Prose Poetry* (New Rivers Press, 1996) eds. Robert Alexander, Mark Vinz, and C.W. Truesdale.]

"Lake Superior" by Lorine Niedecker was published in *Collected Works*, ed. Jenny Penberthy (University of California Press, 2002). Reprinted by permission of University of California Press.

["What horror to awake at night"] by Lorine Niedecker was published in *Collected Works*, ed. Jenny Penberthy (University of California Press, 2002). Reprinted by permission of University of California Press.

"Dusk" by Stellanova Osborn was published in *Summer Songs on the St. Marys* (North Star Communications, 1982), reprinted from her earlier collections *Balsam Boughs, Iron and Arbutus*, and *Beside the Cabin*. Reprinted courtesy of the Bentley Historical Library of the University of Michigan.

"Censors" by Stellanova Osborn was published in *Beside the Cabin* (Northwoods Press, 1957) and *Summer Songs on the St. Marys* (North Star Communications, 1982). Reprinted courtesy of the Bentley Historical Library of the University of Michigan.

"Postscript" by Stellanova Osborn was published in *Beside the Cabin* (Northwoods Press, 1957) and *Summer Songs on the St. Marys* (North Star Communications, 1982). Reprinted courtesy of the Bentley Historical Library of the University of Michigan.

"Eighteen Maple Trees" by Jane Piirto was published in *A Location in the Upper Peninsula* (Sampo Publishing, 1995, grant from the Finlandia Foundation). Reprinted by permission of the author.

"Here" by Jane Piirto was published in *Saunas* (Mayapple Press, 2008). Reprinted by permission of the author.

"All I know of white" by Saara Myrene Raappana was published in *32 Poems*. Reprinted by permission of the author.

Dandelion Cottage by Carroll Watson Rankin was first published in 1904 by Henry Holt and Company and later by Marquette County Historical Society in 1977. Public domain.

"Imprinting" by Janeen Rastall was published in *Heron Tree*. Reprinted by permission of the author.

"Lake Superior Confesses to the Shore of Keweenaw Bay" by Catie Rosemurgy was published in *My Favorite Apocalypse* (Graywolf Press, 2001). Reprinted by permission of the author.

"Love, with Trees and Lightning" by Catie Rosemurgy was published in *Verse Daily*, *River Styx*, and *The Stranger Manual* (Graywolf Press, 2009). Reprinted by permission of the author.

"Winter in Gold River" by Catie Rosemurgy was published in *Prairie Schooner* (2006) and *The Stranger Manual* (Graywolf Press, 2009). Reprinted by permission of the author.

"New Year's Eve" by Catie Rosemurgy was published in *Alaska Quarterly Review* (2008) and *The Stranger Manual* (Graywolf Press, 2010). Reprinted by permission of the author.

"Billy Recalls It Differently" by Catie Rosemurgy was published in *My Favorite Apocalypse* (Graywolf Press, 2001). Reprinted by permission of the author.

"Summer in Gold River" by Catie Rosemurgy was published in *Prairie Schooner* (2006) and *The Stranger Manual* (Graywolf Press, 2010). Reprinted by permission of the author.

An earlier version of "Sleeping in Spirit's Room" by Diane Moon Sautter was published in *Why Heron Is Blue* (March St. Press, 2006). Reprinted by permission of the author.

An earlier version of "Persephone" by Andrea Scarpino was published in *Linebreak* and revised in *Once, Then* (Red Hen Press, 2014). Reprinted by permission of the author.

"The Break Away," "The Inventory of Goodbye" and "The Lost Lie" are from *45 Mercy Street* by Anne Sexton, edited by Linda Gray Sexton. Copyright © 1976 by Linda Gray Sexton and Loring Conant, Jr., Executors of the Estate of Anne Sexton. Reprinted by permission of Houghton Mifflin Harcourt Publishing Company. All rights reserved.

"You Aren't Sure & I May Not" by Emily Van Kley was published in *Iowa Review* (2011). Reprinted by permission of the author.

"Vital Signs" by Emily Van Kley was published in *The Florida Review* (2009). Reprinted by permission of the author.

"Paradoxical Undressing" by Emily Walter was published in *Cedilla* (Autumn 2011). Reprinted by permission of the author.

Once on This Island by Gloria Whelan was published by HarperCollins (1996). Used by permission of HarperCollins Publishers.

"Incomer" by Gloria Whelan is from *Living Together*. Copyright © 2013 Wayne State University Press, with the permission of Wayne State University Press.

"How to Draw a Crow" by Anne Ohman Youngs is from *Poems from the Third Coast: Contemporary Michigan Poetry* [eds. Michael Delp, Conrad Hilberry, and Josie Kearns]. Copyright © 2000 Wayne State University Press, with the permission of Wayne State University Press. [It was also published in *Recognizing Ever-Changing Landscapes* (Northern Michigan University Press, 2004).]

Contributors

ELLEN AIRGOOD lives and writes in the Upper Peninsula of Michigan, near Lake Superior, where she runs a diner with her husband. Her goal in writing *South of Superior* was to illustrate the strength and humor that characterize so many inhabitants of the U.P., and to show the lake and landscape as characters within themselves.

Born in Sault Ste. Marie, one of the very first Native American authors, BAME-WA-WA-GE-ZHIK-AQUAY (Jane Johnston Schoolcraft) (1800–1842) is a key figure in the history of American literature. Her short stories were important source material for the famous epic poem *The Song of Hiawatha*. Robert Dale Parker, in *The Sound the Stars Make Rushing Through the Sky: The Writings of Jane Johnston Schoolcraft*, described her as the "first known American Indian literary writer" and "the first known Indian woman writer." More continued research needs to be done on the significance of her writing. Her public domain papers are kept at the Library of Congress.

JULIE BROOKS BARBOUR is the author of *Small Chimes* (2014) and a chapbook, *Come To Me and Drink* (2012). Her poems have appeared in *Waccamaw*, *diode*, *storySouth*, *Prime Number Magazine*, *The Rumpus*, *Midwestern Gothic*, and *Verse Daily*. She is co-editor of the journal *Border Crossing* and an Associate Poetry Editor at *Connotation Press: An Online Artifact*. She teaches composition and creative writing at Lake Superior State University.

ELINOR BENEDICT, raised in Tennessee, has lived in the Upper Peninsula of Michigan for nearly forty years. With degrees from Duke University, Wright State University, and Vermont College, she served as founding editor of *Passages North* from 1979 until 1989. She is winner of the May Swenson Poetry Award for her collection *All That Divides Us*, and she has five chapbooks and another collection, *Late News from the Wilderness*.

MARY BIDDINGER's newest poetry collection is *A Sunny Place with Adequate Water* (2014). Her poems have recently appeared in *Crazyhorse*, *Guernica*, *Gulf Coast*, *Denver Quarterly*, *Pleiades*, and *Sou'wester*, among others. Though she now calls Akron, Ohio, home, Biddinger left much (if not all) of her heart in Michigan, where she lived for over ten years.

SALLY BRUNK (Ojibwa/Lac du Flambeau) is a writer and poet who centers on the bond of family and the American Indian way of life. She was proudly born and raised in the Keweenaw Bay Indian Community; this is where she still lives now. Sally has work in *The Way North: Collected Upper Peninsula New Works*, *Voice on the Water: Great Lakes Native America Now*, *Cradle Songs: An Anthology of Poems on Motherhood*, and *Sharing Our Stories of Survival: Native Women Surviving Violence*. She has her own book of poetry, *The Cliffs: Summer Soundings* (featuring Jim Denomie's art).

BONNIE JO CAMPBELL is the author of the bestselling novel *Once Upon a River* (2011) and a 2011 Guggenheim Fellow. She was a 2009 National Book Award finalist and National Book Critics Circle Award finalist for her collection of stories *American Salvage*. Campbell is also author of the novel *Q Road* and the story collection *Women and Other Animals*. She lives in Kalamazoo, Michigan, with her husband and two donkeys.

Clara Corbett is a member of the Keweenaw Bay Community-Ojibwe Tribe. She lives and works in Baraga, Michigan. She continues to be inspired by the natural world around her, enjoying the shores of Lake Superior and the surrounding forest.

Lisa Fay Coutley is the author of *Errata*, winner of the 2014 Crab Orchard Series in Poetry Open Competition, and *In the Carnival of Breathing* (2011), winner of the Black River Chapbook Competition. Her poems have been awarded a fellowship from the National Endowment for the Arts, scholarships to the Sewanee Writers' Conference and the Bread Loaf Writers' Conference, and an Academy of American Poets Levis Prize, and have appeared in *Kenyon Review*, *Gulf Coast*, *Crazyhorse*, *Best of the Net*, and *Best New Poets*.

Echoe Deibert, a deep woods woman, was born and raised "up North." She followed the geese south to earn a certificate to teach, taught trolls a dozen years, met others who left only footprints on the land, and then journeyed home again to twenty-three face-cord winters and a life of learning. Now in her mid-seventies, she shelters in towns, writes, reads, teaches anyone available, and still wanders where there are no trails.

Sharon Dilworth is the author of two collections of short stories, *The Long White* and *Women Drinking Benedictine*, and a novel, *Year of the Ginkgo*. Though she is a Detroit native, her short stories mainly take place in Michigan's Upper Peninsula. She currently lives in Pittsburgh, Pennsylvania, where she is director of the creative writing program at Carnegie Mellon University. She also serves as the fiction editor of Autumn House Press. Her play *The Far Travelers* was part of Terra Nova's 2013 summer reading series.

Manda Frederick holds an MFA in nonfiction and an MA in literary studies. She has published poetry, nonfiction, fiction, and interviews in a number of journals and anthologies, and was recently nominated for a Pushcart Prize. She currently serves as the Editor in Chief for *Glassworks*, the literary journal for Rowan University's MA in Writing Arts Program, where she is also an assistant professor.

ROXANE GAY's writing has appeared in *The Best American Short Stories 2012, Best Sex Writing 2012, Oxford American, American Short Fiction, West Branch, Virginia Quarterly Review, NOON, The New York Times* "Sunday Book Review," *Bookforum, Time, Los Angeles Times, Nation, The Rumpus, Salon, Wall Street Journal's* "Speakeasy" culture blog, and in many other publications. She is the co-editor of *PANK* and essays editor for *The Rumpus.* She teaches writing at Eastern Illinois University. Her novel *An Untamed State* and her essay collection *Bad Feminist* were published in 2014.

BARBARA HENNING is the author of three novels and seven books of poetry. Her most recent book, *A Swift Passage* (2013), is a collection of poetry and prose. Born in Detroit, she has lived in New York City since 1983. As a longtime yoga practitioner, she brings this knowledge and discipline to her writing and her teaching at Naropa University, writers.com, and Long Island University in Brooklyn, where she is professor emerita.

CAITLIN HORROCKS is the author of the story collection *This Is Not Your City.* Her stories have appeared in *The New Yorker, The Best American Short Stories, The PEN/O. Henry Prize Stories, The Pushcart Prize, The Paris Review, Tin House,* and elsewhere. She is fiction editor of *The Kenyon Review* and teaches at Grand Valley State University in Grand Rapids, Michigan.

AMÉLIE JUMEL was born in Lille in the north of France. After studying engineering, she became an expatriate, living in Asia, Vietnam, and then China. Passionate about travel, she has been a vagabond throughout Southeast Asia and Europe, always accompanied by a travel book and a camera.

CHARMI KERANEN is the author of the poetry chapbook *The Afterlife is a Dry County* (2011). Her poetry has appeared in *Passages North, The Salt River*

Review, JMWW, Stirring, blossombones, elimae, The Dirty Napkin, Ouroboros Review, Sugar House Review, inter|rupture, Grasslimb Journal, and *Hot Metal Bridge.* She and her husband live in Northern Indiana, where she works as a freelance writer and proofreader of court transcripts.

JANET LOXLEY LEWIS's (1899–1998, born in Chicago) books include *The Indians in the Woods*; *The Ancient Ones: Poems*; *The Invasion: A Narrative of Events Concerning the Johnston Family of St. Mary's*; *The Wife of Martin Guerre; The Trial of Soren Qvist*; *The Ghost of Monsieur Scarron*; *The Friendly Adventures of Ollie Ostrich*; *The Selected Poems of Janet Lewis*; *The Wheel in Midsummer*; *Against a Darkening Sky*; *The Earth-Bound, 1924–1944*; *Good-Bye, Son and Other Stories*; *Poems, 1924–1944*; *Keiko's Bubble*; *Poems Old and New 1918–1978*, and *Late Offerings*. Her work has been labeled as "significant" and "courageous."

APRIL LINDALA (Grand River Six Nations) is the director of the Center for Native American Studies and an associate professor of English at Northern Michigan University. Lindala co-edited *Mikwendaagozi—To Be Remembered*, a showcase of photography by Anishinaabe youth from Michigan's Upper Peninsula. Lindala's "For the Healing of All Women" appears in *The Way North: Collected Upper Peninsula New Works.* Lindala's poetry has appeared in the anthology she co-edited, *Voice on the Water: Great Lakes Native America Now.*

BEVERLY MATHERNE is a member of the creative writing faculty at Northern Michigan University, and she has read across the United States, Canada, Wales, Belgium, France, Germany, and Spain. She is one of eight authors, including Samuel Beckett and Vladimir Nabokov, whose bilingual writing is the subject of a doctoral dissertation from the Sorbonne. She translates from French to English (including Charles Baudelaire and Arthur Rimbaud) and English to French (including Stanley Kunitz). Widely published, she has received seven first place prizes, including the Hackney Literary Award for Poetry, and five Pushcart Prize nominations.

U.P. native AMY MCINNIS's collection of poems *Cut River* was the 2006 winner of Logan House Press's Holland Prize. Her poems have been published in *The MacGuffin*, *Cimarron Review*, *Mid-American Review*, and other journals. She holds an MFA from Western Michigan University.

JUDITH MINTY's books include *Yellow Dog Journal*, *Walking with the Bear*, *In the Presence of Mothers*, *Dancing the Fault*, and *Lake Songs and Other Fears*, which received the United States Award of the International Poetry Forum. She has been awarded *Poetry*'s Eunice Tietjens Award and the Villa Montalvo Award for Excellence in Poetry. She lives near the shoreline of Lake Michigan and spends time on the Yellow Dog River in the Upper Peninsula.

LORINE NIEDECKER's (1903–1970, born in Fort Atkinson, Wisconsin) books include *Lorine Niedecker: Collected Works*; *The Granite Pail: The Selected Poems of Lorine Niedecker*; *Lake Superior*; *Between Your House and Mine: The Letters of Lorine Niedecker to Cid Corman, 1960 to 1970*; *Harpsichord & Salt Fish*, *New Goose*, *North Central*, *My Life by Water: Collected Poems, 1936–1968*, and more.

Born in Hamilton, Ontario, STELLANOVA OSBORN (1894–1988) wrote the books *Schoolcraft, Longfellow, Hiawatha*, *Hiawatha with its Original Indian Legends*, *Eighty and On: The Unending Adventurings of Chase S. Osborn*, *Summer Songs on the St. Mary's*, *A Tale of Possum Poke in Possum Lane*, *IRON and Arbutus*, *Beside the Cabin*, and more. Her extensive diaries are kept at the University of Michigan's Bentley Historical Library and are open to research.

Author of twenty books and chapbooks, JANE PIIRTO is a Finnish-American native of Ishpeming, Michigan, and spends summers there in her childhood home in Cleveland Location. Northern Michigan University awarded her a BA and an honorary Doctorate of Humane Letters. She is Trustees' Distinguished Professor at Ashland University.

SAARA MYRENE RAAPPANA's poems have appeared in such publications as *Blackbird, Cream City Review, Harvard Review Online, Iron Horse Literary Review*, and *The Gettysburg Review*, and she has been featured on *Verse Daily*. She grew up in the Upper Peninsula of Michigan and served as a Peace Corps Volunteer in southern China. She is an editor for *Cellpoems*, a poetry journal distributed via text message.

Born in Marquette, Michigan, the prolific CARROLL WATSON RANKIN (1864–1945) wrote the books *The Adopting of Rosa Marie, The Castaways of Pete's Patch, The Cinder Pond, Finders Keepers, The Girls of Gardenville, Gipsy Nan, Girls of Highland Hall: Further Adventures of the Dandelion Cottagers, Stump Village, Wolf Rock*, the classic *Dandelion Cottage*, and more.

JANEEN RASTALL lives in Gordon, Michigan (population 2). Her poetry has appeared in several publications including *The Raleigh Review, Dunes Review, Prime Number Magazine, Heron Tree*, and *The Midwest Quarterly*. Wayne State University Press nominated her poems in *The Way North: Collected Upper Peninsula New Works* for a Pushcart Prize. Her chapbook *In the Yellowed House* was published in 2014.

CATIE ROSEMURGY is the author of two poetry collections, *My Favorite Apocalypse* and *The Stranger Manual*. She is the recipient of a Rona Jaffe Foundation Writers' Award, a National Endowment for the Arts Fellowship, and a Pew Fellowship in the Arts. She lives in Philadelphia and teaches at The College of New Jersey.

DIANE SAUTTER is a professor in the English Department at Northern Michigan University, teaching creative writing, myth, and literature courses. Her poetry book *Why Heron Is Blue* was published in 2006. A group of her poems appear in the anthology Greenhouse; other poems were recently included in a hand-printed book, *Passages North*, and in Paterson Literary Review. She is presently involved in consolidating two books of poems.

Andrea Scarpino is the author of the poetry collection *Once, Then* (2014) and the chapbook *The Grove Behind* (2009). She received an MFA in creative writing from Ohio State University and has published in numerous journals including *The Cincinnati Review, Los Angeles Review,* and *Prairie Schooner.* She contributes weekly to the blog Planet of the Blind.

Anne Sexton's (1928–1974, born in Newton, Massachusetts) books include *The Complete Poems: Anne Sexton, Transformations, Selected Poems of Anne Sexton, Anne Sexton: A Self-Portrait in Letters, Love Poems, The Awful Rowing Toward God, The Death Notebooks, 45 Mercy Street, Words for Dr. Y: Uncollected Poems with Three Stories, To Bedlam and Part Way Back,* and *All My Pretty Ones,* which has been called a "work of genius." In 1967, her *Live or Die* won the Pulitzer Prize for Poetry.

Alison Swan's anthology *Fresh Water: Women Writing on the Great Lakes* was named a Michigan Notable Book. An award-winning poet, writer, and environmental activist, she teaches environmental and sustainability studies at Western Michigan University.

Emily Van Kley's poems have appeared in *The Iowa Review, The Florida Review, Salamander,* and *The Mississippi Review,* among others. Her work has won the Iowa Review Award and Florida Review Editors' Award, and has been a finalist for *Narrative*'s Below 30 Contest. Most recently, Brenda Shaughnessy chose her work for inclusion in *Best New Poets 2013.*

Emily Walter is from Leelanau County, Michigan, and currently lives and writes in Missoula, Montana. She's been published in *32 poems, Blue Earth Review, Coe Review,* and other publications. She teaches poetry and runs a cooking school.

Gloria Whelan's short stories have appeared in numerous literary quarterlies and anthologies including *The O. Henry Prize Stories.* Whelan also writes for young readers and her young adult novel *Homeless Bird* received a National Book Award.

The award-winning poet ANNE OHMAN YOUNGS wrote the collection *Thirty Octaves above Middle-C: Poems* and the chapbook *Markers*. Her work has been included in *Passages North* and *New Poems from the Third Coast: Contemporary Michigan Poetry*.